ENGINE TROUBLE

K. Subramannya

Rupa & Co

Copyright © K. Subramannya 2008

Published 2008 by

Rupa & Co

7/16, Ansari Road, Daryaganj
New Delhi 110 002

Sales Centres:
Allahabad Bangalooru Chandigarh Chennai
Hyderabad Jaipur Kathmandu
Kolkata Mumbai

Typeset in 3Stone Informal by
Mindways Design
1410 Chiranjiv Tower
43 Nehru Place
New Delhi 110 019

Printed in India by
Rekha Printers Pvt. Ltd.
A-102/1 Okhla Industrial Area, Phase-II
New Delhi-110 020

For my parents,
K. Damodara Bhat and Padma D. Bhat

1

FRIDAY, 5 DECEMBER 1947

Yadu Ranganathan sat on the steps of the Parthasarathy temple tank watching the cricket match being played below. The light in the sky was fading rapidly, and the bowling team seemed desperate to wrap up the match. Only one last wicket stood between them and victory. The fielders had all moved in close to the batsman in a bid to intimidate him. But the batsman, who was substituting for Yadu, hung on bravely in the middle. Usually he lasted only three or four balls, but today he was playing more determinedly. The umpire was expected to stop the match any minute now because of poor light, and the batsman obviously didn't want to lose the match for his side by losing his wicket.

Yadu watched with bated breath as his teammate stonewalled each ball. He understood it only too well that if they lost the match now, his teammates would surely blame him for it. He was supposed to have arrived there to play at half past two, and he had turned up ten minutes back, when the game was nearly over. The truth was, Yadu had completely forgotten about that afternoon's match with the neighbourhood boys. He had been so busy preparing for his forthcoming exams that the cricket fixture had somehow slipped his mind. Yadu's lips curled into a smile. He couldn't believe this: it was not like him to forget such an important thing as a match fixture. Cricket was his life, his passion. It was what his life revolved around. At least that's how it had been till last month. Now he was not so sure. Over the past few weeks, cricket had been forced to give way to a tearing priority: academics. In a way he felt he had to thank his cousins for this dramatic shift in his life. The previous month, tired of their snide remarks and sarcastic comments about his academic performance, Yadu had challenged his cousins that he would out-perform them in the mid-term examinations. In order to win this challenge he had focused all his energy and time over the past month towards his school studies, even ignoring his favourite pastime – cricket. And if all went well the following week, he would have the last laugh.

Yadu Ranganathan was an above average student, always had been. But in his family being 'above average' was just not good enough. He sometimes cursed his luck for being born into a family of achievers. His family on his mother's side was a super intelligent breed, at least half of whom featured regularly in the city's who's who list. One of his uncle was a cabinet secretary, another a leading surgeon. He had an aunt who was an ICS officer, and her husband was the principal of a leading city college. Yadu had eight cousins, five of them of the same age group as he was: sixteen. One of his cousins played cricket for the state; two others were gold medalists from their respective colleges, and two more (twin sisters studying in the same class as Yadu) sang regularly in kutcheries and on the All India Radio. Yadu sometimes wondered how they did it. Their report cards resembled a set of binary numbers against every subject except English and Tamil, and yet they found time to sing in kutcheries and play for the state. Unfortunately for him, he was neither extraordinarily gifted in academics, nor did he stand out in extracurriculars. It was for this very reason that Yadu hated attending family functions. Since five of his cousins studied in the same pre-university college as he did – of which three were his classmates – his academic and extracurricular under-achievements could not be kept a secret. Conversation during these get-togethers would invariably veer towards who scored how much in what, and his classmate-cousins derived intense pleasure in announcing his marks to all and sundry. At this point, one of his uncles, usually the one who was college principal, would *tch-tch* sympathetically, and then lecture him for an hour about the importance of taking one's studies seriously. The function he had attended the previous month in his cousin's house had been the proverbial last straw. Almost everyone who had come had taken potshots at him. Their sympathy-coated cynicism had made him want to throw up. He had felt so humiliated that he had decided then and there that he was going to do something about his '*just* above average marks'.

So, over the past month, he had struggled hard in order to prepare for his half yearly exams, even neglecting cricket matches with the neighbouring street boys. Perhaps Yadu might not have studied so hard if he had known that there was going to be a major upheaval in his life in the next couple of days. His best efforts were destined to go to waste because of certain events happening that very instant in other parts of Madras.

~

On the tank bed below, the umpire finally stopped the match, much to the delight of Yadu's teammates. He declared the match a draw, as the light was insufficient to complete the game. The fielding side, who were by now completely exhausted, accepted the verdict without a murmur and shook hands graciously with the last two batsmen. Some of them had already collapsed onto the hard surface and were now relaxing contently, while a few others dashed off towards the exit gate and home. Yet another game of cricket had ended at the temple tank. Yadu sometimes wondered what the young boys in the locality would do without their 'stadium' – the temple tank. It was the only place in the vicinity where they could play cricket unhindered.

Triplicane, the area where Yadu lived, was one of the most densely populated parts of Madras. Over the years, poor town planning and a huge population had ensured that there were very few open grounds in the area where youngsters could play cricket. Yes, there were a couple of big grounds, but one had to walk a long distance to get to those grounds. Unlike other parts of the city, street cricket was not a viable option in Triplicane. The streets were very narrow and almost always crowded with people. Sunday afternoons were the only time when the streets were empty, and when cricket was possible. Thus, for the teenagers in the area, the tank-stadium was a godsend. Literally. Yadu and his friends had even given their 'stadium' a name. They called it the Lord Parthasarathy Cricket Stadium. Lord's for short.

He now watched as his teammates collected their gear and headed up to the exit gate. He considered for a moment whether he should intercept them and apologise for not turning up, but decided against it. He would see them later that night during the rathotsavam anyway. He could apologise then. That way he would be able to save an hour or two and use it for studying. After all his hard work and the sacrifices there was one thing Yadu fervently hoped for: that it wouldn't rain over the next few weeks.

That was the one thing that could destroy his carefully planned Christmas vacation.

In Madras, the monsoon arrived late. October to December were the rainy months. This year, there had not been much rain, which was why the tank bed was dry as cinder and made a perfect pitch. But the moment the rains started the tank would start filling. A couple of weeks of continuous downpour was usually sufficient for the tank to fill right up. And that usually meant that there would be no more cricket until March or April the following year. Christmas vacations would end up being a disaster. It had happened to Yadu in the past. The previous year he had spent all ten days of his vacation cooped up in his house because it had been raining heavily. What a waste that vacation had been! He just hoped this vacation would be better, since he had put in such an enormous effort into his exams. Yadu sprang up on his feet, climbed the five-six steps to the exit gate, and sat down on the tank bund. The lights on Car Street (the lane running around the perimetre of the tank) had just been turned on. A few seconds later, the floodlights erected on poles for the rathotsavam later that night, were switched on. A powerful blast of light now illuminated Yadu's house, which was across the tank, directly opposite to where he was seated. He could make out the silhouette of his paati through the kitchen window. She was tending to some task, holding Archana – Yadu's four-year-old sister – in her left arm.

As he watched, a familiar car drove up and stopped opposite his house. Ranganathan, Yadu's father, had arrived from office. Yadu watched as his father brusquely waved the company car away and then trudged slowly past the gate towards the house. Yadu stayed where he was to see if the second car would arrive today.

It didn't.

Perhaps it's not coming today, he thought. It was really a pity, because he had planned a nice little surprise for the occupants of that car today. His gaze now went back to his father. He felt a tinge of disappointment seeing him plod laboriously to the door. He had hoped that his father's depression would have lifted at least today, but his hunched back and general demeanour suggested otherwise. Ranganathan had not been his usual jovial self this past one week. He had withdrawn into a kind of a shell for some reason. Many a time this past week, Yadu had caught him looking deeply agitated. It was not just Yadu; paati had noticed it too. In fact they both had asked Ranganathan what the problem was. Something was troubling him no doubt. Usually his father told them if there was trouble. But this time no matter how many times they had asked he refused to tell them anything. He just kept mum. Preoccupied as he was with his studies Yadu didn't pursue the matter further with his father. He let things be hoping his father would be alright in a few days. But this morning he'd had two conversations, back to back, and what he had learned from them had shaken him to his very bones. So immersed had he been in his studies that he had failed to see certain things happening around his house for the last few days.

The first of these conversations he'd had was with Nadar, the grocery merchant, whose shop was three doors away. Yadu got chatting with him that morning when paati had sent him to the shop for provisions. He had casually mentioned his father's troubled appearance over the past one week. Nadar had said he'd noticed it too. The shopkeeper told him about the car he had seen following Ranganathan for the past one week or so. He claimed that this was the cause of his father's anxiety.

'It's a black Morris,' Nadar explained. 'You might have seen it too. It's been parked outside your house for the past three days.'

Yadu remembered seeing the vehicle. He had thought that the car had broken down or something. But Nadar claimed that nothing was wrong with it. He believed the occupants of the car had been spying on the house. Yadu had, of course, been shocked to hear this. He couldn't believe that he hadn't noticed all this. He had wanted to verify this immediately with his father, so he had run home with the provisions. Ranganathan, however, had already left for his office by then. He had asked his grandmother about the car. It came as a surprise that she had seen it too. Apparently, she had asked her son about it and he had asked her to mind her business. So she had dropped the matter and hadn't brought it up again. After his chat with Nadar and his paati that morning, Yadu had come to the conclusion that his father's agitated behaviour this past week was no doubt caused by the occupants of this car. He had decided to confront them if they ever came back. He had expected to find the Morris tailing his father's car this evening, but that hadn't happened.

Perhaps that's the last of the Morris and its occupants, he thought.

Yadu looked at his watch; it was five minutes past six. The tank bed and the steps wore a deserted look. Almost everybody had left. He decided it was time that he too went home. He jumped off the tank bund and started walking. The lane that Yadu had to take to reach his house was bustling with activity today. The pavement was already occupied by flower-sellers, beggars, hawkers, cloth merchants and toy sellers. They were all busy laying out their wares for business. The night of the rathotsavam was usually good for business because a lot of people gathered

on Car Street every year for the event. Yadu noticed that the place was teeming with police today. Though most of them were in mufti he had no problem recognising them. He passed by the Triplicane police station everyday on his way to school and he knew almost all the constables by sight. Yadu wondered if it was just his imagination but he thought he saw a hint of cautiousness about their activity this evening. They usually arrived only at 8 o'clock for crowd control duty. However, they were already here today, two hours early. They probably expected a larger crowd this year. Yadu watched as the constables carried the barricades to both ends of the lane on instructions from their inspector. In about an hour or so they would cordon off Car Street. No vehicles would be allowed inside for the duration of the procession. He understood well what this meant: even if the Morris arrived now, it would be evicted within an hour by the police. The occupants of the car wouldn't be able to spy on them from the comfortable confines of their vehicle today. They would have to come out into the open. If they came back today, Yadu knew he had a good chance of seeing these men face to face....
His reflections came to a screeching halt by what he saw at the other end of the lane. The car he had just been thinking about – *was back.*

2

The car cruised smoothly down the lane, slowed down near Nadar's shop, took a U-turn, and then came to a halt fifty metres from his house.

Yadu stopped walking and observed the car. The rascals were not done yet with their spying! They had come back for more. The confrontation he had just been thinking about seemed inevitable now. He had to find out what these men were up to. Why had they picked their house of all the houses to spy on? Yadu started walking towards the car with quick and long strides. One thing that gave him confidence was the timing. It couldn't have been better – with the lane swarming with policemen in mufti and all. Even if the car's occupants tried anything stupid he could call for help. He had nothing to be afraid of. A few minutes later, he was near the car. He couldn't see anything from behind as the rear window had been curtained off. He moved a little forward to see if he could peer through the side windows. But all he could see were the festival lights reflecting off the tinted glasses. He stood next to the car for a few seconds preparing his verbal assault. What happened next happened with such speed that it took Yadu completely by surprise.

All of a sudden the back door of the car opened abruptly, a hand reached for the scruff of his neck and pulled him inside with such force that it took the wind out of him. Yadu found himself inside the dark interiors of the car staring at a pair of cold, grey eyes. The man who held him – a bald Englishman with bushy eyebrows – looked menacing in the darkness. He was tall, powerfully built and his complexion was a sickly pinkish-yellow.

'You just saved us the trouble of coming after you,' the Englishman hissed in a low whisper. Yadu felt a chill run up his spine as he stared at the evil-spewing eyes of the stranger. It took him roughly ten seconds to get adjusted to the darkness inside. Besides the Englishman, there were two others in the car, both locals. Both were seated up front with their heads cocked straight ahead. The man in the driver's seat had long flowing hair and a thick beard. He had a slim frame and looked quite tall. The man seated in the passenger seat next to him was shorter but more robustly built. His shirtsleeves were folded right up to the top of his arms, and it revealed his bulging biceps. An amulet adorned his right arm.

'You are Ran-ga-natan's son, aren't you?' the Englishman asked. The man threw off a whisky-tobacco stench that Yadu found unbearable. He felt like throwing up and had to curb the instinct quickly.

'Let go of me,' Yadu shouted, struggling to get out of the Englishman's grasp.

Still holding Yadu by his scruff, the Englishman pulled out a switchblade from his back pocket, flicked it open and held it under Yadu's neck.

'You move so much as a muscle and I'll slit your throat,' the Englishman warned. 'Stay still.'

Yadu stopped struggling, even breathing for a few seconds. Then mustering up his courage, he asked, 'Who are you people? Why are you spying on us?'

'Name's Hardaker,' the man said in a tone that sent shivers down Yadu's spine. 'Ring a bell? Your father probably mentioned it over dinner last night, or the night before.'

The name did ring a bell, but it wasn't because his father had mentioned it. Yadu vaguely remembered reading a newspaper article about the man – an article he had not been able to finish because of the revulsion he'd felt. From what he remembered, this man was wanted by the police for torturing a witness in a case.

'He didn't?' Hardaker asked, surprised. 'It doesn't matter. What's important is your father knows who we are and what we are after.' After a brief pause the Englishman went on, 'Tell him we are done with him dilly-dallying things. We are coming for the details at six tomorrow morning. If we don't find him outside, at the front gate with the details, or if he attempts to go to the police, then the consequences will be *most* severe. His son might be run over by a car; his daughter, kidnapped. We can make his life a living hell and he knows that.'

The Englishman made a small slit on Yadu's neck from which blood instantly ran. Yadu winced in pain.

'Will you tell him that?' The Englishman was about to add something more, but at that moment things suddenly started going wrong for them. The man behind the wheel whipped his head around looking ashen-faced.

'Brian! *Police!*'

The Englishman frowned on hearing this. 'Where did the police come from?' he scowled.

He turned towards Yadu and stared at him, as if he suspected him of setting this up. 'They are in mufti and all over the street.'

Hardaker looked in front. 'They are putting up barricades.'

'Cool down, Sethu', said the man seated in the front passenger seat. 'The barricades are being put up for the function tonight. It's not for us.'

'Function?' Hardaker asked.

'It's the car festival, Brian. They usually cordon off the street for the night. Nothing to worry about.'

Sethu, the man in the driver's seat, didn't seem convinced by his friend's words. 'But the function doesn't start for another three hours, Dorai. They don't put up barricades so early. I have a bad feeling about this. Something's definitely wrong.'

'Nothing's wrong. You are imagining things,' said Dorai.

Sethu turned back in his seat to face Hardaker. 'Brian, take a look outside. Do you see those two moustaches who are looking this way? I am sure they are constables in mufti. I have seen them before.'

Hardaker lowered the glass halfway and peered outside. He still had not let go of Yadu's scruff. The Englishman was quiet for a couple of minutes. Then, upon seeing a man dressed in civil clothes approach the car, he suddenly jerked into action.

'You are right, Sethu. Start the car,' he barked with an urgency. 'Let's get the hell out of here.' As he spoke, he pushed open the door behind Yadu with his free hand. The car started, and Hardaker kicked Yadu hard on his chest, forcing him to tumble out of the moving car.

For a moment Yadu didn't know what hit him. One second he was seated inside the car with a switchblade at his neck and the next instant he was lying on the cold platform, the breath knocked out of him. He watched as the car picked up speed. It turned out that the man in civils who had been approaching the car was indeed a constable. The constable recognised a getaway immediately and threw himself onto the bonnet. Sethu swerved the car left and right in a bid to throw off the man. The constable held on bravely for about twenty seconds. When he eventually fell off, it was not because of Sethu's swerving, but because of the state of the road. The car hit a pothole and he got thrown to one side because of the unexpected jerk. A few constables now started running after the car. They swung their batons and tried to connect with the car's windows but weren't successful because it already had a head start. Yadu could feel blood trickle down his temple. He had hurt himself during the fall but he was least concerned about that. His eyes were locked on the fleeing car as it sped towards the barricades. A couple of more constables dressed in mufti, who were hanging around in vantage points, tried to bring the speeding car to a halt, but they too were unsuccessful. The car then slammed against the metal barricade sending it somersaulting to the left. Passersbys who were in the car's path ran helter-skelter.

Yadu was growing weaker and weaker. By the time the car reached the end of the lane he couldn't keep his eyes open any longer. He shut his heavy eyelids and passed out.

~

Yadu struggled to open his eyes. He could hear voices around him and guessed that a curious crowd had gathered around him. He felt claustrophobic and wheezed for air. Finally, he opened his eyes and his gaze fell first on Nadar. The grocer was using his hand cloth to stem the flow of blood from the wound on his forehead. Somebody else offered him a soda, which he was in no position to drink. He mumbled weakly to Nadar asking him to disperse the crowd so that he could get some fresh air; but his voice was lost in the crowd.

Yadu noticed a couple of they constables nearby trying hard to push the crowd back, but they were fighting a losing battle. Then, to Yadu's great relief, a police inspector arrived on the scene. He shouted and tried to shoo away the curious onlookers. But not a soul budged. The inspector then raised his voice and screamed harder, pushing them away from the pavement. But they came back, like fruit flies to a bruised mango. Yadu wondered what it was about an injured person that made people crowd around and gawk. He felt like a street performer performing in the nude. When stern warnings failed to disperse the crowd the inspector finally resorted to his baton. He started swinging it wantonly striking at whoever was nearest to him. The crowd stretched like an amoeba in different directions, depending on where he was attacking. After a few minutes the inspector gave up the lathi charge too because it did not have the desired effect. Panting slightly, he looked down at Yadu and grinned, 'Time for desperate measures,' he said, and winked. He stepped a little forward, cleared his throat, and then addressed the crowd. 'Listen up everybody. I need five volunteers from among you; five people who can come with me to the police station to sign a witness statement.'

Now, *this* had the desired effect. The words worked like magic. Even before the inspector had finished his sentence the people began to move away.

'Five volunteers. Just five volunteers,' the inspector repeated. The crowd of about twenty dwindled to less than five people within seconds.

'How about you sir, and you madam?' the inspector asked, but the last few people cast a quick glance at Yadu and then started rushing away pretending to be in a great hurry.

Only one man was still around. Nadar. He was helping Yadu sit up. Yadu looked up at the inspector and smiled wanly. 'Nice work, inspector.'

'Works every time,' he said dropping onto his knees beside Yadu. The inspector was a healthy looking man, middle-aged, and balding prematurely. He had a friendly face that Yadu warmed up to immediately.

'Are you hurt badly, young man?' the inspector asked. The nameplate on his chest read: Rafeeq Ahmad.

Yadu shook his head. The blood had stopped trickling from his forehead now, but Yadu still felt a heaviness inside his head. 'I am alright, thanks,' he said with a weak smile.

The inspector then turned to the shopkeeper. 'Nadar, do you know this boy?'

'Of course! He is Yadu, lives just across the street, there, in that house,' Nadar said pointing at a white building.

The inspector lit up a match and examined Yadu's wound and simultaneously issued a myriad orders to his constables. Yadu had by now sat up straight and was still feeling a bit groggy from the fall, but otherwise he was okay. The inspector patted Yadu lightly on his back and said, 'I have to talk to you about this incident, Yadu, but perhaps this is not the right time,' he said.

'I am alright, inspector. You can talk to me now if you like.'

'No, don't strain yourself. You go home now and relax for a few minutes. I'll come over to your house as soon as I am done here.'

Yadu shrugged. 'Okay.'

He got up. He was glad to find that other than the bruise on his forehead he hadn't had any injuries at all.

'I can get a couple of my constables to carry you to your house, if you can't make it on your own,' offered the inspector.

'Oh, no, there is no need for that,' Yadu said quickly. He surely didn't want to be carried to his house, temple-deity style. No way. He was not that badly injured anyway. 'I can manage on my own, thanks.'

Yadu thanked Nadar and the inspector and then started walking to his house. He reached the gate on the other side of the street and turned back. He noticed that the inspector and Nadar were still at the same spot. They were deeply engrossed in a conversation and didn't notice him. Yadu closed the gate and entered his compound.

3

Yadu was taken aback to see all three members of his family at the front door. His father, his grandmother, and his sister, Archana, had come out a few minutes earlier, having heard the commotion on the street. He walked past the garden towards them even as his father switched on the lights outside.

On either side of their front door was a thinnai, a raised platform with a roof, like a verandah but only much smaller. Ranganathan was leaning against one of the wooden pillars that kept the red-tile roof of the thinnai in place. His arms were folded in front of his chest. He was a decent looking man, forty-three years of age, lean, and fairly tall. His face was clean-shaven, and his black hair was neatly trimmed. He wore a pair of round, steel-rimmed glasses and had already changed from his work clothes into a *dhoti* and a full-sleeved white banian.

'What happened to you?' Ranganathan asked, seeing the bruise on his son's forehead. 'You are bleeding!'

Yadu sat down on the thinnai with his back resting against the wall. 'Don't worry. It's not as bad as it looks.' He noticed that his sister was on the verge of tears seeing the smears of blood on his face. He pulled her to him and patted her head playfully.

'That's what happens when you play cricket on the street,' paati scolded him.

Yadu gave her a bewildered look. 'I didn't get that playing cricket,' he said, but paati wasn't listening.

'How many times have I told you not to play with a *cover* ball?' she continued. She had taken Ranganathan's hand towel from his shoulder and had pushed him aside. She now stood in front of Yadu dabbing at the bruise with the towel. 'Now, would you have got that if you had played with a tennis ball?'

Yadu didn't even bother arguing. There was no point in trying to argue with his paati; he had learned that a long time back. Paati was examining the wound carefully. Realising that she needed some cotton wool, she disappeared inside taking Archana with her.

The moment paati went in, Ranganathan asked, 'What happened on the street, Yadu? What was all that commotion about?'

'I got kicked out of a speeding car.'

'You can't be serious!' Ranganathan said with an incredulous look on his face.

Yadu stared at his father for a few seconds. 'You know the car that you have been avoiding the last few days...' Ranganathan instantly looked away confirming Yadu's suspicions.

'I was just standing beside this car when all of a sudden the back door opened, and a hand pulled me inside. It was this Englishman, Brian Hard...Hard...'

'Hardaker. Go on; what did the rascal want?'

After a pause Yadu said, 'He wanted a message passed on to you.'

Ranganathan's apple bobbed up and down.

'He said he is coming for the details at six tomorrow morning,' Yadu repeated Brian Hardaker's threat verbatim.

Ranganathan moved back a little and sat down heavily on the thinnai on the left side. He began to sweat in spite of the cool evening breeze.

'Was there anybody else in the car?'

'Yes. Two local edupudis.'

'Then what happened?' Ranganathan asked.

'He wanted to say something else to me, but at that moment the guy in the driver's seat saw a policeman approaching the car, and he panicked. He started the car on Hardaker's instructions and as the car picked up speed, Hardaker kicked me out.'

'And you fell onto the pavement,' Ranganathan completed.

'That's exactly how it happened.'

'What about the car? Was the policeman successful in stopping it?'

'No,' said Yadu. 'He tried, but he got thrown over to one side. The lane was full of policemen today. Seeing me fall, the other policemen tried to bring the car to a stop, but they too were unsuccessful. The car just crashed right through the barricades like it happens in American films.'

Disappointment was writ large on Ranganathan's face. 'So Hardaker escaped then,' he murmured unhappily.

Yadu nodded. Ranganathan fell silent as he absorbed this piece of information.

Paati returned with the medicine chest. She took out some cotton and a couple of small bottles. Yadu watched in horror as she soaked a cotton ball thoroughly with some tincture solution. She then dabbed this ball on his wound. The pain shot through his body like lightning. Yadu grit his teeth to stop from screaming. Paati soaked another ball of cotton with tincture, and this time placed it on his neck wound. Again, the pain was unbearable.

'Looks like the ball hit you in two places,' paati commented, as she threw the cotton blobs away.

'Yes, paati. It ricocheted off my neck and then hit my forehead,' Yadu said dryly.

Paati stared at her grandson for a second wondering whether he was making fun of her. Seeing the deadpan expression on Yadu's face she decided that he was not and continued with her work. She now removed the cap off a bottle and applied some balm liberally to his wounds. Ranganathan and Yadu kept quiet for the next five minutes, waiting for paati to finish up and go inside. Once the balm was applied paati left for the kitchen with a firm warning to her grandson. 'If I ever catch you playing on the street with a cover ball you have had it, Yadu.' Yadu nodded to make her happy.

He turned to face his father. 'Are you going to tell me what all this is about?'

Ranganathan waved the question away, irritated. 'You are better off not knowing anything.'

'I am NOT better off, pa. I want to know who this man is and what he wants from you. Why are they spying on us? What is this "dilly-dallying" he was referring to?'

'Not now, Yadu. I'll tell you later.'

'No way, appa. You are going to tell me *right now* what this is about.'

Ranganathan happened to look up just then. His eyes drifted to the street and he noticed that a police inspector was approaching their gate.

'What's he coming here for?' Ranganathan asked.

'That's Inspector Rafeeq. He told me he was coming to see me about the car incident.'

Ranganathan's face changed colour immediately when he heard this. 'Oh my God! Yadu, have you told him anything about what happened inside the car?'

'N...No. I didn't get a chance,' Yadu said.

Ranganathan looked relieved upon hearing this. 'Thank God for that,' he said. He then turned serious. 'Now listen very carefully, Yadu. The inspector is bound to ask you questions about what happened inside the car. Under no circumstances will you tell him about Hardaker's threat.'

Yadu couldn't believe what he had just heard. 'But that's ridiculous,' he protested. 'It's a *death* threat, pa. We ought to tell the police about it so that they can nab Hardaker.'

Ranganathan shook his head vehemently. 'I repeat, Yadu, do not tell him anything Hardaker told you inside the car. The inspector shouldn't suspect that I know Hardaker.'

'But why?'

'I have my reasons, believe me. I'll explain everything to you later; I promise.'

'I...I just don't believe that you are asking me to do this. That man has been hounding you all week, appa. Have you forgotten? This is our chance to tell the police and have him nabbed.'

Ranganathan was positively angry by now. 'Yadu, you just do what I say. I know what I am doing,' he said, gritting his teeth.

Yadu shrugged his shoulders in resignation. He decided to obey his father and see what happens. He mumbled out the words, 'Okay, as you wish. I won't tell the inspector about the threat. Are you happy now?' and turned his face away to watch the approaching policeman. But the very next instant something occurred to him and he turned back and asked, 'But what do I tell him then? He'll surely want to know why Hardaker pulled me into the car.'

Ranganathan sighed as if he was disappointed with his son. 'Use your imagination, Yadu. Lie to him. Tell him...tell him that he pulled you in to kidnap you. I am sure he'd believe that.'

Yadu wasn't sure whether that approach would work with Rafeeq. He would have to wait and see.

4

'Good evening. My name is Rafeeq Ahmad,' the inspector said, extending his arm to Yadu's father.

'I am Ranganathan.' They shook hands.

Yadu went inside and fetched a wooden chair for the inspector.

'How are you feeling, young man?' he asked Yadu as he took his seat.

'A lot better, thanks.'

Ranganathan sat down on the thinnai opposite the policeman and Yadu, with his back to the wall.

Rafeeq looked at Ranganathan briefly. 'Did he tell you what happened out there?' he asked.

Ranganathan nodded.

'Let's get straight to business then. Yadu, I want to hear your version of what happened.'

'Were you in the vicinity when it all started, inspector?' Yadu asked tentatively. He wanted to know how much the inspector had seen before he started lying.

'I was very much there but at the other end, by the barricades. I didn't see what happened opposite your house. That's why I want you to fill me up on what happened here.'

Yadu said, 'Well, I was returning home from the tank when I saw this car parked in front of our house. I was curious and just as I was walking past it, somebody pulled me into the car.'

'Go on, what happened after that?' the inspector asked.

'The man who pulled me inside removed a switchblade and held it to my neck, and asked me to remain quiet. Then...'

The inspector interrupted Yadu. 'How many people were inside the car?'

'There were three of them: one Englishman and two locals.'

'Do you know their names?'

'The Englishman's name was Hardaker...Brian Hardaker. One of the men in front was called Dorai.' Yadu thought for a few seconds. 'I can't seem to recall the other man's name.'

'Never mind. Have you seen any of these men before?'

'No'

'What did they want from you?'

'I didn't have the chance to find out. They had chosen the wrong moment to pull me in, because just a couple of minutes later a policeman approached the car.'

'What do *you* think they wanted from you?'

Yadu glanced momentarily at his father who nodded his head ever so slightly. 'I...I don't know. I think their intention was to kidnap me. It didn't work out though, because of the policeman's unexpected arrival.'

'You mean they saw the policeman and decided to abandon the attempt.'

'Yes. It was not just the policeman. The driver saw the barricades being put up and he panicked. He thought it was a trap meant for them. And when moments later the policeman came towards the car, they just abandoned the attempt, kicked me out of the car and fled.'

The inspector frowned upon hearing this. He uncrossed his legs and leaned forward. 'Tell me Yadu, did you have a good look at these men? Would you be able to identify them if the necessity arose?'

'The Englishman I can identify, I am quite confident of that. But the other two, I am not so sure. It was dark inside and I just had a fleeting glimpse of their faces.'

'And you think their intention was to kidnap you?'

'Yes.'

The inspector now turned his attention on Ranganathan. Yadu let out a quiet sigh of relief.

'What do you do for a living, Mr Ranganathan?'

'I am an officer with the RBI.'

'You work for the Reserve Bank? That's interesting,' the inspector said with raised eyebrows. 'Now, sir, do you know anybody by the name of Hardaker or Dorai?'

Ranganathan shook his head. 'No.'

Rafeeq Ahmad rubbed his brow thoughtfully. 'Are you sure you don't know this Englishman?'

Ranganathan grimaced. 'I've told you already, I don't know who he is. This is the first time I've heard this name.'

The inspector held out his palms in a pacifying gesture. 'Relax, Mr Ranganathan. I only asked you that question again for confirmation. I find your statements contrary to my findings, so it's my job to check.'

Ranganathan leaned forward. 'What findings? What are you talking about?' he demanded.

The inspector scratched his cheeks lazily, wondering what the best way to put the information across was. 'Just before I came here,' he began, 'I had a quick chat with Nadar. He told me that this particular car has been following you around for nearly a week now. He said the car stood opposite your house for over twenty-four hours the other day. He believes that the car's occupants have been spying on your house. And you say that you don't know who they are. Do you expect me to believe that, sir?'

Yadu watched his father fidget nervously.

'I have seen these men from a distance, that's all. But I don't know who they are or what they want.'

The inspector now pulled out a notebook from his back pocket and went through its contents for a brief moment. 'So why were these men camped outside your house, Mr Ranganathan? Why were they camped here for twenty-four straight hours?'

'How would I know? They didn't tell me why they were hanging around here.'

'But you knew they were outside your house, didn't you?'

Ranganathan admitted to this. 'Yes, I did.'

'Then why didn't you confront them and just ask?' the inspector asked matter-of-factly. 'If somebody had parked a car outside my house and had stood there for twenty-four hours, I would surely have gone outside and asked them what they were up to.'

There was a pause as Ranganathan thought of a reasonable answer to this reasonable question. He took his time. Once he decided his course of action he sighed heavily.

'I was afraid of approaching them because they looked like thugs to me. I didn't want any trouble, that's all.'

'Okay. Even so, why didn't you approach the police if you were afraid of confronting them? We would have knocked them around a bit and found out what they wanted.'

Ranganathan paused once again. It was obvious that he felt like a trapped rabbit. And Yadu could see that these frequent pauses were making the inspector suspicious.

'I...,' Ranganathan cleared his throat, and continued, 'I just thought that if I ignored them for long enough they would get fed up and go away.'

The inspector spread his arms wide. 'What can I say, Mr Ranganathan... You don't sound very convincing.' He pulled out a pen from his pocket and started scribbling something into his notebook.

Yadu knew that his father had made a big mistake by lying to the policeman. His father had tied himself into a nice little knot.

The inspector now turned his attention on Yadu. 'Yadu, are you sure you have told me everything that happened in the car?'

'Yes, I have,' said Yadu confidently.

'You have not held back anything?'

'No, I haven't.'

Inspector Rafeeq nodded. He remained quiet for a while looking from father to son, then son to father. Yadu could sense that the inspector knew that they were both lying. He was very annoyed with his father for having put him in such a tight spot. He hated lying, especially to the police. And if there was one thing he hated more than lying it was getting *caught* at it. He promised himself that he would get to the bottom of what it was that his father was hiding. Yadu, tired of sitting with his back against the wall, moved away from the wall to the edge of the thinnai and sat with his legs dangling. The inspector too got up to stretch his legs. Suddenly he spotted something that interested him. He pushed back his chair and walked up to the place where Yadu was seated.

'That slit in your neck looks fresh. How did you get that?'

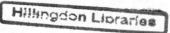

Yadu froze. He had hoped the inspector wouldn't notice it. His mind raced to find a suitable answer to the question.

'I...uh...I attempted foolishly to escape out of Hardaker's hands. This was the prize I got for it,' Yadu said, laughing nervously.

There was not a flicker of emotion in Rafeeq's face. He stared at Yadu wondering whether or not to believe what he was saying.

'Why did you not tell me about this before?' the inspector queried. 'You never mentioned about your escape bid until this moment.'

'I thought it was obvious,' Yadu said, recovering his wits in time. 'I told you already that Hardaker held a switchblade to my neck. I thought you would put two and two together and conclude that Hardaker slit my neck slightly when I tried to escape.'

Yadu was relieved to find that Rafeeq seemed to accept this answer, however shoddy it was. He hoped that the inspector would now walk back to his chair and sit down because the inspector's presence near him was quite unsettling. He had shed his friendly mask and was interrogating them as if they were common criminals. Yadu hoped this ordeal would end soon. The inspector finally moved away from Yadu. He thrust both his hands into his trouser pockets and walked to where Ranganathan was seated.

'Why are you wasting your time like this?' Ranganathan asked the inspector. 'This is an open and shut case. My son explained what happened: Hardaker tried to kidnap him, but to his bad luck a policeman appeared on the scene, so he abandoned the attempt and sped away. All is well that ends well. Why are you breaking your head over it?' he said in one breath.

Inspector Rafeeq smiled. 'I really wish it were that simple, Mr Ranganathan. My instinct however tells me it

is not. There is more to this incident than meets the eye.'
He glanced at his watch then went back to sit down on his
chair. 'Forgive me for asking, Mr Ranganathan, but how
are you doing financially? Are you quite wealthy?'

Ranganathan smirked. 'No, I am not. I am a salaried
civil servant, like I told you earlier.'

'That's what I thought. Your son suspects that Hardaker
tried to kidnap him. I think we can safely assume that
kidnapping was not the motive here. I know from experience
that Hardaker takes only big jobs. If his motive was to
kidnap for money, then he would have rather picked a
boy from a wealthy family, don't you think?'

Ranganathan had to admit: the inspector had a valid
point. 'Quite true,' he said nodding his head. 'He wouldn't
have got much from me by way of ransom, that's for
sure.'

'Yes. And if kidnapping was his motive why did he kick
him out of the car? He could have held onto Yadu and
could have still made the getaway.'

Ranganathan and Yadu remained silent.

'See? I told you there is more to this than meets the
eye. Kidnapping Yadu for ransom couldn't have been the
motive. So why was Hardaker here then? Why did he pull
Yadu into the car?'

The inspector paused. 'What did he want from you,
Yadu?' he asked moments later.

Yadu subdued his urge to squirm and struggled to
answer this question. 'Like I said before inspector, I don't
know. I never had a chance to find out.'

The inspector removed his cap and laid it to rest on his
lap. 'Both of you listen very carefully to what I am about
to say. This man, Hardaker, is no ordinary criminal. He is
evil...*seriously* evil. Hardaker is the most wanted man in
the state today. And if he has been hanging around your

house all this while then rest assured he is up to something.' The inspector waited for this piece of information to sink in, then said, 'I have told you who you are up against. I'll ask you one last time: Why was he camped outside your house?'

Ranganathan maintained a straight face. 'My answer remains the same inspector. I haven't a clue.'

The inspector shook his head in disgust. 'You are a stubborn man, Mr Ranganathan,' he declared angrily. 'You are going to regret this sooner or later.'

Ranganathan snorted at this threat. 'Tell me inspector, if that man is so dangerous what is taking the police so long to put him behind bars?'

'We are doing our best, Mr Ranganathan. But this man, he is an ex-British spy. Knows all the tricks of the trade. Trying to catch him is like trying to catch an eel in a tub of oil.'

'But he is British and most of the British have left. So he must stick out like a sore thumb wherever he goes. It must be easy capturing him now.'

'It is not, let me assure you. It is never easy catching a criminal as professional as Hardaker. Most of the time he works behind the scenes. He gets all his footwork done by his local associates. How can we capture him when we don't even see him for months? Today was one of those very rare occasions when he graced the streets of Madras, and luckily I found out about it.'

Yadu did a double take. 'You mean you knew Hardaker was coming here today?'

'Yes. I got a tip this afternoon from an anonymous informer. That's how I was able to set up a trap for him.'

It all made sense to Yadu suddenly. 'Is that why you brought the barricades up so early today?' Yadu asked.

'Yes. The barricades, the policemen in mufti, the extra policemen on Car Street – they were all arranged for nabbing Hardaker. It was not for the procession as everybody on the street thought.'

Yadu now realised that the driver of the car had indeed been right in his assumption that it was a trap. What a sharp man! thought Yadu.

The inspector was saying, '...but in spite of all my effort and preparation...he escaped. It won't be long before he gets caught though. I have alerted the police control room and have given them the vehicle registration number.'

'You think they might be able to intercept him?' Yadu asked hopefully.

'I hope so. In the meanwhile if the car comes back, Mr Ranganathan, I want you to inform the police. Will you do that?'

Both Yadu and his father nodded. The inspector seemed satisfied. He spent the next couple of minutes writing something into his notebook. Having done that he thrust the note into his back pocket and got up from his chair. 'I must be going now,' the inspector said, placing his cap back on his head. 'But before I go, Yadu, I need a favour.'

'Tell me, inspector,' Yadu said, getting up.

'I want you to pay a visit to the police station when you are feeling better.'

'What for?' Ranganathan asked, springing to his feet.

'I need him to sign the F.I.R. and identify Hardaker's henchmen from our file photos. Is that okay with you, Yadu?'

'Sure, no problem,' Yadu said. 'I can come with you now if you like.'

'Alright, come on then,' said Inspector Rafeeq.

Yadu asked his father if it was okay for him to go to the police station with the inspector. Ranganathan didn't seem too happy with the idea. But since he had no grounds on which to object he mumbled an okay. He shook hands with the inspector perfunctorily and then went into the house. Yadu put on his chappals and then followed the inspector back to his jeep.

5

The formalities at the police station took Yadu twenty-five minutes. He was back on the street opposite his house by a quarter past eight. He walked slowly down the street looking for the car. He was glad when he couldn't spot it anywhere. Good riddance! he thought as he opened the front gate of his house.

The house was nearly fifty years old. His grandfather had built it at the turn of the century. It had a sloping red tile roof, and its walls had just recently been whitewashed. It was a pretty large house, single storied, but spread over a large area. Ranganathan had given away one portion of the house on rent since the house was too big for just the four of them. He knocked forcefully on the heavy door. It took about five minutes for paati to finally open the door. She was a little hard of hearing, and if she was in the kitchen she sometimes couldn't hear the front door being knocked. Many a time visitors waited in vain for the door to open. Yadu had told his grandma in the past not to keep the front door locked all the time. Paati's health was failing. She was just over seventy and he feared that she might fall ill or collapse one of these days. If the front door was locked then no one would even know that she required medical help. Yadu's father too shared this fear. But paati was unmoved by their arguments. She was a woman of a different era and was mortally frightened of keeping the front door open all the time. Paati had heard the knock this time though. She unbolted the door and threw it open.

'Go straight to the bathroom and have a bath,' she instructed him, even before he had set foot inside. She looked every bit over seventy. She had already lost most of her teeth and the many years she had spent leaning over the kitchen fires had made her a hunchback. She was heavily dependent on her walking stick now. And, like most older widows of her community, she too had tonsured her head. Paati's preferred garment was a faded peach, cotton saree which she wore without a blouse, part of which she draped over her shaven head. Yadu called it her uniform because every single saree in her possession was of the exact same colour.

'Why should I have a bath?' Yadu asked, bewildered.

'You have been to the police station, that's why. You have treaded the same ground that murderers and criminals have. You are polluted now and you need to have a bath.'

Yadu gave her a bemused look, but didn't say anything. He walked past her and went straight to the sunken courtyard at the centre of the house. He washed his hands and feet by the well. Paati, who was standing by a wooden pillar, watched him with a look of disbelief on her face. 'You are not going to have that bath then,' she said. 'There is no respect for age and wisdom in this house. Nobody ever listens to me these days.'

'Oh paati, don't get dramatic. Of course I respect you,' Yadu said in a placatory tone.

'But sometimes you take your tradition a bit too seriously. Imagine if everybody had a bath every time they went to a police station there would be a water crisis in Madras. Inspector Rafeeq would have to carry a bathtub around with him all the time.' Yadu found this image rather funny and laughed, irritating his grandmother even more.

'Tease me, Yadu. Tease me all you like. That's what I am here for – to be poked fun at.' Saying this, paati walked off in a huff in the direction of the kitchen.

'Paati,' Yadu called out behind her, but it fell on deaf ears. Partially deaf ears, actually.

Yadu sat down on the corridor that ran around the perimetre of the courtyard and wiped his hands and feet. He noticed his father and sister coming out of the kitchen hand in hand. Yadu was greatly relieved to see a smile on his father's face. At last, he thought. It looked like his cute little sister had achieved the impossible. Ranganathan seemed to have forgotten all his worries – at least momentarily. Yadu watched as his father scooped Archana up and flung her into the air. His sister gave a whoop of joy when he caught her inches off the ground. She demanded an encore and her father readily gave in. Deep inside, Yadu always felt intensely sorry for his kid sister. He was twelve when his mother had died, but he was thankful that he had at least known her. Archana, the poor girl, had never even seen her mother. There wasn't a day that passed without Yadu seeing his kid sister and feeling a pang of guilt. In a way he was responsible for Archana not having a mother. Though others gave it a different name, he knew that it was he who had killed his mother. If he hadn't played that nasty trick on her that evening, perhaps she would still be alive...

Four years back, Yadu and his mother – who was then heavily pregnant with Archana – had gone to the temple tank one evening. Yadu had just completed his swimming lessons. Taking him to the swimming pool everyday was physically impossible for his pregnant mother, so she would take him to the temple tank opposite their house for him to practice. The water was just twelve feet deep and there were always people about, so safety was not an issue. On that fateful evening, Yadu swam quietly under the watchful eyes of his mother. After some time though he got bored, because he was the only one swimming in the tank that evening. In a fit of boredom Yadu decided to play a prank on his mother – a prank that was to cost her her life...

When she was not looking, Yadu slipped farther and farther away from the steps. About twenty feet away from the steps he suddenly started flaying his arms wildly, pretending that he was drowning. His mother didn't notice it for the first few seconds because of the fading light. But then she heard his cry for help. She shot up from the steps like a spring, panic flooding through her veins. At this point, Yadu, glad that he had frightened his mother, stopped flaying his arms. But she did not notice this. Perhaps it was the low light or the low turnout of people on the steps that evening – he couldn't be sure, but his mother had *completely* flipped. She ran down the steps blindly, her mind in turmoil, and slipped on the green moss covering the steps. Yadu, floating a little distance away, watched in horror as his mother fell heavily on the steps, half her body in the water, and the other half on the step. Blood drained from his face as Yadu swam furiously towards the steps hoping and praying that his mother was not hurt badly.

But she was.

Mrs Ranganathan had hurt her abdomen region very badly. The doctors informed them that she had to be operated upon immediately. It was initially assumed that the baby would die and Yadu's mother would survive. But the opposite happened. The baby – Archana – survived miraculously, but Yadu's mother died during delivery.

Yadu shuddered involuntarily. He did that every time he thought of those terrible few moments. He wiped away the thin film of tears that had begun to blur his vision. It had been four years since his mother's demise but he still hadn't come to terms with the tragedy. He could see that his father and paati had recovered substantially and went on with their lives. But his guilt made it difficult to forget his mother. Sometimes he wondered how different life would have been if only he hadn't played that prank on his mother. In all these years Yadu had never been able to muster up the courage to tell his father and paati what really happened that evening. Both of them were still under the impression that she had accidentally slipped and had fallen. They still didn't know that it was he who was responsible for her fall. He was too ashamed to tell them about his role in the whole tragedy. And so, to this day it had remained his secret. Nobody, not even Shaji, his closest friend, knew of this.

Archana's tinkling silver anklets jerked Yadu out of his reverie. Having noticed her brother, she loosened herself from Ranganathan's grasp and rushed straight into Yadu's welcoming arms. She quickly clambered on top of his legs and then started pinching his cheeks. Yadu howled in mock-agony to the delight of his little sister. She then methodically started pulling at his facial parts: first the nose, then the ear and then the eyelashes. Yadu obliged by screaming in a different pitch each time. She played with her brother for about ten minutes but soon lost interest and went looking for paati. He watched as she danced her way into the kitchen to trouble her grandmother. Yadu decided to go up to his room. Halfway to the staircase he remembered that he didn't get a chance to talk to his father because of Inspector Rafeeq's untimely arrival.

Yadu reached his father's study a few seconds later. He knocked and then entered.

6

Ranganathan was seated in his swivel chair, his back facing the door. His eyes were fixed blankly at the wall opposite him. Yadu walked up to the chair and plopped down noisily on it forcing his father to snap out of his thoughts.

Ranganathan swiveled around, mildly irritated. 'Oh, it's you. How did it go at the station?'

'It went okay. I identified Hardaker's henchmen for the inspector.'

'Did he trouble you?'

'He treated me rather well, actually.'

Ranganathan looked surprised upon hearing this. He murmured something under his breath that didn't quite reach Yadu's ears.

'Don't you want to know the names of Hardaker's henchmen?' Yadu asked, placing a cushion behind him so he could rest his back on it.

'What are their names?' Ranganathan asked. His tone suggested that he didn't care what their names were.

'The driver was a man by the name of Sethu. The one by his side was called Dorai.' Yadu watched his father nod sagely upon hearing the names. 'You already knew that, didn't you?' Yadu asked. Ranganathan nodded again.

'You know, while I was at the police station, Rafeeq showed me the police reports on Dorai and Hardaker. He was telling the truth. These people are extremely dangerous.'

Ranganathan smiled mournfully. 'I know.'

'So tell me, pa, what are these dangerous criminals doing outside our house?'

Ranganathan looked away, evading his son's gaze deliberately.

'I am beginning to think that you are involved in some nefarious scheme with Hardaker,' said Yadu flatly.

Ranganathan brought his gaze back on his son. His eyes looked deeply hurt. He studied his son's face for a second, deliberating, debating whether to tell or not to tell. He then sighed heavily in a gesture of resignation.

'Hardaker is *blackmailing* me, Yadu,' Ranganathan said softly.

Yadu felt a lump take shape in his throat.

'Hardaker is after some confidential information I have in my possession. The man knows I work for the Reserve Bank,' his father said. 'For the past one week he's been threatening to kill you and Archana if I don't provide him with the details he seeks.'

A chill shot through Yadu's body the moment he heard his sister's name. '*Aiiyo Kadavule*,' he cried.

'He wants the information within the next couple of days. That's why he has been stalking me night and day.'

Yadu's brow furrowed in perplexity. 'What kind of information is the man seeking?'

Ranganathan was silent. Yadu stared at his father not knowing what to make of this silence.

'He has somehow got to know of a 'reissuables' transfer and he wants me to give him the date of transfer.'

Yadu stared at his father blankly.

'The Reserve Bank has to routinely transfer large amounts of cash from city to city, from branch to branch, based on market needs. I am in charge of all such transfers from Madras.'

'Since when?' Yadu asked.

'Since August. I have been working in the Issue department as a currency officer for the last four months. I am the one in the bank now who decides the date and time of these physical transfers, the mode of transport, and I coordinate security for the transfer. In short, I am solely responsible for the movement of all heavy cash in and out of Madras.'

'You never told us about this new responsibility of yours,' Yadu complained.

It had been four months since his father had been entrusted with this responsibility and he hadn't mentioned this even once.

'I am sworn to secrecy, Yadu. When you have a job like this you don't want the world to know what you do. I shouldn't have told even you this, but I can't keep this a secret after what happened to you this evening.'

'It's a *huge* responsibility,' Yadu remarked.

'It is. Can you imagine the consequences if word leaked out about a huge city-to-city transfer? Criminals are always all ears for information such as this. The moment they hear of such a shipment they will prepare for an ambush and before you and I can bat an eyelid they'll vanish with the money.'

Considering the tension and the vagaries of the job he held, Yadu wondered how his father's hair was still as dark as it was. 'So, this is the confidential bank information that Hardaker is blackmailing you for,' Yadu said.

'Yes,' said Ranganathan with a sigh. 'There is some money being transferred from the Madras RBI to Coimbatore next week. He wants to know the date and time of transfer so that he can rob the cash.'

Yadu shook his head in disbelief. 'But how did Hardaker find out that you dealt with these transfers?'

Ranganathan shrugged his shoulders lamely and said, 'Only God knows how he found out. I suspect he's got a source inside the RBI, somebody very high up who's given him this information.'

Yadu sat with his fingers on his mouth. He couldn't believe what he had just heard. 'Do you suspect anybody in particular?'

'It must be one of my superiors. I don't know which one though.'

Yadu removed the cushion from behind him and dropped it on his lap. He placed his elbows on the pillow and leaned forward, deep in thought. 'Have you discussed your situation with anyone at the office?'

'You don't understand the implications, Yadu. Hardaker has warned me that if I breathe a word about him to the police, or anybody else, he will have Archana's throat slit. Now just picture this: what if I go to my boss and explain my situation and he's the one who put Hardaker onto me in the first place? I can't put Archana in harm's way, ever,' he said firmly.

Yadu threw the cushion aside and sat on the bed in the corner of the room with his legs pulled up. He thought quietly about what his father had just said. He was right of course. Yadu felt a stab of pity seeing his father seated forlornly on the chair. Now that he knew what was troubling his dad, Yadu felt that his father's behaviour over the past week was entirely justified. With one eye fixed on his dad Yadu mulled over the problem. He still felt that the police and Inspector Rafeeq were their best bet. He tried putting this thought across subtly to his father.

'You know, appa, Inspector Rafeeq asked me to remind you that you are free to approach him anytime, if at all you decide to open up.'

Ranganathan snorted upon hearing this. 'That's never going to happen.'

'I wonder why you mistrust the police so much. They are here to help us. You must understand that first.'

Ranganathan got up from his chair and pushed it behind. He pulled up his dhoti and folded it so that it came up to his knees.

'I mistrust them because they are inept, inefficient, and incapable,' he said. He started pacing up and down the room now. Yadu couldn't help noticing that the very word 'police' had sent his father into a tizzy.

'You ought to give them a chance before you pass a judgment like that. They are not all that bad you know,' Yadu countered.

Ranganathan walked up to the bed, bent down, and looked squarely at Yadu. 'I already gave them a chance and they blew it.' He walked away deciding not to say anything more. All of a sudden he changed his mind and came back to the bed. 'Inspector Rafeeq mentioned getting a tip this afternoon from an anonymous police informer. Who do you think the informer was?'

The way Ranganathan had framed the question, there was no doubt in Yadu's mind as to who the informer must have been. But he kept quiet allowing his father the satisfaction of answering the question himself.

'It was *me*!' Ranganathan said, stabbing at his chest with his forefinger. 'I risked Archana's life and called to tell him of Hardaker's whereabouts. I gave him the exact location and the exact time. I even told him how many people there were in the car.' Ranganathan's face looked flushed now. He started pacing the room once again. 'And what did Rafeeq do with this chance that I gave him? He blew it *sky-high*,' he said, sending his hands flying up into the air once again.

Yadu felt like he had just been hit by a bouncer. In the light of this revelation though, a lot of things suddenly made sense to him. He now understood why his father had refused to cooperate with the inspector. Ranganathan was obviously angry with the policeman for having let Hardaker slip away.

'So *you* tipped off Rafeeq then,' Yadu said.

'Yes, I was hoping that he would be caught and put away once and for all. But I underestimated Hardaker and overestimated police capability. So many policemen on the lane and they couldn't stop *one* car. They'll never get a better chance than this to capture Hardaker. I had defied Hardaker's warning and informed the police and nothing came of it. I didn't want to antagonise Hardaker any further. That's why I clammed up.'

Ranganathan stopped pacing and sat on the bed, a couple of feet away from his son. He had a worried look on his face. 'Yadu, you don't know how afraid I am right now. If Hardaker figures out that I was the one who informed the police...and you say he is coming at six...'

Yadu could see that his father was on the verge of cracking up. The pressure he was feeling was palpable. Yadu felt inadequate for not knowing what to say to console his father. For want of better words to break the awkward silence Yadu asked the first question that popped into his mind.

'This shipment that Hardaker is after – is it a huge one?' This question was like a life buoy thrown to a drowning man. Ranganathan latched onto it gratefully and plunged into an explanation, narrowly escaping the embarrassment of crying out in front of his son.

'It is a huge one,' Ranganathan said, sniffing back his tears. 'About twenty-five lakh rupees worth of reissuables and fifteen lakh rupees of brand new currency and coins ore being transported. Hardaker, through his source, has found out where it is headed, but he doesn't know when and how it leaves.'

'How is it being transported? By van?' Yadu asked.

'No. Since the shipment is huge we are sending it by a special coach. The coach is being attached to the Mangalore Express. The coach will be dropped off midway, at Coimbatore.'

'What about security personnel?'

'There will be two armed escorts on the train. I don't know how effective they will be though if Hardaker comes with a big gang.'

'When is the coach being sent to Coimbatore?'

'Tomorrow evening.'

'*Tomorrow evening?*' Yadu asked surprised. 'And Hardaker still doesn't know this?'

'No,' said Ranganathan.

'Why don't you dilly-dally for a couple of days?' suggested Yadu. 'And then you can tell him the shipment has already gone to Coimbatore.' He realised how silly his words sounded the instant they left his mouth.

'How do you think Hardaker will react to being foiled thus? Do you think he'll take it lying down? Who do you think he'll take it out on?'

'On Archana,' Yadu admitted in a whisper.

'Exactly. And don't forget, there are always other shipments leaving for other cities. He'll just bide his time and one fine day I'll have to give him the transfer details of some shipment or the other. There is no escape – even if I resign from my job now. I am trapped.'

Yadu scratched his head in irritation. Was there really no way out? Did he not know anybody who could provide a solution to this problem of theirs?

His thoughts were interrupted by another consideration. He looked up at his father. 'What if you gave Hardaker the information? What will be the repercussions then?'

Ranganathan smiled ruefully. 'The day after the robbery the police will be at my door to arrest me, because it'll be obvious to them that it's an inside job. They'll know somebody inside the RBI has provided the exact date of the transfer to the robbers. That somebody can be only me because I decide the dates.'

Yadu asked, 'Is there no way out of this situation then?'

'The only way out is for me to commit suicide,' said Ranganathan gravely.

'Don't talk like that, pa. We'll find a solution soon.' To an eavesdropper this would have sounded comforting, but in reality Yadu's insides had turned to ice upon hearing his father's solution. He knew that his father wasn't kidding. Ranganathan had in the past displayed a suicidal streak. In his lifetime, every time events had spiralled out of his control he had contemplated suicide: when his wife had passed away, for instance. And Yadu knew another aspect about his father that increased his fear. Ranganathan was a man who valued his self-respect more than his life. If he got jailed he would surely take his life, unable to bear the shame.

For the next fifteen minutes father and son discussed every one of their options thread bare. It was decided in the end that their one and only choice was to stall Hardaker when he came the next day. Yadu suggested that he should ask for a two-day grace period to find the transfer dates. By that time the Coimbatore consignment would have gone. They would then have at least till next month to plan their next move. Ranganathan was not sure whether this would work, but he decided to try nevertheless.

Their conversation ended when Ranganathan looked up at the clock and noticed that it was half past nine.

'You better go have dinner, Yadu.'

Yadu nodded and got up. He straightened the pillow and set right the bedsheet. 'Aren't you coming?' he asked.

'I told your paati that I'll be skipping dinner tonight. You go ahead,' Ranganathan said. Yadu got up and then walked towards the door. Just as he reached the door Ranganathan called out to him. 'Listen, Yadu. Not a word about all this to your paati. I don't want her upset, do you understand?'

Yadu nodded.

'And rub that gloomy expression off your face. Look happy and try to keep her in good humour. She already suspects that something's wrong.'

Yadu wanted to tell him that if he had practiced this himself paati would never have suspected anything in the first place. But it was not his place to advise his father. So he murmured saying he would try his best, and then walked out of the door.

7

Inside the spacious but dimly-lit kitchen, paati was busy
serving rice and vegetables onto a plantain leaf laid out
on the floor.

Inside the spacious but dimly-lit kitchen, paati was busy
serving rice and vegetables onto a plantain leaf laid out
on the floor. Archana was lying on a blanket in one corner
of the kitchen. She was yet to fall asleep. His grandmother
wasn't making eye contact and Yadu realised that she was
still angry with him. Yadu pushed away all his tension
and worries for the moment and decided to have a little
fun with his grandma.

'You are looking very tired, paati. Another long day in
the kitchen?' Yadu asked in a teasing manner.

'Of course it's been a long day,' patti lashed back. 'One of
these days I'll die in the kitchen cooking for all of you.'

He heard Archana giggle.

Yadu had learnt a long time back not to take his
grandmother's whining seriously. In the beginning he used
to get extremely worried every time his paati moaned
about her workload. After the death of his mother, not
only did paati have to handle the running of the house
but she also had to shoulder the responsibility of bringing
up little Archana. She was, of course, helped considerably
by Yadu and his father. But she always moaned that what
they were doing was just not enough. And Yadu felt very
sad every time she said that. But as the months passed
by, Yadu realised that paati's moaning was actually an act

put on by her to persuade her son to remarry. Paati's idea was that Yadu – and more importantly -- Archana, needed a mother. She had been shrewd enough to realise that her son would never remarry for his own sake but there was a slim chance of him remarrying if she complained constantly about the amount of work she had to do all day. Her reasoning had been that, Ranganathan unable to see his mother suffer would consider remarrying to reduce her burden. But so far, Ranganathan had turned a blind eye to her 'suffering'.

Even as he gulped down the food, Yadu, who *loved* making his grandmother angry, continued to tease her. 'Have you made any paayasam for dinner paati?' he asked, anticipating a whiplash reaction.

'No,' came the curt reply, as paati squatted on the floor a little distance away.

'Oh paati, you are becoming very lazy these days. All day long you do nothing but sleep. Can't you at least make some paayasam once in a while?' Yadu asked with a mischievous glint in his eyes.

Paati grabbed a stick lying by her side and tried to hit Yadu's thigh with it. 'Ungrateful wretch. All day I slog inside the kitchen to feed you and this is what I get in return?'

Yadu who had pulled up his legs to escape the stick, smiled benevolently at his paati. 'Of course I know how hard you work paati. In fact, I was just telling appa this evening that you needed help in the kitchen...'

'I don't need any help in the kitchen,' retorted paati instantly. Being very conservative, she wouldn't allow any servants to enter the kitchen.

'No servants inside my kitchen. Have I made myself clear?' she barked.

'No paati, we are not talking about servants here,' said Yadu trying to pacify her.

'Then what?' she demanded. 'Your father doesn't want to remarry. So who is going to come to help me in the kitchen? You?'

Yadu said with a deadpan expression on his face, 'I was thinking, maybe I should get married...'

Archana – who was standing beside Yadu now – started clapping her hands. Paati picked up her stick again and flung it at his legs this time.

'You shameless rascal! You are barely sixteen and you want to get married already?' paati exploded.

It took a great deal of effort on Yadu's part not to burst out laughing. He maintained a straight face, then said, 'What's wrong with that paati? You married when you were fourteen, didn't you? I have waited for two more years than you. What's good for you is good enough for your grandson,' he declared. 'And you forget that I am not marrying for me; I am marrying for *you* – so that *your* burden will be eased. Ask appa. Even he thinks it's a good idea.'

'You are mad – the both of you,' paati said shaking her head vigorously. She opened her betelnut box and removed a few betel leaves. She applied some quicklime onto the leaves, folded them into a triangle and then tucked it effortlessly into her mouth. 'And who do you think will give his daughter to you in marriage anyway?'

'Oh...you don't worry about that paati. I have seen this nice girl. Her name is Rachel and she is from a nice Christian family...'

Paati finally blew her top when she heard the word 'Christian.'

'Scoundrel!' She opened her betelnut box and started pelting Yadu with whole arecanuts. 'Did you hear that Ranga? Your son wants to bring a Christian girl into this house. *Panduranga...*'

Since there was no response from her son, paati picked up a couple of more arecanuts and pelted her grandson with it. Yadu dodged the nuts skilfully and Archana clapped even more loudly, amused at the show that was being put up for her.

'Paati, you can be so narrow-minded at times,' Yadu continued. 'Rachel is such a nice girl. Wait till you meet her. She even made me a nice mutton curry the last time I went to her house.'

By now paati had got up on her feet. She scampered to where Yadu was sitting, took hold of Yadu's left ear and squeezed it hard.

'*Aiiiiiiyooooooh!*' Yadu screamed.

'*Abhistu!* Shameless creature! So you have started eating non-veg as well?'

'No...no...Paati. I was just joking,' Yadu pleaded as his grandmother squeezed his ear harder. 'I am sorry,' he said trying to wrench his grandmother's hands away.

Paati thwacked Yadu's head lightly, and then finally let go off his ear. 'Don't *ever* talk about non-veg food inside my kitchen again. Now finish your food and scoot. I have to clear up here.'

~

After dinner Yadu went back to his textbooks only to discard the attempt because he couldn't concentrate. His mind kept flitting back to the conversation he'd had with his father a while back. He had to do some heavy-duty thinking, so he walked along the corridors for half an hour or so trying out the various options for size. After much thought Yadu decided that the only sane option was to defy Hardaker and go to the police. If he found out they would be done for, of course. But there was the possibility that the police would give them protection after hearing about the blackmail. Yadu decided to persuade his father to take this risk. He went into his father's study a short while later and had a long discussion with him.

Ranganathan, at first, was averse to the idea, but Yadu managed to somehow convince him at the end.

'I'll go to the police first thing tomorrow morning,' Ranganathan said.

'I think you ought to go there tonight itself pa,' said Yadu. 'The car might be back tomorrow. There is a possibility that they will follow you around. You don't want them to see you enter the police station, do you?'

'Absolutely not,' said Ranganathan.

'Then go to the police tonight itself. I'll come with you if you want me to. In two hours we can be back in our beds. And who knows, we might even get a couple of constables as security.'

Yadu didn't expect his father to be taken up by this idea, but surprisingly he relented. After all the thinking he had done he too had arrived at the conclusion that the police were still their best bet.

'I have decided to go with your idea,' Ranganathan said some five minutes later, to Yadu's delight. 'But you are not coming with me to the police station.'

'Why not?' asked Yadu.

'What if Hardaker decides to barge in here? It's not safe to leave just paati and Archana in the house.'

That made sense, so Yadu complied without putting up any resistance.

'I'll go to the balcony and see if the coast is clear. Meanwhile you get dressed,' Yadu told his father. Ranganathan nodded.

Yadu took the narrow wooden staircase that went upstairs to his room and to the large balcony next to it. Reaching the balcony he walked to the edge and looked out onto the road. He felt relieved to see that the car was not around. In the distance he could see the temple gopuram. He assumed that the car festival had wound up because he couldn't hear the nadaswarams and the mridangams anymore.

He looked up at the sky. It looked like it would rain any minute now. Earlier during the day he had heard a weather forecast on the radio, and the newsreader had said rain was expected all over the Madras presidency in the next couple of days. Apparently there was a low-pressure depression in the Bay of Bengal. The front door opened and Yadu saw his father step out. He looked up at the balcony and waved to his son.

'They haven't come back,' Yadu said.

'I thought so. I'll be back in an hour,' Ranganathan told his son. He then started walking the fifty-odd metres to the front gate. The neighbourhood was silent as a graveyard, which was normal considering that it was nearly half past eleven at night. Today, it seemed even more quiet than usual. Even the streets seemed darker than usual for some reason. Then it struck him that it was because of the temple festivities. Throughout the day the loudspeakers had been blaring carnatic music. The streets had looked brighter all evening because of the extra lights that had been placed on the roads. Now that they had all been switched off the street felt even more silent and dark than usual. Ranganathan had by this time reached the gate. He opened it, went out and put the latch back. Barely had Ranganathan taken five paces to the left when a sound – that of a car engine being started – reached Yadu's ears. The blood in Yadu's veins froze to ice.

There was a car outside. *Only, it wasn't visible from up here.* The moment Yadu heard the car engine he yelled out to his father.

'*Appa, come back!*'

In a fit of panic he leapt from the balcony onto the sunshade and from there on to the ground. Even as he hit the ground his ears picked up two distinct sounds. One was his father's sharp cry for help. And the other was a dull thud. With his heart thumping wildly Yadu started running towards the gate. This wasn't good. It looked like Hardaker and his men had returned and had been waiting in the dark just for a moment like this. All kinds of wild thoughts ran through his head as he ran towards the car.

Yadu removed the latch and pulled the gate open and was just in time to catch a familiar car wizz past him towards the main road. It was the same black-coloured Morris Minor.

With a thumping heart he looked to his left.

There was no sign of his father there.

Yadu felt his heart sink to the pit of his stomach as the realisation struck him: *his father had just been kidnapped.*

8

Two hours later the mood in the Ranganathan household was predictably somber. None of them could sleep and that included four-year-old Archana.

Yadu had run after Hardaker's car like a mad man though he had no chance of catching it. He ran up to Tram road, and then finally gave up, because he didn't know which way the car had turned at the junction. He had collapsed on the road, with tears streaming down his cheeks, and with his heart hammering inside his ribcage. The weight of the guilt he felt crushed his spirit. He felt responsible for what had happened. His father had been very reluctant about the idea of going to the police, but *he* had forced him to do it. Heartbroken, Yadu had trudged back home. Feeling overwhelmed with fear and guilt he had told paati everything. He had told her about the blackmail; about the details Hardaker and his men were after and about how they had just kidnapped her son right from their gate.

'What do we do?' he asked her now. He had no idea what to do next. Should he go to the police? Would that be the right thing to do? Or would that make Hardaker more furious? Yadu had no intention of upsetting Hardaker any further. It was his father's life that was at stake. If he made a wrong move now and if his father got killed, then he would never be able to live with that guilt – of causing the death of both his parents.

Paati cleared her throat and said calmly, 'Let's not take any rash decisions.' Her voice was a lot steadier than his. Just listening to her gave him a little bit of confidence. 'We'll wait until tomorrow morning,' paati continued. 'After finding out what they want they might release your father. God willing, he might even be back home by tomorrow morning, so don't worry.'

Listening to his grandmother's calm voice brought tears to his eyes. He was glad to have her around. Such a puny size, yet such inner strength!

Paati said that they better shut the door and retire to bed. There was no point in staying awake. She then took Archana and went into her room. Yadu stayed back in the living room saying that he wasn't feeling sleepy. He stayed out on the swing all night hoping to hear the front gate creak open.

~

SATURDAY, 6 DECEMBER 1947

The next morning Ranganathan didn't turn up like paati had expected. There however was a note tucked into the folds of their newspaper. Yadu opened the note and read it.

Yadu,

Don't even think about going to the police. Unless you want your father dead.

(signed)
Brian Hardaker.

Yadu showed his paati the note and told her what was written.

'There is still hope,' said paati optimistically. 'Once they have robbed the coach they might release your father.'

Yadu didn't feel all that confident about it. From what he had heard so far from Inspector Rafeeq, this man was ruthless. Yadu had his doubts if the goons would spare his father even if the robbery went off successfully. Of course it was another matter whether his father wanted to live at all after that. He wouldn't want to go through the humiliation of a police arrest and a jail term and all the brouhaha that went with it.

Paati suggested some time later that he ought to go seek the counsel of one of his uncles. They were all well-read men. Surely one of them would help. Yadu thought about it for some time but decided not to pursue the matter with his uncles. He knew what they would do if he told them his problem. They would drag him straight to the police station. That's the one thing he didn't want at the moment because that would seal his father's fate. Yadu explained this to paati and she agreed that they couldn't go to the police. For the same reason it was decided that they wouldn't approach his father's friends as well.

~

All morning, Yadu sat on the swing thinking, trying to figure out what he should do next. He found out from the *Hindu* that the Mangalore Express was scheduled to leave Madras Central at ten past seven that evening. He remembered his father telling him that the RBI coach Hardaker was after was being sent to Coimbatore on that particular train. Now that his father was kidnapped Yadu wondered how successful Hardaker would be in prying out the details from him. Would his father crack under pressure and divulge the details, or would he hold out bravely?

Even if the Englishman managed to get the information out of his father, would he go after the RBI coach at such short notice? Would he be prepared mentally, or otherwise, to go after the coach in just a few hours? Yadu wished he knew for sure if Hardaker was going to rob the coach tonight only then he could warn the RBI with confidence. He didn't want to end up raising a false alarm without being sure. He had the same reservations about informing the police. But what would happen if he informed Inspector Rafeeq that the RBI coach on tonight's Mangalore Express was going to be robbed and if his father hadn't divulged the details to Hardaker? Rafeeq would make arrangements in preparation for an attack that would, in the end, never take place. But then again, if his father had told Hardaker about the RBI coach and if the Englishman decided to rob it, then Rafeeq's preparations might pay off. Maybe he ought to tell the police...

Yadu decided to give this a little more thought. Suppose he told Rafeeq about the blackmail and the robbery, the inspector could be expected to do one of three things to prevent it. One, he might call up the RBI and cancel the coach's trip to Coimbatore. Two, he might organise for extra escorts for the coach. Three, he might send the coach to Coimbatore that same night but on another train. Whatever Rafeeq did, one could safely assume that the robbery would be averted. But Yadu couldn't help thinking how Hardaker would react if the robbery was foiled thus. If he boarded the train and found the Reserve Bank coach missing, how long would it be before he jumped to the conclusion that Ranganathan had duped him? Or how long before he put two and two together and surmised that Yadu had gone to the police? Yadu feared that the Englishman's retaliation would be swift and brutal. He would blow his father's brains out in anger.

It struck him that there was nothing to gain and everything to lose if he told Rafeeq about the robbery. Rafeeq would focus his attention on stopping the robbery, not on nabbing Hardaker.

On the other hand, if he took a leaf out of his father's book, the prospects appeared a bit rosier. His father had made an anonymous call to Rafeeq to tell him where he could find Hardaker and his gang. What if he did the same? What if he made an anonymous call and told Rafeeq that he could find Hardaker at Central tonight? What if he deliberately refrained from telling him about the robbery? Rafeeq would still rush to Central to see if he could nab Hardaker. If he succeeded, the robbery would be averted and all would be well. Even if Rafeeq messed up again, the Englishman would be none the wiser that he, Yadu, had gone to the police. The RBI coach would still be on the train so Hardaker wouldn't suspect anything.

Yadu decided that this was the right course of action, considering the circumstances. There was one change, however, that he made to his plans. He decided to send a letter to Rafeeq instead of making the call. He feared Rafeeq would recognise his voice if he made the phone call.

With a letter there was no such thing to fear.

~

The rains that the Met department had warned about started lashing Madras at 5.20 pm, ten minutes after Yadu's letter reached the hands of Inspector Rafeeq.

For two rupees Yadu had found a beggar willing to go up the steps of the police station, to hand over the letter to the constable standing outside. Yadu had watched from a distance as the beggar delivered the letter and then scooted. The constable opened the letter, saw it was addressed to Inspector Rafeeq and took it inside. Yadu had given very clear instructions in the letter as to where the inspector could find Hardaker. He had mentioned the name of the train, the time it was to depart and the date. Yadu had asked the inspector to rush to the station immediately.

He waited for about five minutes to see if Rafeeq would take off immediately. But he didn't. Yadu would have waited for some more time, but the rains started. He gave up his cover and then ran home.

No sooner had he opened the front gate to his house, than the clouds opened up and it poured. This downpour would continue to lash most of Madras Presidency for the next twelve hours, something the Met department failed to mention in their broadcast. Yadu found his paati washing vessels in the kitchen. He helped himself to four idlis, left over from that morning's breakfast. While paati made coffee for him he told her about the letter he had just sent to the inspector. He explained to her the rationality behind his decision. Paati nodded her approval.

'I'll be going to the railway station now,' Yadu informed her.

'What for?' asked paati.

'To look for Hardaker and his gang,' said Yadu.

'The police will be doing that now that they have got your letter. What need is there for you to go?' paati asked.

'How else am I going to find out if appa has given these goons the details or not? If I find Hardaker in the station then it will be confirmed that appa has told them about the Coimbatore consignment. It will be confirmed that Hardaker is boarding the train tonight to rob the coach. Even if Inspector Rafeeq fails to apprehend them at Central I can still call up the RBI and inform them of the impending robbery.'

'But it is raining heavily, Yadu,' paati protested.

'Frankly, paati, this is not the time to be worrying about inane things like the weather.'

Paati watched him drink his coffee. 'I hope you'll be careful,' she said finally, which was her way of saying, yes, he could go.

Yadu finished his coffee and tiffin and then washed up. He took a look inside his wallet; there wasn't much money in it. He stuffed it into his pocket anyway, put on his raincoat, bid goodbye to his grandmother, and stepped out into the rain.

The departure of the Mangalore Express was just ninety minutes away.

9

The Madras Central railway station was a single-storied structure from which a trio of towers shot up. While the centre tower looked quite tall and majestic, the ones at either end were rather short and looked stunted. All three towers had aluminium girdle work done atop them, the kind that looked like crowns from a distance. There were two more towers at the back, hidden from view.

Yadu was in a foul mood as he breezed into the railway station. There had been heavy water logging on all the major streets – and that had resulted in the tram service from Triplicane to George Town getting cancelled. He had waited forever for some kind of transport to get him to the station. A tram, a bus, a cycle rickshaw...anything, but eventually he had to settle for a tonga which wasn't the greatest transport when one is in an awful hurry.

It was twenty minutes to seven when he finally made it to the station which meant that thirty minutes was all he had to comb the station for Hardaker and his men. In thirty minutes he had to search the ten-odd bogies on the train, the platform, the waiting lounges *and* the lobby. Impossible, his brain screamed at him.

The station was jam-packed, as was usually the case at this time of the evening. Nudging his way past the waiting passengers he walked up to the departures board. He found out that the Mangalore Express was scheduled to leave from platform three, so he headed off in that direction.

Outside, the rain continued unabated. He could hear the loud clatter of raindrops on the asbestos sheet above. Yadu still had his raincoat on. He thought of getting rid of it, but then had a better idea. He decided to keep it on – the coat as well as the cap. If he tied the cap a certain way it could serve another purpose – as a makeshift disguise. He removed the cap and tied it in such a fashion that only his eyes and nose were visible. There. He was feeling a little safer already. Even if Hardaker or Rafeeq walked past him accidentally, they wouldn't recognise him.

The train had already arrived on platform three; there were still a few stragglers boarding it. From the platform entrance Yadu started walking towards the engine. He kept to the shadows mostly. He walked, allowing his eyes to scan the area. There were well over a hundred people on the platform already. Yadu was on the lookout for two different sets of people here. Hardaker and his men were of course the first lot. They were wanted men in the city so it was likely they would be here in disguise. Yadu was confident he would recognise Hardaker even with a disguise. He was not so sure about Dorai and Sethu though. Then, he had to watch out for Rafeeq and his policemen. If they did come here he hoped they would be in mufti. Having such a large area to cover – the platform, the many compartments, etc. – they would be better off in civil clothes. They wouldn't stick out like sore thumbs and frighten Hardaker away. There was something else that he had to look for: the RBI coach. Till now though, every car he had passed was a passenger car, save one, which was the mail van.

Yadu had, by now, reached the front of the train. So far he hadn't caught sight of any of the men he was looking for. However, he was now walking towards what he reckoned was the RBI coach. There was the engine spewing out thick billows of smoke, hissing and sighing in turns, and just behind it was a boxcar. From the activity going on, it appeared as if the engine and the boxcar had just been attached to the rest of the train. A man stood on the track coupling the boxcar behind the engine to the first coach of the train. The boxcar itself looked insignificant. It looked like any other goods carriage. The only difference was the number of locks that were in place. There were four of them in all. Each of these massive locks was wrapped in white cloth, and a government wax seal had been embossed on it. Inspecting the coupling operation were three men. Two of them were dressed in khakis, and had rifles slung on their hefty shoulders. A belt of cartridges hung around each of their hips. Yadu guessed that they were the armed escorts, the men escorting the RBI coach to its destination. The other man was probably a RBI representative, one of his father's colleagues, surely. Once the coupling operation was complete the armed men walked up to the engine and started talking to the engine driver. Yadu stood observing the escorts for a few minutes. After their chat with the driver the escorts walked back and boarded C1, the coach just behind the RBI carriage. The RBI representative started walking away towards the exit.

Yadu started walking back towards the mouth of the platform. He observed that the Mangalore Express comprised thirteen coaches in all. Behind the RBI coach were three second class coaches (C1, C2, C3). Then there was F1, the first class coach, after which there were seven coaches (C4, C5, C6, C7, C8, C9 and the mail van). C10, the unreserved bogie, brought up the rear of the train. He walked past the coaches one by one with little success. Then, when he had just passed by C6 Yadu noticed a flurry of activity at the platform entrance. Yadu's heart missed a beat as he recognised Rafeeq's familiar figure. Behind him were over a dozen policemen. The inspector has taken my note seriously, Yadu thought with a sigh of relief. For a moment he had thought that Rafeeq wouldn't show up, that he had ignored the note. Yadu now positioned himself behind a steel girder that supported the roof.

Rafeeq was about two hundred metres away, barking instructions at his men, who were all in civils, incidentally. He placed two constables at the entrance and sent one to the other side of the train. Six of his men he sent to the front of the train and four more he pushed towards C10. The policemen started boarding the compartments in two's. One took the forward exit and the other the aft. They worked their way through each compartment until they ran into each other. Anyone who even remotely resembled Dorai or Sethu was hauled out of the train and in front of Rafeeq, who stood rock-like on the platform. One of the policemen rounded up all the white men travelling on the train. There were four of them in all. Rafeeq had a good look at them and then sent them back to their compartments. The passengers on the train sensed that there was trouble brewing somewhere. A few of them tried to enquire what was happening, but the policemen were too busy to bother replying to their questions.

The minutes ticked by as the search wore on without success. Yadu started to sweat with the building tension. This was not going the way he had imagined. They had just five minutes before the train's departure. There was still no sign of Hardaker or his men on the platform. Yadu was now beginning to think that Hardaker didn't know about the RBI coach. Had his father held onto the details? If they still had not boarded the train, could there be other reasons? There was, of course, the possibility that Hardaker would deliberately arrive at the last possible minute to board the train. A wanted criminal that he was, he wouldn't arrive early and risk getting caught by the police. Yadu could see the frustration and disappointment on Rafeeq's face. The policemen were all returning to him now, telling him they hadn't found the gang. He watched on as the inspector kicked the side of the train in anger. Yadu wasn't sure how he was supposed to feel. Was he supposed to feel elated or depressed at the Englishman's non-arrival? Partly, he felt elated; because it looked like the RBI coach on tonight's train wasn't going to be robbed, after all. And if Hardaker needed the details for the next consignment he had to release his father, so he could go to the Reserve Bank to get it. It looked as if they had just had a reprieve. On the other hand he felt depressed because he would have liked Hardaker and his men to have been here so they could have been caught by Rafeeq and his men. As things stood at the moment, the bandits were still out there somewhere, with his father still held hostage, and that made him very uncomfortable.

The tannoy above came alive with a burst of static. A man with a hoarse voice announced the departure of the Mangalore Express in a few minutes. Yadu turned his attention back to Rafeeq. He could see that the inspector had given up hope. He instructed two of his men to patrol the platform; the rest he asked to go outside and board their vehicle. A railway employee started ringing the departure bell. Rafeeq followed his men out of the exit door. Yadu stood still for the next thirty seconds or so looking at the last few passengers board the train. The peddlers started disembarking, expecting the train to start any moment. The TTEs got into their respective compartments. From somewhere in front he heard the shrill whistle of the engine. Yadu's eyes were glued to the entrance even as he hoped fervently that Hardaker wouldn't arrive now. That instant, out of the blue, Yadu had an insight that sent a chill up his spine.

What if Hardaker and his men had never intended to board the train in Madras?

What if they were to board the train in one of the smaller wayside stations? It felt like a tight slap on his face. Yadu gulped anxiously as he realised that this was indeed likely. Hardaker and his men were wanted men in this city. Why would they board the train in Madras and risk getting caught by the police? Wouldn't it make more sense for them to board the train in a smaller station, where police presence was minimal? Coimbatore – where the coach was meant to be dropped off – was nine hours away. Even if they boarded the train at the next station or the station after that they would still have ample time on their hands to rob the coach.

Yadu had a look of wild desperation in his eyes now. His gut instincts told him that this was it; this was what Hardaker intended to do. His eyes instantly flitted to the exit, but there was no sign of the inspector. He was probably in his jeep by now. He then looked around for the two policemen the inspector had left behind. But he couldn't see them in the crowd of bystanders. The coarse voice returned on the tannoy informing passengers that the Mangalore Express was pulling away now. Yadu's mind was completely blank for a few seconds. He watched in a rather detached sort of way as the train jerked to life. Well-wishers standing on the platform were waving to their friends and family as the train reluctantly started to move forward. Watching the train move Yadu snapped back to consciousness. *What was he going to do?* He was still not sure if Hardaker would rob the RBI coach tonight. All he knew was that it remained a possibility. Then Yadu took a sudden decision: *he was going to board the train.* If he was on the train he could be on the lookout for Hardaker in the wayside stations. If they *did* board the train at one of the next few stations he could be certain that they were going ahead with the strike tonight. Once he was sure of this he could inform the police and get them nabbed. If he was on the train he still had an outside chance of preventing the robbery – *if* and when it happens. There was no point in him being here in Madras tonight.

Having made the decision, Yadu broke forth into a sudden sprint. The last bogie was already thirty metres away, but he knew he could catch it if he put his mind to it. Yadu ran like a man possessed, pushing people out of his way, sidestepping trolleys, leaping across trunks and gunny bags.... Less than thirty seconds later he came abreast of the C10 handrail...

And then he leapt.

10

For the first few seconds he couldn't even believe that he had done it, that he had made it aboard the coach safely. And when the feeling finally sunk in, he felt such a surge of relief sweep through his body that his skin had broken out into a sea of goose pimples.

Yadu Ranganathan looked up and thanked his stars, then collapsed onto his knees in sheer exhaustion. Sweat trickled unchecked down both his cheeks. His legs felt leaden and his face looked all flushed. His heart was still hammering wildly against his rib cage.

Yadu had never ever attempted anything as dangerous as this before. And he made a spot decision that this would be the first and last time he would board a train in this fashion. It was far too dangerous. One false step and he could have been under the wheels of the train. He gave an involuntary shudder. Never again, he promised himself.

He removed the raincoat he was wearing and threw it out of the door. The less baggage he carried, the better. Of what use was the raincoat going to be anyway, now that he was inside the train? He now hunched forward and concentrated on getting his breath back.

A quarter of an hour passed. His sweating had still not stopped, but his breathing rhythm was back in order. The back of his shirt was fully damp and his nape felt sticky and wet. He pulled out his handkerchief and dried his face and neck with it. He then sat down on the floor with his back resting on the coach door. Squatting in this fashion he watched disinterestedly as the train swept past shacks, slums, sheds and myriad industrial buildings. The night time sky erupted every now and then in brilliant flashes.

Soon the train was clipping at top speed. Buildings gave way to fields and wide expanses of wasteland. Without even being aware of it Yadu withdrew into himself. He fell deep into thought, oblivious of the countryside whizzing past, oblivious of the slanting rain splattering the coach steps by his side. His mind had lapsed back to the events of the past fifteen minutes. He was, quite expectedly, in a state of mild disbelief. On a whim he had boarded the train. And now he was headed out of his hometown to God knew where. He didn't possess a ticket, didn't have enough money on him to buy one, and hadn't even informed his paati.

Pure madness, he thought.

His gaze wandered up to the dark sky above. Looking at the rain-pregnant clouds it struck him that the weather might end up playing a crucial part in the proceedings tonight. Even if the Englishman and his gang boarded the train in the next station it would be interesting to see if they go ahead with their plan of robbing the coach. If the rains continued to lash all night he wondered how Hardaker would board the RBI coach, let alone rob it. The way he saw it they would attempt robbing the coach only when the train was in motion. They wouldn't dare draw attention upon themselves by trying to rob the coach while the train was in a station. But if the train was speeding like a bullet and if the winds were as fierce as they are now, would they risk their lives atop the train, he wondered. Of course there was no telling with a master criminal like

Hardaker. The Englishman might play it either way. He might decide to risk all their lives and go for the booty, as it was a huge one. Or, he might just abandon the attempt knowing fully well that he could blackmail Ranganathan into giving him the details for the next consignment.

It would be interesting to see what he would do.

Yadu had been on this line to Coimbatore a few times in the past. He now tried to recollect the stations that the train passed. He was fairly certain that Arakkonam was the first station where the train would stop. He reckoned they would be there in another thirty minutes. After that there was Katpadi, and then Jolarpet junction. The stations after that he wasn't very sure about. He knew the train would pass through Salem at some point.

Yadu felt that it was important he knew the exact duration of the train's halt at each station. If he knew the amount of time he had on his hands he could plan his moves accordingly. For example, in Arakkonam, he not only had to watch out for Hardaker and his men on the platform, he also had to go buy himself a ticket at the booking office. If Hardaker and his men did board the train in Arakkonam he would have to see which coach they boarded. Then he would have to make his way to the station master's cabin and inform the officials about the impending robbery. It was all going to be touch-and-go.

The next half hour passed with Yadu still deep in thought. Then, at ten past eight he saw the faint twinkling lights of an approaching town. Arakkonam.

Yadu stood up by the door and put his hand into his trouser pocket. He pulled out his wallet and checked the amount of money in it. Three rupees and four annas. He sighed. It was probably not enough to buy a ticket even to the next station. He now wished he had brought his father's wallet instead of his own. He had seen it in the drawer at home when he had taken his own wallet, but he hadn't had the foresight to carry it.

He watched now as the platform came up to hug the side of the train. The Mangalore Express had managed to arrive at Arakkonam on time in spite of the bad weather.

He was feeling a bit nervous. He had a strong feeling that Hardaker might board the train here at Arakkonam, since this station was closest to Madras. It was just over an hour away, was well connected to the city by road and rail, and best of all, it was a small station not meriting a major police presence. Yadu believed Hardaker couldn't choose a better station than Arakkonam to board the train. He would know shortly if his assumption was right.

The train slowed down gradually.

Yadu had a good first look. The station was a small one. It had a roof, but not much else. The station building from what Yadu could see consisted of a station entrance flanked by four rooms, two on either side of it. On the right hand side of the entrance was the booking office with a cage like façade. Yadu noticed that the light inside the office was switched off. It appeared as if the booking office was already closed for the day.

Next to the booking office was a room that Yadu guessed was the station master's cabin. On the left hand side of the entrance was a room that contained all kinds of mechanical levers. The room next to it Yadu guessed was the parcels office going by the huge wooden cases lying outside its door.

A random rove of the platform confirmed Yadu's suspicions that this station did not have any police patrolling it.

The train slowed down further.

Yadu's gaze had now moved to the passengers waiting to board the train. There were not many, which was to be expected in a small station like this. Most of the passengers were spread out near the centre of the platform. They were roughly about three hundred metres away from where Yadu stood, and the distance was getting shorter every second. As they drew nearer Yadu started checking out the faces and the profiles of the waiting passengers. It took him just a few seconds to search the crowd.

He didn't like what he saw. Not one bit.

The first thing he noticed was that none of the waiting passengers were of foreign origin – which ruled out Hardaker immediately. And from what he could see from this distance, none of the men standing on the platform resembled Dorai or Sethu either. None of them sported a flowing beard; none of them had a bulky frame the likes of which Dorai possessed.

Just to make sure Yadu looked at all their faces once again. The train had come a little closer now. And this time he was sure Hardaker and his men were not on this platform.

Besides this small group of people, the only other people on the platform were a couple of waiters and a few railway employees. The waiters holding tea-kettles in one hand and a tray of glasses in the other, were running alongside the train, ready to board it the moment it stopped. Two railway employees meanwhile were pushing a gunnybag laden trolley towards the back, where they expected the mail van to stop. Apart from these men there was nobody else about on the platform.

The train jerked once and then came to a halt.

Yadu jumped off the coach and then started walking towards the forward end of the platform. He now wondered what he should do next.

Behind him the platform now looked empty. Almost all of the passengers who had been waiting for the train had boarded it by now. It was usual for some passengers to get down at a station to smoke a cigarette or stretch their legs. Here in Arakkonam not a single passenger got down.

As he walked he was aware of the raindrops on the roof above. He noticed that the din was really loud if he actually focused his attention on it. He was looking up and thinking along these lines when a thought suddenly struck him. So far he had been assuming that Hardaker and his men would board the train from the platform side of the station. What if they had planned to board the train on the other side?

This thought stopped Yadu dead in his tracks.

He thought about it for a second and realised that this was indeed likely. Since there was no platform on the other side it was usually dark. And since it was dark, nobody usually ventured there. These seemed like perfect conditions for someone wanting to board the train surreptitiously. Why would Hardaker board the train on the platform side and risk being noticed when he could take the easier route?

Yadu decided that this theory was definitely worth pursuing. He decided to have a quick look on the other side.

He took one last glance at the station entrance, then set off towards the nearest coach door. He got onto the coach, walked over to the door on the other side and drew it open.

The place was pitch dark just as he had expected. The only lighting for this side of the station was a fluorescent lamp some two hundred metres away from where he stood. For some seconds he stood there and stared into the night to get his eyes accustomed to the darkness. Slowly he could make out the landscape. He could see that there was another track running alongside this one. Beyond that were thick shrubs, and further beyond that was a line of trees.

Yadu could have seen better if it hadn't been for the rain, which cut visibility by at least fifty per cent.

Once his eyes were a bit accustomed to the darkness he stepped down cautiously from the coach. Within seconds he was fully drenched. He cursed himself for prematurely throwing away his raincoat. Why couldn't he have just kept it on? The things he did sometimes, he wanted to hit himself with a stick.

He made his way now towards the forward end of the train. He stepped on rocks, gravel, and fishplates as he made his way up the track. As he progressed forward he found it easier to see in the dark. He learnt to use the light pouring out of the coach windows to negotiate the bigger puddles. Once he got the hang of it he walked faster. He kept looking to his left every now and then in the hope of catching sight of somebody. But either they weren't there or they weren't coming out yet. And every time he arrived at a coupling gap his eyes darted to the right, towards the station entrance. But the station entrance looked as empty and lifeless as the rest of the platform.

Yadu didn't like walking on this side one bit. The darkness, the rains, the silence that enveloped the place and the eerie atmosphere made him kind of edgy. He felt a strange sense of loneliness, as if this was a moonscape he was walking on and as if he was the only human being on it. He reminded himself that there were a few hundred people eating, sleeping and chatting right next to where he was walking. But the feeling of loneliness persisted.

He had arrived by the RBI coach by this time. He stood there for some time looking at the shrubs, trees, hoping to see a shadow move. No such thing happened. He looked at himself. He was soaking wet from the rain. He was sure he looked like a sparrow that had taken a dive into a pond.

Then he heard the departure bell ringing in some corner of the station. A little distance in front of him the engine was hissing angrily and spewing out smoke in short bursts. Yadu had to admit to himself that this exercise too had turned futile. He felt extremely disappointed. Disheartened and depressed, he turned around and started walking back the way he came.

Beside him the train started to move. He started to jog now. The last thing he could afford right now was to miss this train. Even as he jogged he started checking off the coaches at they went past him.

C1...C2...C3...F1...

He was just preparing to get aboard C4 when suddenly he heard a dull 'thump' from behind him.

Yadu swivelled around and was just in time to notice a man pick himself up from the adjoining track and run towards the train. It looked as if he had stumbled on the track in the dark. Yadu stared gape-mouthed as the man, who was about fifty metres from where he stood, got to the train, caught hold of a handrail, and then clambered on top of the steps.

Until this moment Yadu had no idea about the identity of this figure. But now the man threw open the coach door and Yadu watched as the light pouring out of the coach illuminated his face.

Yadu recognised him instantly.

It was Dorai.

11

He had been right.

Yadu almost collapsed onto the ground in sheer relief. So happy was he at having caught sight of one of his father's kidnappers that if the train hadn't been moving, he would have surely dropped on his knees and thanked God.

However, the train *was* moving, so Yadu had to curtail his celebrations and thanksgiving until later. There were decisions to be taken. Quickly.

He had seen the bandit board what appeared to be C1, the coach right behind the RBI carriage. He wondered if he ought to try and board the same coach. Now that he had found Dorai he didn't want to let him out of his sight. It would be the right thing for him to do: to board C1. The only problem was that C1 was three coaches in front. He would have to run *really* fast to get there.

For just a second Yadu was tempted to go for it. The very next instant though, he decided not to. He could have made it to the coach if it had been daylight, and if it hadn't been raining so hard. But to go after the coach in this kind of weather would be stupid. The place was so dark he wouldn't even know where he was stepping while he ran. He decided that instead of running like that and hurting himself it was more prudent to wait until the next station to get to that coach.

Once this decision was taken, he caught the next handrail that came along and boarded the train.

~

Seeing Dorai board the train had cleared a few things in his head. Now he was certain that his father had divulged the details of the Coimbatore consignment to Hardaker. Also, he was now certain that they were going ahead with the robbery. It cleared up his own position in the scheme of things. His job now was to inform the railway authorities of the impending robbery and thwart it somehow. It was not going to be easy, because he had to do this without falling into Hardaker's eyes. It had to be done though; otherwise he would fall in his own eyes.

Yadu stood by the door for a few minutes wondering what he was going to do next. He had an hour before the train reached Katpadi. He decided that first of all he would get into a toilet and do something about his drenched state. If he remained in his wet clothes for any longer he was sure to catch a cold. Besides, he was aware of the mess he was making on the coach floor. The toilet was the best place for him right now, the *only* place for him right now. He shut the coach door and made his way towards the toilets.

Like most coaches of the time C5 too had two toilets at the back. Yadu reached them in four short strides. He had to wait for his turn as both booths were occupied.

He waited patiently.

A few minutes later the door on the right opened and a young girl stepped out. She was dressed in a black blouse and a parrot green, full-length skirt. Yadu guessed that she was about the same age as he was. Very pretty, he thought. It looked as if she'd just had a face wash, and it no doubt enhanced her appearance.

As she went past him she stared wide-eyed at the state of his clothes. Yadu ignored her gaze, went into the toilet and slammed the door shut. The moment he was inside he began taking his clothes off. The shirt came off first. He folded it tightly and then started wringing it real hard. He wrung it until no more water oozed out. Then he used the shirt like a towel to wipe his head and his upper body. He wiped energetically until he felt fairly dry. Then he wrung his shirt once more and hung it on the window vent for drying. He started on his trousers next.

He took off his trousers and was just starting to wring it when he heard a soft knock on the door. *Come on*, he thought. He had barely been inside a couple of minutes and somebody was waiting to get in already. He decided to ignore the knock. To hell with whoever is on the other side, he thought. They have three other toilets. Let them use one of those.

He started on his trousers once again and worked in silence for a few minutes.

And then he heard the knock once again. This time it was a tight-knuckled rap. Yadu ignored it this time too. He continued with what he was doing. Once he had squeezed the trouser to his satisfaction he made some place for it on the window vent and then hung it there. The small vent in the toilet proved to be a boon for Yadu. It not only helped him air his clothes a bit, it also kept the cold winds out. Whatever little air entered through the vent was smothered by his clothes. It was just as well, because he was standing in his underwear, and even the slightest breeze made his body shiver and his teeth chatter.

The person outside knocked yet again. Whoever is standing outside is extremely desperate, he thought. But he still had no intention of giving up the toilet so soon. He was beginning to like it in here. It was warm, cozy, and it didn't smell all that bad. Perhaps, he had got used to the smell. Anyway, it didn't bother him and that's all that mattered. If he went out now he would have to stand by the coach door in his wet clothes. The cold winds and his damp clothes would surely combine to freeze him numb. No. He decided that he would rather stay here. The person outside would have to make alternative arrangements.

~

Almost at the very instant that Yadu locked himself inside the toilet Dorai too locked himself inside a toilet further up the train. But unlike Yadu, Dorai didn't stay inside the toilet for long. He was in and out in a jiffy, going inside just to wipe his face and comb his hair. Unlike Yadu he had been wearing a raincoat.

Coming out of the toilet Dorai kissed the amulet in his right arm, then got to doing the dirty work assigned to him. He had to find the armed escorts and render them useless. This was the task Hardaker had entrusted him with.

Dorai found the escorts in the second bay from the front of the coach – their rifles and their uniforms a dead giveaway. The two burly escorts were seated next to each other, with one of them occupying the window seat. Besides these two there were two more passengers in the bay, a middle aged man and a young man in his early thirties. Both of them had already climbed onto their berths. The young man was reading a book.

Dorai walked into the bay and took the empty seat opposite the escorts. He looked at them to see if they minded him taking the seat, but they didn't seem to care, so he settled back.

Without making it too obvious he then allowed his eyes to rove around. He noticed that the escorts were not carrying much by way of luggage. Between the two of them they had two small bags – that, he guessed, contained no more than a fresh set of clothes – and one jute bag. Dorai didn't care too much for the two small bags. But the white and brown jute bag held his attention, because, peeking out of the top was a roll of banana leaves. Dorai guessed that this was their 'sappad' bag, the one with their dinners. The banana leaves suggested that they were yet to have their dinners, which was perfect for what he had in mind.

All he needed now was to be alone in the bay for a few minutes. But from the look of it, this was going to be difficult. The escorts didn't look as if they were going to get up from their seats anytime in the near future.

He decided that all he could do at the moment was to wait patiently for an opportunity to present itself.

~

Yadu had expected the knocks to die away with time, but as the minutes ticked by, the knocks kept growing louder and louder. When the knocks had no effect on him, the person outside – it was a girl – started shouting and screaming at him to open the door.

Yadu didn't budge from his place and kept mum. That was his ploy – to refrain from reacting. That way he was sure the girl would feel frustrated and leave.

But she didn't.

The next forty-five minutes proved to be a battle of wits between Yadu and the girl outside. He couldn't understand why the girl was so hell-bent on getting into this particular toilet. This was one stubborn girl. And when he was up against someone stubborn then *he* became stubborn. He decided that he was not going to open the door until the train arrived at the next station.

Then the knocking stopped. And the banging and the kicking began.

'Open the door, goddamn it. This is a public toilet, not a bedroom.'

Yadu ignored the sarcasm. He was not going to bite the bait. Nothing was going to make him open the door. Nothing. But the girl's very next words had him struggling to get into his wet trousers. She said in a loud and clear voice that if the door wasn't opened in thirty seconds then she was going to bring the TTE to the door.

Now, the ticket examiner was the last person Yadu wanted to see. It would lead to unnecessary complications since he didn't possess a ticket. So he quickly got into his clothes and opened the door, extremely angry with the girl for being so stubborn about getting into *this* toilet.

When he opened the door he found out it was the same girl, the one who had been in the toilet before him, the one wearing the black blouse and the parrot green skirt. Yadu assumed that she must be having a bowel problem or something, otherwise, nobody would have knocked and kicked at a door that desperately.

'And what did you have for lunch today?' the girl asked as he stumbled out of the toilet. She was standing with her hands on her hips. Her eyes blazed with anger.

'I...I am sorry,' Yadu mumbled and tried to move away.

'You have been inside there for nearly an hour, do you know that?' she screamed. 'Didn't you hear me knocking all this while?'

Until this moment his mind hadn't registered the fact that the toilet opposite was empty. So he had looked apologetically at the girl. But now he noticed the empty toilet, and a rush of blood shot up to his temple.

'Hey, if you were that desperate why couldn't you have used *that* toilet? Why did you have to bring me out of this one?' he demanded.

The girl brushed past him into the toilet in answer. Yadu watched as she put her hand into the tray below the mirror and picked up something. She then shuffled out of the toilet the next instant.

'I had to get into *this* toilet because *this* is where I left my ring.' She displayed the ring to Yadu and made a show of putting it on her finger.

'Oh!' said Yadu stupidly. That's all he could manage.

'You could have asked for the ring and I would have passed it out to you,' he said.

'I didn't want to take the risk,' said the girl.

Yadu stared at her.

'Let's say I brought your attention to the ring. What if you decided to keep it yourself? What if you told me there was no ring in the tray? You could have been a thief for all I know.'

Yadu remained silent. The girl had a point.

'Now you are free to go inside and continue with your...er...unfinished business,' she said sarcastically.

'I was not...,' he started defensively, but stopped himself. 'I was drying my clothes. That's why I didn't open the door.'

The girl eyed his wet clothes briefly.

Yadu felt that he owed the girl an apology. He said, 'I am genuinely sorry for keeping you waiting for so long. I didn't realise...'

Hearing this apology the girl's features softened a little. Pointing at his shirt she said, 'Wouldn't it be easier for you to change into a new set of clothes?'

Yadu smiled ruefully. 'I don't have another set with me. I boarded the train in a hurry, you see. I am not carrying any clothes.'

'Oh,' the girl said. 'Well, you better get back to your drying then.' Saying this she moved away.

~

Yadu had no intention of going back to the toilet just yet. He wanted to go to the exit door first, to check if they had arrived at Katpadi. He glanced at his watch. It was a quarter past nine. They ought to have arrived at Katpadi by now. He took a couple of steps and he was by the exit doors. The one to the left was already taken by the girl in the green skirt, who was busy looking out. Yadu went to the one on the right.

No sooner had he arrived by the door, than he caught sight of somebody standing about twenty feet away to his left. Alarm bells started ringing inside Yadu's head as he recognised the uniform the man was wearing. It was the TTE of the coach, and he was obviously on his rounds examining tickets. From the way he stood it seemed as if he was advancing in this direction. And the speed at which he was progressing suggested that he would be there in another ten minutes.

Trouble.

He had to get out of there somehow.

Yadu looked outside to see if they had neared the town yet. If they had, and if the train slowed down, then he could at least jump off the train. But the train was still passing through wilderness. They hadn't reached the outer edges of the town yet, so that option was ruled out. The other option was to get to the front of the coach. That area had been checked already. But he would have to pass the TTE for that of course. If the TTE didn't stop him then he would be fine. But if he did stop him and ask him for his ticket, he was done for. Too risky, he decided. Another option was to spend the next twenty minutes on the roof of the coach, but that again was too risky. There was nowhere else he could go – except the toilet, that is. Even that was ruled out because the TTEs these days checked the occupants of the toilets as well for their tickets.

While he was weighing all these options he turned around, and his eyes now fell on the girl in the green skirt. Looking at the girl an idea occurred to him. For the next few seconds he played it out in his mind wondering whether it would work. It seemed to him as if it would. The big question was, would the girl agree to help him?

What's the harm in trying, Yadu thought, and walked towards her.

The girl was closing the door and preparing to go when Yadu got to her. Sensing his presence she whirled around.

'Yes?'

'Look Miss...'

'Vandana,' the girl said.

'Miss Vandana, I have a favour to ask of you. Will you help me?'

The girl looked at him suspiciously.

'Look, I boarded the train without buying a ticket, and I just noticed that the TTE is coming this way...'

'So?'

The moment he heard the tone in which the 'so' was delivered he knew this was not going to work. Nevertheless, he continued.

'Can you help me evade the TTE?'

Vandana looked at him with a stern expression on her face. 'You shouldn't have boarded the train if you didn't have a ticket,' she admonished.

'I know,' said Yadu. 'I had to get aboard because of an emergency. That's why...'

Yadu could see that the girl didn't seem impressed with his explanation.

'So just pay a fine and I am sure the TTE will let you off,' the girl suggested.

'I don't have much money on me. That's the problem,' Yadu said. He pulled out his wallet and showed its contents to prove that he was telling her the truth.

The girl stared at him for a long time. Then it suddenly seemed to dawn on her what this was all about. 'You want *money*. That's what you are after, right?'

'No...no,' said Yadu hastily. The girl had misunderstood his motive. 'I don't want any money. All I need is a few minutes of your time.'

The girl thought some more. Then she said, 'What have I got to do?'

Yadu let out a sigh of relief. He had succesfully cleared obstacle one. Now for obstacle two.

'Are you carrying your ticket with you?' he asked.

'No, it's with my sister, up there,' said Vandana, pointing towards the front of the coach. She was still looking at him with suspicious eyes, but that was only to be expected.

'That's okay. I expected that,' he said. After a pause he got to the point. 'The only way I can evade the TTE now is by hiding inside the toilet. But if I am in the toilet on my own then I can't escape the TTE. But if both of us get into the toilet, then I have a chance of escaping.'

The girl's eyes grew wide upon hearing this. The look on her face said it all. She had an expression that was a mixture of disbelief, suspicion and curiosity. Luckily for Yadu her curiosity was more powerful than her other emotions. So she asked, 'How would my being inside the toilet help?'

'You'll be my decoy,' he said.

'Decoy?'

'Yes. The TTE when he ends up here is bound to knock on the toilet door. When he knocks you get out of the toilet, while I remain hidden inside. Now, he wouldn't expect two people to be inside the toilet, so he wouldn't come inside and check. And I can escape. Of course he is bound to ask you to produce your ticket, but all you have to do is take him to your sister. That's my plan.'

Vandana raised her eyebrows, thought about it a bit.

'Well, what do you say?' Yadu asked eagerly.

Vandana was looking at him with pursed lips. 'Are you saying that the two of us are going to be inside the toilet *together*?'

'Yes,' said Yadu, quickly understanding the apprehension going through the girl's mind. 'But only for a few minutes,' he hastened to add.

The girl smiled sweetly at him. 'No baba, I can't do that.'

Yadu panicked on hearing this. 'Wait! Just listen me out. It's just for three or four minutes maximum. I promise.'

Vandana just shook her head. 'I am sorry, but do I look like the kind of girl who gets into toilets with strangers?'

'Please don't misunderstand me,' Yadu begged. 'If I weren't desperate I wouldn't ask this favour of you, believe me.'

Vandana shook her head firmly.

Yadu wasn't one to give up that easily. 'Miss Vandana, how can I make you understand...?' In a desperate bid Yadu decided to blurt out what the emergency was, hoping the girl would stop acting so coy.

'Look Miss Vandana, I boarded this train to stop a robbery. I *cannot* get caught and be detained at Katpadi. Try to understand.'

Vandana raised her eyebrows in mock-surprise. It was apparent that she was not taking this very seriously. 'Bravo!' she said.

'I am serious. Please trust me. They are a gang of four headed by an Englishman. I have already caught sight of one of them. If I get caught now...'

Vandana cut him off with a wave of her hand. 'Don't feed me any more nonsense, please,' she said. 'I am sure you'll find some other willing passenger to join you inside the toilet.' Wishing him luck she walked away towards the aisle.

Yadu watched her disappear and then threw up his hands in frustration. 'Girls!' he muttered, rolling his eyes.

~

In the meantime, on C1, Dorai's patience was finally rewarded. The armed escorts got up from their seats and walked away towards the vestibule, presumably to wash their hands before dinner.

Dorai wanted no witnesses to what he was about to do next. He looked up to see what the other two passengers were up to. The middle aged man was fast asleep, and the young man still had his nose stuck inside a book.

Now or never, Dorai thought.

He slid towards the window, to where the escorts kept their sappad. Inside the jute bag there were two aluminium tiffin boxes, four bananas and a flask.

Dorai fished in his trouser pocket and pulled out a bottle and a syringe. In less than a minute he had jabbed the needle of the syringe into all four bananas. He did it so professionally that nobody handling the bananas would ever suspect anything. Just to make sure, he spiked the coffee in the flask as well. He threw the syringe and the bottle away, cast a look around to make sure nobody was watching. Then quietly he slipped away.

That should take care of the escorts, he thought.

12

Yadu waited by the door for a couple of more minutes hoping some other passenger would come this way. When nobody else came he resigned himself to getting caught by the TTE. There was not much he could do. He was trapped, cornered, with nowhere to go and no routes of escape.

He didn't want to give up without a fight though. So he went back into the toilet, bolted the door from the inside and hoped that the TTE wouldn't come this way.

He must have stood there for a few minutes when he heard a knock. Like he had done with the girl, he ignored it. He was not sure whether it was a passenger who knocked or whether it was the TTE. Whoever it was he decided to open the door only when the train had come to a complete standstill.

After a couple of minutes there was one more loud knock. And that was it. There were no more knocks until the train stopped a few minutes later at Katpadi junction.

Through the window vent he could see that they had arrived beside a platform. Yadu now opened the door, peeped to make sure no one was about and then stepped outside. He got to the door stealthily and was just about to get down when somebody seized his arm.

'Not so quickly,' said the man pulling Yadu back up the coach. 'I have been waiting for you.'

Yadu's heart skipped a beat. He didn't even have to turn back. He knew it was the TTE. The wily man had been waiting for him to get out of the toilet to pounce on him.

Yadu slowly turned around. It was indeed the TTE. He was a medium-sized, dark-complexioned man who was wearing an ill-fitting black coat over his white shirt. His runway top of a head glistened with a combination of oil and sweat. He held a pad in his left hand.

'You didn't hear me knock?' he asked, rather brusquely.

Yadu tried to look as innocent as he could. 'No,' he answered.

'Show me your ticket,' he ordered. He was standing very close to Yadu and was holding him in an iron grip. Every time he spoke he sprayed Yadu's face with spit.

'I...uh...I..."

'You don't have a ticket, do you?'

'Actually, I am booked on another coach,' Yadu lied. 'I got here...'

'Save your breath, you rascal,' the TTE interposed. 'I have come across hundreds like you in my career. It's always the same story: getting into the toilet when I am on my rounds and then claiming you got into the wrong coach. Just tell me, are you in possession of a ticket or not?'

Yadu sensed that lying was not going to take him anywhere with this man. 'I don't have a ticket,' he admitted.

The TTE placed his right leg on the opposite wall to serve as a barrier for Yadu. He then let go of Yadu's hand, and took out his receipt book.

'Pay a ten-rupee fine and get off at this station,' he ordered.

'*Ten rupees*! But I don't have that much money.' Yadu pulled out his wallet and showed him what he had.

The TTE dropped his right leg and caught hold of Yadu's arm once again.

'Well, come with me to the station master then. You people will learn a lesson only if you are jailed for a few days.'

'Jailed?' Yadu's heart sank faster than a pebble thrown into a pond. 'Sir, please don't do that,' he pleaded.

The TTE pulled Yadu onto the platform and started dragging him towards the station master's cabin.

'Can't you pardon me this once? I usually don't travel ticketless.'

'Just shut up,' the TTE snarled

'But mine is a genuine case,' Yadu appealed. 'I was forced to board the train because of certain unavoidable circumstances. If you would only listen for a second...'

The TTE butted in once again. 'I don't want to. Just keep moving.'

Yadu continued boldly. 'One of the coaches on this train is going to be robbed tonight. I boarded the train to try and stop it. I didn't have the time or the money to buy a ticket.'

The TTE turned sharply to look at him. 'Now that's a new one,' he sneered. 'I haven't heard that excuse before. You have a very vivid imagination, I must say.' The man's comments dripped with sarcasm, and Yadu felt like slapping him across his face.

'Will you please allow me to finish what I am saying?' Yadu asked, his temper rising.

'Shut your mouth and keep walking,' said the TTE rudely.

Yadu fell silent. He could see there was no point. The man just didn't want to listen. It was his bad luck that he got caught by a TTE with a really bad temper. And such bad timing! He had just caught sight of Dorai, and here he was about to be jailed.

The thought of Dorai made him turn instinctively towards C1, to see if he was about. He was there alright, standing by the back door, surveying the platform. Yadu quickly turned away so he wouldn't be noticed.

The station master's cabin was only a short distance from where C5 had stopped. They went directly in, only to find it empty. Neither was the station master around nor the night clerk. This made the TTE all the more furious. He banged one of the desks angrily and then pulled Yadu out.

'Let's wait here. At least I can catch the station master's eyes if he is wandering about.'

Yadu said nothing. He stood silently beside the TTE, with his eyes riveted on Dorai, who was around two hundred metres away. The TTE was getting very restless, looking here and there, hoping to catch sight of the station master. Yadu had already caught sight of him. He was standing at the far end of the platform, very near the engine. It appeared as if he was having a conversation with the engine driver. Yadu didn't bother mentioning this to the TTE. His eyes now fell on a railway employee as he made his way towards a bell. It looked as if they weren't stopping here for long. Yadu could see that the TTE was well aware of this going by the way he kept looking at his watch every ten seconds.

'You better leave me here and get back to your coach,' Yadu suggested cheekily. 'Unless you want to miss the train.' Now that he was caught he didn't care about being nice to the man.

The TTE grunted at this suggestion.

Yadu was keen to find out what the TTE intended to do. There was no way the station master was going to arrive here in the next few minutes. The bald man would have to swallow his pride and let go off him. But what if he didn't?

Yadu gave himself another minute. If the man didn't leave him by then he was going to sock him off his feet. He knew he could do it. The man wouldn't even know what hit him. But Yadu was deliberately putting it off for the last minute because he couldn't get himself to do it. After all the man was just doing his duty. It somehow didn't seem right to hit him for that.

So Yadu started to pester the TTE to leave him. The man kept ignoring him.

Time ticked by slowly. He knew the train might start to move any minute now.

He started preparing himself mentally for the assault.

At that moment things started to happen, all at once.

Dorai suddenly jumped off the coach and started walking towards the station entrance. His usually grave face now wore a broad smile. Yadu's eyes followed his gaze and went to the station entrance where three men had just made an entrance. His heart started to beat faster as he recognised the men. The man in the middle was none other than Hardaker! Walking on his left was Sethu, and to his right was an Englishman. An associate of Hardaker, no doubt, thought Yadu. This man was as tall as Hardaker, only much younger, probably in his early twenties. He had blond, spiky hair, had arms that were a bit too long for his body, and walked like a gorilla.

Yadu could hardly take his eyes off Hardaker. So, here it was, proof that they were indeed going ahead with the strike.

Meanwhile, the noose around his neck was tightening. The TTE had finally managed to spot a railway employee passing by. While Yadu's attention was focused on Hardaker and his men, the TTE called the man over and started explaining to him that Yadu was a ticketless traveller who had to be handed over to the station master on his arrival.

Yadu was aware of what was going on beside him, but he was more riveted by what was happening in front of him. He watched as Dorai and Hardaker approached each other. They met in the middle of the platform and shook hands perfunctorily. Dorai said something to Hardaker, and then all four of them started walking towards their coach.

Beside him, the railway employee who was dressed in khakhi shorts and khakhi shirt, nodded dutifully to whatever the TTE said. The ticket examiner now released his grip on Yadu's hand, and the employee took over custody.

At the far end of the platform the station master now blew his whistle. He started waving his green flag. As if on cue the man by the bell started ringing it. Yadu watched with bated breath as Hardaker and his men jogged up the platform and boarded the coach just in front of C4.

The TTE, happy with the way things had worked, gave Yadu a dirty smile and then started running in the direction of his coach.

Now or never, Yadu thought. He had to get back on to the train immediately. He waited until the TTE was out of sight, and then he turned to the man holding him. He saw his face for the first time. So far he had just registered as a man dressed in khakhi. He was dark-skinned and sported a brush moustache.

Yadu decided to appeal to his reasoning.

'Look my friend, I have nothing against you, and you have nothing against me. Just leave me so that I can go catch the train.'

The man dressed in khakhi shook his head. 'I can't do that,' he said categorically. 'The TTE asked me to hand you over to the station master. '

'*Ayya*, I am in an emergency, *please.*'

The man stared at him, said nothing.

'Take a look at me. Do I look like the kind of guy who travels ticketless?' Yadu asked.

The man grinned. 'That's what they all say. You better talk to the station master when he comes.'

'I can't do that,' said Yadu desperately. 'I can't afford to miss this train.'

'And I can't afford to lose this job.'

'But nobody needs to know about it. I won't tell anybody. Just leave me, please.'

'Will you stop bothering me now?'

Yadu bit his nails. This one seemed like another hard nut to crack. He decided to try a different approach. He was just wondering whether he should try bribing the fellow, when the man himself broached the subject.

'Maybe if you greased my palm a bit, my grip on you might loosen,' he said with a wink.

Yadu was mighty relieved to hear this. He pulled his wallet out of his trouser pocket and gave it to the man. 'There is not much money in there, but keep the wallet. That's worth a lot of money.'

The man looked around stealthily, then pocketed the wallet without even looking inside. His grip on Yadu loosened immediately. Yadu thanked the man, who walked away without even looking back. Yadu heaved a huge sigh of relief. He was free again.

The train had started to move, and Yadu made a run for it. He couldn't help feeling that all this train chasing was becoming a habit with him.

He felt good as he ran up the platform, and not without reason. He had finally managed to find his father's kidnappers. Now all that remained was to have them nabbed. Piece of cake.

Even as he ran Yadu decided that he would board the same coach that Hardaker and his men had boarded. That way he could have an eye on their movements until Jolarpet. But how was he going to tackle the TTE of this coach? Perhaps he could take him into his confidence and brief him of the situation. Of course that depended on the kind of person the TTE was. If he was a moron like the one in C5 then he wouldn't risk telling him anything. But if he turned out to be an understanding type then he could explain everything to him and seek his help in apprehending the criminals.

Yadu had covered quite a distance by this time. As he drew closer he realised that the gang had boarded F1. They were travelling first class; he should have known.

He was soon alongside F1. He caught the handrail and got aboard the train. Yet again.

13

The next ten minutes unfolded in a rather bizarre fashion for Yadu.

As soon as he got aboard the coach he found the coupe that Hardaker and his men had got into, courtesy the wet footprints they left behind them. So it had started off quite promisingly.

Having found their coupe Yadu decided to eavesdrop on their conversation to see if he could pick up any details about the forthcoming heist. His reasoning went something like this: if he knew exactly where they were going to strike then he could plan his moves accordingly. That was the basic idea.

So Yadu got to their door, and after making sure the door had been bolted from the inside, he got down on his knees, and then peered inside. There was a tiny slit, just a little thicker than a pencil line where the two doors met. Yadu had to jam his eye close to the door to see.

But see he did. He saw the blond Englishman lying on a settee to his left. Hardaker was standing opposite him with his hands tucked into his trouser pockets. They were talking to each other in low whispers. Yadu heard Hardaker address the man as Icy. What a peculiar name, thought Yadu.

Yadu couldn't see the other two. He guessed that they were seated on the settee to his right, which was out of his view.

He now removed his eye from the slit and placed his left ear there, in the hope that he could hear their conversation.

This is when things started to go wrong for Yadu.

Since Hardaker and his men were talking in low voices he couldn't hear very clearly. Every now and then he heard a stray phrase like 'signal router' or 'the linesman's duty', or something like that which made no sense to him. He decided to counter this by concentrating harder. So he jammed his ear to the crack and focused on the conversation intensely.

Engrossed as he was in this fashion, Yadu failed to pick up a sound that came from behind him. Somebody had just come out of the toilet at the back, and the click of the toilet door failed to register in his mind. If he had heard the door and if he had leapt up to his feet immediately then there was a chance that he could have escaped without being noticed. But it didn't happen that way.

The man came out of the toilet and walked up the aisle. No doubt he noticed the young boy crouched suspiciously outside a coupe. He started walking briskly towards him. Yadu was unaware of the man until he was just about twenty feet away from him. He suddenly heard the man's frenzied footsteps and whirled around to see who it was. His face registered shock and bewilderment as he recognised the man.

Dorai.

Gripped by panic, Yadu couldn't think straight. How the hell? he wondered. He had taken it for granted that all four of them had got into the coupe. It now looked as if he had jumped to the wrong conclusion. He realised now what must have happened. Dorai had probably gone straight to the toilet upon boarding the coach while the rest of them had gone to their coupe.

He could see Dorai's eyes boring through him; the goon had already recognised him. Yadu shot up to his feet and sprinted towards the forward end of the train. If Dorai pulled out his gun now and shot him he was not liable to miss. He was a sitting duck as long as he remained on the aisle. Even if he reached the door he didn't have that many options. The train was moving too fast for him to try jumping out.

He turned back even as he ran, just once, to see what Dorai was up to. The hoodlum hadn't whipped out his gun for some reason. Having reached their coupe he started to bang loudly on the door. It looked as if he was going to warn his colleagues first before he came after him.

By now Yadu had reached the front of the coach. Until this moment he had been thinking of getting into a toilet to save himself. But now he decided that even that was unsafe. The only chance he had of getting out of this situation alive was by getting onto the roof.

~

Hardaker opened the door in response to Dorai's frantic banging.

'We have a problem,' Dorai said bluntly. 'Yadu is on the train.'

A shell-shocked silence ensued for a few seconds.

Icy's face had twisted into a nasty scowl. 'Yadu?'

Dorai nodded. 'He was by this door just now eavesdropping on your conversation.'

'Are you sure it was him?' Hardaker asked. His voice had suddenly acquired a steely timbre.

'Yes,' Dorai replied. 'I got a good look at him.'

'But what's that boy doing on this train?' Sethu wondered.

'He must have come here to stop us from carrying out our little heist,' said Dorai, chuckling.

'He must have followed us here. The gall...wait till I get my hands on him!' Sethu bellowed.

'Where is he now?' Hardaker asked.

'He ran towards the front. I thought I'd inform you before I go after him. He can't go very far now, can he?'

'Good thinking,' Hardaker murmured. 'But don't go alone. Take Icy and Sethu with you.'

'You want us to bring him back here?' Sethu asked.

'What for? Just shoot him and throw him off the train.'

Dorai started walking towards the front, with Sethu following close behind him. Icy brought up the rear.

'Come back quickly,' Hardaker hissed. 'We have work to do.'

~

By the time Dorai, Icy and Sethu arrived by the toilets, Yadu had already clambered onto the roof of the coach. He had got a thirty-second head start on them and he had made the best use of it.

The climb to the top had been pretty arduous, but that seemed nothing compared to what he was experiencing on the roof now. He was being hit on the chest by gale-force strength head winds that threatened to blow him right off the top of the coach. He had never felt winds of this magnitude in his life before. He found it hard even to breathe.

In a way Yadu was unlucky because this was probably the worst night anybody could have chosen to get atop a train. It was a stormy night with prevailing winds reaching speeds of up to sixty kilometres per hour. This, combined with the fact that the train was travelling at almost seventy kilometres per hour, resulted in wind velocities in excess of one hundred and thirty kilometres per hour on top of the train. This was good enough to throw an average-sized man right off his feet. This was what Yadu was up against. Not just that, his face was being relentlessly stung by rain pellets, so much so that he could hardly see in front of him. As it is he couldn't see clearly because the rooftop was pitch dark.

Yadu's first decision upon arriving on top was that, no matter what, he was not going to run towards the forward end of the train. He wouldn't last twenty seconds on the roof if he tried that. He started running towards the tail end of the train. This way it was his back that bore the brunt of the head wind and breathing was a bit easier.

As can be imagined, running was not easy in the prevailing conditions. The coach was swaying madly underneath him, first this way, then that way. Yadu had to get his body rhythm in tandem with the movement of the coach. He had to anticipate when it would sway next and adjust his balance accordingly. And, he had to do this even as he ran at top speed on a rain-slick, treacherous surface.

For the first few seconds he ran cautiously trying to get used to it all. But then he heard a grunt from somewhere behind him. He glanced around and noticed that somebody was already climbing onto the rooftop! This made him run faster, his clothes now flapping under the pressure of the wind.

He had an intense desire to turn back and see who the person behind him was. But right now every second counted. He had to put as much distance as possible between him and his pursuers; so he resisted the temptation to look back.

But something happened the very next second that forced him to slow down and turn around.

He heard a gunshot.

'There he is,' Dorai shouted. The stockily-built man with the bulging biceps had already made it to the roof. He was now running in Yadu's direction holding a gun in his right hand. Behind him there were two others who were clambering onto the roof.

Yadu had covered perhaps less than hundred metres when he heard a cry that scythed through the air. 'Stop or I'll shoot!' Dorai screamed.

Yadu ignored the warning. He had arrived at the coupling gap that separated this coach from the next one. He concentrated on clearing the four feet wide chasm in front of him.

Clearing four feet on ground was one thing, but having to clear it under these conditions was something else. He had to take into consideration the sway of the coach, the speed at which the train was travelling, and most importantly, the slippery nature of the surface he was landing on.

He put on a fresh burst of speed, prayed, and then leapt.

He landed on the roof of the adjoining coach with a thump. Amazingly, he didn't skid off to one side or lose his balance. On touch-down he began to run once again. The wind was still screaming in his ears. The train was passing through a barren landscape, not that Yadu had eyes for it. His entire focus was on not slipping. It was tough, because every now and then he had to leap across some contraption that jutted out of the roof. He guessed that they were light tops. They looked harmless, but if he stumbled on one of them that would be good enough to send him careening into the night.

Yadu turned to see how far back the men were. The other two men were quite far away, but Dorai had caught up with him incredibly fast. The man was running as if he was running on land; he was literally charging down the coach like a bull. Yadu however noticed something that gave him a little hope. The gun that was in his hand a while back was gone. The man must have accidentally dropped it while he ran. One thing less to worry about.

A few seconds later he heard a thump behind him. Dorai was now on the same coach as he was. He was probably less than twenty metres away from him now. And he was gaining on him rapidly. Yadu's heart was hammering wildly inside him.

Yadu reached another coupling gap and he leapt across it cleanly. So did Dorai, who landed just seconds after him. He could now feel Dorai's hands reaching out to grab him. He knew that this was it. Any minute now the man would lunge at him and bring him down. Or worse still he might push him off the coach. He shuddered at the very thought of flying through the air and landing on the ground. The sheer speed at which the train was moving would ensure that every bone in his body would break on impact.

They were running atop C6 now. When they were about halfway down the coach Yadu's luck finally ran out. Dorai lunged forward and brought Yadu down onto his knees. He quickly tried to pin him down, but Yadu slipped out of his grip. He turned around and punched Dorai sharply on his chin.

Dorai's retaliation was immediate and severe. He punched him in his stomach. Such was the power behind Dorai's punch that Yadu doubled over in pain. Seizing this opportunity Dorai locked his fingers together and brought his hands down like a club onto Yadu's back. Yadu felt as if he'd just been hit by a tree trunk. The pain that shot through his back was sharp and searing.

Before he could even recover from this blow Dorai struck again. And again.

Yadu was in no position to block the blows or prepare for a counter-attack. What was worse, from the corner of his eyes he noticed Sethu and Icy approaching fast.

Dorai could see that he had the situation well under control, so he got to his feet.

'Eavesdropping on us, were you? Do you want to know how Hardaker deals with nosey pests? Well, find out.' Dorai kicked him again, and Yadu groaned in pain.

Dorai now pulled Yadu up on his feet and then delivered a powerful right upper cut. Such was the force of the blow that Yadu was airborne before he came crashing down. Luckily he landed in the centre of the coach. Blood dripped from a wound in his left forehead.

Dorai now walked up to him and prepared to kick Yadu once again. He was staring at him and was blabbering about how Hardaker usually dealt with people who came in his way. Yadu saw Dorai's right foot swing. He watched as it swung towards his stomach. In a flash he moved out of its way, and made a grab for the foot. He managed to catch it, and then held on tightly to it. It happened so fast that Dorai was completely taken by surprise. Yadu now kicked at Dorai's left shin so hard that the man's leg gave way. A stunned Dorai landed on his left knee with his right leg stretched and in Yadu's hold. The man howled in agony as his groin region landed on the edge of a light top.

Yadu swiftly got to his feet, and then kicked him hard on his groin once more. He then leapt over the man and started running.

Dorai, who was embarrassed, angry and in agony, pulled himself up with considerable effort. He kicked his legs to rid them of the pain. Then he started chasing Yadu as if nothing had happened. And this time he started running even faster than before.

Yadu's sense of relief at having escaped from Dorai's clutches didn't last all that long. In fact, it lasted just thirty seconds. That's all the time it took for Dorai to catch up with him once again.

This time Dorai got behind Yadu and then gave him a solid push. Yadu went sprawling on the roof. He would have ended up sliding off if it hadn't been for his presence of mind. Even as he slipped he saw a light top in a blur and held onto it. He hung onto it for dear life as his lower body swayed with the inertia of the fall.

In the end all this turned out to be most fortunate, because when Yadu fell, Dorai who was right behind, lost his balance and toppled over his legs. Yadu had fallen directly in Dorai's path.

Whereas Yadu had the chance to catch a light top, Dorai had nothing to hold on to. For a second he lunged madly at Yadu's legs but that swung out of his reach and Dorai found himself sliding down the side.

For a brief moment Yadu thought that was the end of Dorai, because he slipped out of view. But when he got to his feet he noticed the man's hands gripping a lip-like protrusion on the roof. He had half a mind to go to the edge and stamp the man's fingers until he let go. But he looked back and noticed the other two advancing rapidly towards him.

Yadu turned around and started running again. Survival came first.

~

The way it turned out, Yadu needn't even have bothered running so hard, because Sethu and Icy had suddenly lost all interest in him. They saw Dorai hanging for his life and went to his help.

Yadu didn't notice this until he had gone some distance. He stopped near the next coupling gap to see how far back his pursuers were. Only then did he notice that they weren't behind him at all. The two of them were lying flat on their stomachs with their arms stretched towards Dorai.

Here was his chance to disappear out of view. They were too engrossed in rescuing their partner to bother about him now.

He took a quick decision. He would head back directly to the coach he had first boarded (C10) and would hide there until Jolarpet.

14

For a long, long time Vandana debated with herself whether she had done the right thing by refusing to help the boy. It had been a tough call to make. She liked to think that she was a helpful kind of person. Whenever an opportunity arose where her help was demanded she usually never refused. In fact, she always went out of her way to help people. But this time, to her own surprise, she had bluntly refused. She now pondered on why she had taken such a decision. Had she been justified in refusing to help him? Or had she behaved like a prude?

The boy, whatever his name was, had looked decent and had seemed to be an honest type. He had asked her very politely and all, and even her instinct had told her that he was telling her the truth about why he had got aboard ticketless. So why had she refused to help him then? Did it have anything to do with the fact that he was male and was of the same age as she was? She thought about this for a while. She had to admit that this could have been one of the reasons. If the person had been an honest sixteen-year-old *girl*, then she would have readily agreed to help her. Or for that matter if it had been an older woman, or an aged man, she would have surely bailed any of them out. She decided that it was his fault that he belonged to the wrong gender and the wrong age group.

She told herself that boys of that age group couldn't be trusted – no matter how innocent they looked, no mater how genuine their case sounded – at least not inside a public toilet. Boys these days had so much adrenalin that they were capable of *anything*. Better safe than sorry, she told herself.

She still couldn't help wondering about what had happened to the boy though. When she had last glanced in the direction of the toilets the boy was not around. But the TTE had been hovering around the place impatiently, as if waiting for one of the toilet doors to open. Had the boy been caught by the TTE? Had he been detained at Katpadi?

Vandana decided to throw her guilt-ridden thoughts out of her head and think about something else. She looked out of the window and promised herself that for the next hour she wouldn't entertain any thoughts about the boy in her head.

She wasn't very successful in this attempt though. Her mind drifted aimlessly for a while, and then came right back to thoughts about the boy. She realised that if she had to get this guilty feeling out of her system, then she had to discuss this issue with her sister. But the trouble was, her elder sister Kanchana with whom she was travelling, was fast asleep. Vandana had already looked in her direction a few times in the hope that she would wake up from her sleep. But knowing Kanchana, she was not going to get up again until they reached Palghat.

This train trip from Madras to Palghat was the first time the two sisters were travelling with just each other for company. The reason for this was that Vandana lived with her parents in Palghat (which was an hour to the west of Coimbatore) while Kanchana lived in Madras (with her husband and two children).

Kanchana was ten years older than Vandana. She had been married for the past eight years. All this while she had lived in Madras, since her husband's job was based in that city. Raghupathy, Kanchana's husband was a journalist who worked for the *Hindu*.

Two weeks back, Vandana and her mother had dashed off to Madras to consult a couple of the city's leading doctors about her father's condition. Harikumar, Vandana's father, had been grievously ill for the past few months. The doctors in Palghat feared that he had cancer. Vandana and her mother had obviously been shocked to hear this news. In panic they had called up Raghupathy. He had asked them to come to Madras with the reports so they could get a second opinion. On their arrival in Madras, the three of them had visited two specialists, who to their extreme relief had told them that the preliminary diagnosis was wrong: Harikumar was *not* suffering from cancer. Upon hearing this good news, Mrs Harikumar had rushed back immediately to Palghat to tend to her husband, while Vandana had stayed back at her sister's place for a week. Now, she was escorting her sister to Palghat so she could visit her ill father. Raghupathy was to join them the next week and he was to take Kanchana back to Madras.

It was due to these complicated circumstances that the two sisters found themselves travelling with each other and with no other escort.

For Vandana, the past three months had been a horrible time. She had just attended two months of her pre-university college when her father had been struck ill. For the past three months she hadn't been able to attend classes owing to her father's illness. Both mother and daughter had to take turns being in the hospital and taking care of the house. The long hours and the chores had sucked all of Vandana's energy away. Only in the past one week, after they had found out her father would recover soon, had she started enjoying herself again. Now she had to go back to school and cram all the lessons she had missed before her exams began.

Vandana cast yet another hope-filled glance at her sister, only to find her sleeping soundly, oblivious of the racket the trains' wheels were making. She couldn't help feeling a bit envious of her sister. Kanchi had this ability to sleep anywhere she wished, for however long she wanted. It didn't matter if the lights were on or if an aeroplane was gearing up for take off nearby. She would sleep through it all. Vandana unfortunately was at the other end of the spectrum. She was an insomniac. She got just four hours of sleep every night – if she was lucky.

She now mentally prepared herself for a long boring night ahead. From past experience she knew that there was nothing more boring in the world than sitting alone in a dark compartment and watching everybody else sleep peacefully.

She wished something exciting would happen on the train tonight – like that robbery the boy had mentioned – that would make the hours fly by quickly. But she told herself that nothing of that sort would happen, because nobody up there ever listened to her requests anyway.

Vandana was to realise only much later how mistaken she was. She was going to get all the excitement she could possibly manage, and a bit more, in just a short while.

15

It all started with Vandana hearing the sound of running feet on the roof above. She heard a 'thump' first as somebody landed on the roof, and then she heard the frenzied 'thud-thud' of running shoes. She got up from her seat and looked around to see if any other passenger had heard it. But almost all of them were already asleep by now, and the sound had not been loud enough to wake any of them.

Vandana got back to her seat and was just about to sit down when she heard another 'thump'. Now somebody else had got onto their roof and was running on it. This naturally baffled her. She couldn't understand why anybody would be foolish enough to run on the slippery roof in this kind of weather. Her curiosity was aroused, and part of her wanted to go to the door and see what was happening on the roof. But she decided against it and re-occupied her seat.

After that, for a couple of minutes, there was complete silence.

And then she heard the sound of more running feet. This time she was really intrigued. She got up from her seat and walked swiftly to the nearest exit door, which was at the back of the coach. She opened the door and was met with a blast of wind and rain. Unmindful of this she leaned out to see if she could see anybody on the roof. From the sound of the running feet she had already guessed that the men were running from the front to the back of the train. So she leaned and checked the back of the train first.

She was just in time to see the silhouettes of two men as they ran atop the next coach. Then they disappeared out of sight. There was no sign of the other two men who had preceded these two.

Vandana wondered whether she had to report what she had seen to the TTE. She decided not to bother for the time being.

She walked back to her seat to find Kanchana still fast asleep. She pulled out a cloth from one of her bags and started wiping her face. Vandana undid her hair, wiped it dry, combed it again, and then folded it into a single plait. She didn't hear any more sounds from the roof above.

Outside, the rains had toned down to a light drizzle but the powerful winds and the flashes of lightning remained.

Ordinarily, Vandana would have remained in her seat for the rest of the night and watched the wet countryside. She wouldn't have given another thought about the men who had run on the roof. But since she was feeling extremely bored, and since she had already spent close to four hours on the hard wooden bench they called a seat, she decided that she would rather stand by the exit door for a while.

For Vandana, that is how it all started – with her decision to stand by the exit door.

Shortly after she arrived by the exit door, the Mangalore Express made an unexpected, unscheduled stop at a small station called Ambur. Vandana had travelled umpteen times on this route before, and she knew that this train never ever stopped at this station.

Wanting to know the reason for the halt she stepped down onto the sparsely lit platform. It drizzled lightly but this didn't bother her in the least. She walked a little distance to see what the matter was. The place looked like a ghost station. One couldn't even call it a proper railway station. It had a raised platform, yes, and an asbestos-sheeted tiny office. But that was it. There was not a soul on the platform: no passengers, no railway employees, not even a station master.

She looked around hoping one of the TTEs would get down so that she could ask them what the matter was. But nobody got down.

She waited patiently for a while. The cold winds, the emptiness of the vast platform and the all-pervading darkness finally played on her nerves. She decided to get back onto the train as she felt very uncomfortable standing there.

She turned around to head back towards the C5 door when something caught her eye. She noticed a dark figure on the roof leaping from coach to coach. The man was headed this way. Vandana stopped right where she was and watched the man. He was now on C3 and was advancing quite rapidly. Since he was still quite far away she couldn't make out his features clearly. The way he was running though suggested that he was in an enormous hurry.

Vandana's eyes were transfixed on him. She watched his every movement carefully. As he came nearer she noticed that even as he ran he was waving at somebody. She looked back instinctively to see who he was waving at. There seemed to be no one behind her. For a moment she didn't get it. Then she realised that he was waving to somebody on the other side of the train.

Her curiosity was further aroused now. The train stopping in no man's land, the men running on top of the coaches for the past twenty minutes.... She wanted to get to the bottom of all this.

Vandana quickly boarded her coach, walked to the door on the other side, and pulled it open. She was about to peep out to see if there was anybody on this side when she heard voices. There *was* somebody on this side. Actually, from the voices she could make out that there were two of them. From the way their voices kept growing louder and louder she guessed that they were walking towards the forward end of the train. They were fast approaching the door near where Vandana stood.

She quietly closed the door, but not fully. She left a gap through which light from the coach fell on the ground below. She now waited for the men to pass the door and hoped the light from the coach would fall on their faces as they passed. Vandana had a feeling that these men walking alongside the train were the same ones who were running atop the roof sometime back.

Shortly, the two men passed by the door. The light pouring out of the coach illuminated their faces. One of them was a vellayan, a white man, and the other was a bearded local with long flowing hair. Both were tall. The white man had blond, spiky hair and looked very young. The bearded man looked a few years older. He was thirtyish, she guessed.

Having seen the foreigner, Vandana grew even more curious. What was this man up to? What had they got off the train for? She decided she wanted to have another look at them so she got up and started running towards the forward end of the coach.

When she reached the exit door at the front, she found the door was closed and she didn't bother opening it. She knelt down so that the window in the mid-portion of the door was at her eye-level.

And then she waited for the men to pass her.

4...3...2...1

The men passed by the door, unaware that a girl was watching them from a window less than three feet away. By now both men had slowed down. Vandana watched them walk a little further and stop by the coupling gap.

At first she didn't realise why. Then she heard a voice ring out: 'What's the matter? Why has the train stopped?' From the accent she realised that it was the foreigner talking.

'We are waiting for a goods train to pass,' someone said. This voice came from atop the roof.

The man on the roof said something else, but Vandana didn't hear that bit. She had to get closer to them if she wanted to hear what they were saying. She ruled out getting down from the coach for safety reasons. They would spot her as soon as she stepped out. She decided that getting into the nearby toilet was a better idea. The toilet was right next to the coupling gap and just a few metres from where the two men stood. She supposed that she had a better chance of hearing their conversation through the toilet window than from here.

She went to the toilet on the left and found it unoccupied. She went in, closed the door shut, and put the bolt into place. She could already hear their voices a little more clearly. She peered through the tiny gap between the window bars and noticed the two men standing side by side. Their heads were cocked up towards the roof, where Vandana supposed the other man was standing.

She heard the bearded one ask, 'How long is it going to take, Dorai?'

'At least another ten minutes,' the man on the roof said.

She heard the Englishman curse rudely upon hearing about the delay.

'You found the boy yet?' the man on the roof asked.

'Not yet,' muttered the bearded man.

'Did you tell Brian what happened?' the Englishman asked.

Vandana couldn't hear what the man said in reply. There was a pause. Then he said, 'I thought he was going to shoot me, I swear.'

The bearded man gave a throaty laugh.

'You are still alive,' the Englishman said sardonically.

'Thank God, it wasn't my job to tell the boss the news,' the bearded man said grinning.

'Don't laugh just yet, Sethu,' the man on the roof warned. 'Hardaker wants to talk with the two of you. He's waiting for you outside his coach.'

The young Englishman muttered something under his breath that Vandana didn't quite catch.

'What about the boy then?' the bearded man asked.

'Let's see what Hardaker's got to say. Then we'll come back for the boy.'

Vandana peered through the window bars. She noticed the two of them exchange glances.

'Alright Dorai, you go ahead. We'll follow behind,' the blond Englishman said.

Vandana's mind had already started connecting the dots. The boy without the ticket had said he had boarded the train to stop a robbery. He had said that the gang leader was an Englishman. She had just caught sight of an Englishman here. Was this just a coincidence, or had the boy been telling her the truth? Had he really boarded the train to stop a robbery? Had she made a grave error by not helping him?

Vandana's guilt came back to her in a rush, smothering her. God, what have I done? she thought. If the boy had indeed been caught by the TTE, and if he had been detained at Katpadi, then there was probably nobody else on the train who knew about the impending robbery. There was nobody else to stop this robbery. She felt responsible for this state of affairs. If she had just listened to the boy and had helped him...

Vandana shut her eyes for a few seconds. She could see the faces of the two men now, the one called Sethu, and the spiky-haired Englishman. They had looked every bit like hoodlums, both of them. It was not just their faces, even the behaviour of these three men looked suspicious. What business had they atop the roof anyway? Why had they been running up and down the train for the past twenty minutes?

Vandana decided she had to get to the bottom of this, if not for her sake, at least for the sake of the boy who she had refused to help. She had to find out where these men were headed and what they were planning. If she knew for certain that these men were the robbers the boy had been after, then she could go to the police and try to stop them.

She craned her neck and looked to her right. She saw the two men walking towards the front. She could see the one on the roof too, albeit far away.

She decided to get off the train and follow them. If she found out what coach they were travelling in then she could inform the authorities. She could give them a physical description and they would take care of the rest.

She got out of the toilet, went quickly to the exit door and pulled it open. The man on the roof had said that it would be at least another ten minutes before the train was on its way again. Ten minutes was enough time to follow them to their coach and get back here. She slipped down onto the track bed.

The ground under her feet felt squishy. It was still drizzling steadily, and the robust wind chilled her to the bone. To her left was a railway track running alongside the one where the Mangalore Express stood. Beyond that was a dilapidated building overgrown with vines, and further beyond that a number of huts. The entire place was reverberating with the croaking of scores of frogs.

Vandana walked as swiftly as she possibly could, so that she could keep up with the men in front of her. The man on the roof was already out of sight. Sethu and the Englishman were about a hundred metres ahead of her.

She now noticed a tall foreigner get down from what looked like the first class coach. The bearing, the posture of the man, the way he stood with his hands tucked into his raincoat pockets – Vandana had no doubts that this man was their ringleader. He was bald; that much she could make out even from this distance. Also, he looked older than the rest of the men.

The man on the roof was now standing on top of F1. Even as she watched he slid down the side of the coach and then joined the Englishman on the ground.

She started to walk faster. Sethu and the blond Englishman had reached the other two. The four of them huddled together and were talking.

Vandana was hugging the shadow of the train, afraid that one of them would notice her if she went any nearer. She had to get closer though. She *had* to know what they were doing on this train.

She walked until she was less than fifty feet away from the four of them. It still wasn't good enough. She couldn't hear a word of what they were saying. All that she could make out from the gang leader's body language was that he was extremely angry with his men.

Vandana was getting desperate now. She had to get close to them – yet not be seen by them. What was she going to do?

She looked at the train on her right side and got an idea. She realised that there was a way for her to get close enough to them. But it was dangerous. Extremely dangerous.

The idea was pretty simple. Hardaker and his men were standing on the ground right next to the track. If she got underneath the train and crawled the next fifty feet, then she would be right beside them without them realising it. She was sure she would be able to hear every word of what they said. But did she dare to do it?

Vandana was in a fix. She found the idea enticing. But when she thought of what she had to do, it churned her stomach inside out.

The four men lit their cigarettes. It looked as if they were going to be there for a while. She looked at the horizon to see if the goods train had arrived yet. It hadn't.

Vandana took a deep breath. She was going to do it; she was going to risk it as repentance for not helping the boy. She got to her knees immediately and then crawled under the train.

An indescribable stink hit her as she crawled under. For the first few seconds it was so bad that she thought she was going to throw up. But she carried on. She moved as quickly as her knees carried her. In some places she had to bend real low so that her head wouldn't hit the under-carriage of the coach. The fifty odd metres felt like five hundred.

A couple of minutes of crawling brought her right beside their feet.

'...you have no idea where the boy is now, is that right?' the older Englishman was saying. The tone with which he spoke suggested that he was trying hard to suppress his anger.

Vandana was truly amazed by the clarity with which she could hear them now. And the best part was, they didn't even know she was listening to every word of what they said.

'Brian, it was an accident. It could have happened to anybody,' the spiky-haired Englishman replied. 'Dorai stumbled on the boy and lost his balance. What were we supposed to do? Leave Dorai hanging like that and go after the boy?'

'Yes, Icy!' shouted Hardaker emphatically. 'One of you should have stayed back and the other should have gone after Yadu. Now look what you people have done.'

'Boss, Dorai could not have been pulled up by one man. It took ten minutes for two of us.'

For the next few seconds Hardaker cursed all of them in the choicest expletives. All three of them stood with their heads hung low. Then he shot a glance at his watch and his demeanour changed dramatically.

'What's happened has happened. Let's move on.'

This suited the three of them just fine. They nodded in relief.

'So what do we do about Yadu?' he asked. 'He knows everything now. He is surely going to head for the station master's cabin in Jolarpet.'

'We'll find him before Jolarpet, Brian. We still have around forty-five minutes,' Dorai piped in.

'It's just five coaches that we have to search. It won't take more than fifteen minutes if we split it between us,' Sethu suggested.

'It's not just five coaches, idiot. You have to search the whole train!' Hardaker barked. 'He might have shifted to one of the front coaches even as we speak.'

'Still not a problem, Brian,' said Dorai.

'As for him going to the station master at Jolarpet, you can rest at ease. The three of us will stand guard by the cabin. If the boy comes anywhere near the place we'll blow his head off.'

Hardaker fell silent on hearing this.

Under the train Vandana was getting edgy. She realised that they were talking about the boy she had refused to help: Yadu. These men intended to kill him. This was indeed serious stuff she was hearing.

She had by now pieced together what must have happened: the boy had somehow found out about the heist. He had boarded the train in a hurry to stop it, but to his bad luck these men had seen him on the train and were now hounding him.

Vandana looked at her watch. She decided that she was going to give this conversation another three minutes then she would start crawling back. She would be putting her life at risk if she stayed any longer.

Hardaker relit his cigar, and then started his tirade once again. 'Just make sure the boy doesn't mess up our plans. He needs to be found by Erode. That's all I care about.'

'Forget Erode, Brian. We'll find him by Jolarpet,' Dorai said confidently.

A period of silence followed this statement.

Then Sethu came up with a query. 'Just for curiosity's sake, Brian, what if we don't find the boy? Do we still go ahead with the hit?' he asked.

There was pin-drop silence for a moment as the Englishman considered this.

'We stick to our plans *no matter what happens*. Is that clear?' Hardaker snarled.

There was a brief silence. Vandana sensed that everybody was nodding their heads respectfully.

As an after-thought the older Englishman added, 'If for some reason we don't see each other for the next couple of hours just make sure you are all atop the RBI coach at Erode. The minute the train leaves Erode we launch our attack. Is that understood?'

'Yes,' they chorused.

Vandana could now hear the goods train arrive on the adjoining track.

The Englishman started giving instructions to his men. He split up the coaches between them and gave all three of them two coaches each to begin with, after which they were to search alternate coaches.

Vandana decided to start crawling back now. She could see the goods engine's headlights in the distance. Then, seconds later, even as she continued to crawl, the goods train shrieked passed her, giving all of Vandana's senses a severe jolt.

So far, Vandana had done everything right. But she had made one fatal error in judgement that she was soon going to pay for. The one thing she hadn't anticipated was the immediacy with which the train above her would start to move. She had expected that there would be a three-four -minute time gap from the time the goods train passed, for the Mangalore Express to start. But no sooner had the last wagon of the goods train passed her, than the Mangalore Express began to move. Vandana found herself hopelessly stuck under the train.

16

Three pairs of feet started to move. However, one pair remained rooted to the same spot. Brian Hardaker didn't move an inch, to Vandana's great dismay.

Oh my God! What have I got myself into? thought Vandana.

She took a crack at crawling back, but soon found out that that was far more difficult than crawling forward. She had no control over where her legs were going. What if it got onto one of the rails?

Vandana was beginning to realise what a death trap she had got herself into. She couldn't escape to her right because the raised platform blocked her. Moving forward made no sense. Rolling to her left would mean falling directly onto the Englishman's feet, which was far worse than getting crushed under the train's wheels. How was she going to get back onto the train now? She could of course remain immobile. That way she could save her life, but then she would miss the train. And she would have to end up spending the night, all alone, in a station that looked more eerie than a cemetery.

The engine's shrill whistle pierced the night.

The Englishman was still very much there puffing away in a leisurely fashion at his cigar. Sweat broke out on Vandana's forehead. She cursed the Englishman under her breath. Move, you scoundrel, *move*, she whispered urgently.

The metal wheels next to her started rolling a bit faster. The sound of the wheels was deafening. It was as if she was hearing it inside a tunnel.

The Englishman took one more long pull on his cigar, then stubbed it. To Vandana's great relief he finally caught hold of one of the handrails and started running after the coach in a bid to board it.

She waited until his feet disappeared from view, then she prepared to get out from under the train. She was gripped with fear looking at the ominously big wheels as they rolled past her. Those wheels, she suspected, were carrying about forty tonnes of weight on them. What if she rolled over the rail and didn't manage to get clear in time? What if her leg or one of her hands got caught? The metal wheels were heavy enough to crush the juice off her limbs.

She watched as a set of wheels clanked past her. Then she counted the number of seconds it took for the next set of wheels to arrive.

Seven seconds. That was all the time she had.

She now edged closer to the rail to her left. She had to time this right. Even if she got it wrong by a split second, all was lost.

She waited for the next set of wheels to pass. In the meantime, she sent a quick, desperate prayer up to Lord Venkatesha. If she rolled out of here unhurt, she promised him that she would roll three times around his temple in Tirupati.

A set of wheels passed by. Vandana held her breath and then rolled over the rail. She closed her eyes shut as she did.

Seconds after she rolled over to the other side the next set of wheels passed by. She didn't notice this as her eyes were still tightly shut.

Then she opened her eyes...

...and the world had never looked more beautiful.

Her limbs were intact! *She had made it!*

The surge of emotions was too much for her heart. She started sobbing uncontrollably. A considerable length of the train had already passed. The coach that had just passed her was numbered C7. If she kept crying then the next three coaches too would pass. She had to get back onto the train. Now.

She lifted her skirt up slightly and then started running alongside the train.

The Mangalore Express was moving at around 20 kmph by now. She now moved closer to the coach. A handrail passed by. She caught it, and then had to immediately let go because she wasn't running at the same speed as the train.

So she increased her speed.

She looked back and noticed another handrail coming her way. She prepared herself better this time. Now she was moving at the same speed as the train. As the handrail came nearer she let go off her skirt and got in position to grab hold of it with both hands.

She caught hold of the handrail, and tried to jump up. But her legs failed to respond. She couldn't get herself to leap! She tried once again, and again her legs failed to respond. The realisation that she was not up to it started creeping in on her now. She let go of the handrail.

Panic began to set in as she ran alongside the penultimate coach. The back of her blouse was soaked in sweat. Her thighs were quivering. She started to run faster, all the time wondering how she was going to make it aboard. Another handrail came by. She ran alongside the handrail, caught hold of it, braced herself and then tried to leap.

Again her legs failed her.

Vandana burst into tears at this point. She now knew that she was not going to make it onto the train. She was not up to it, couldn't do it, was afraid to leap because of some psychosis or God knew what.

This is it, she thought as the last coach came alongside her.

~

All this time, Yadu was watching the antics of the girl, standing at the front exit of C10. He had been standing there for the past fifteen minutes and had seen everything. He had seen the four men standing huddled together outside F1, he had seen the girl follow two of the men up to F1; he had seen her crawl under the train. And finally, after the men had dispersed, he had seen her roll out from under the moving train.

This particular act of the girl had been the most daring and the most foolish thing he had ever seen in his life.

He now watched her as she tried to get back aboard the train. Even as he watched she let go of one more handrail. The girl seemed to be having some problem in leaping up onto the coach steps. Seeing her plight Yadu decided to pull her aboard when she reached C10. But as she came closer he realised who the girl was. She was the one in the parrot-green skirt, the one who had refused to help him evade the TTE on C5.

Vandana...yes, that was her name.

Yadu instantly changed his mind about helping her. 'Serves her right,' he thought.

The girl was now alongside the exit door where he stood. He noticed that she was sobbing uncontrollably. She now looked up and saw him. Her face suddenly lit up as she recognised a familiar face.

'Help me!' she screamed. 'Pull me up please!' she said stretching out her right hand.

Yadu smirked, then ignored her.

For a moment the girl looked shocked. She had seemed so confident that he would help her get aboard. Then, suddenly, she seemed to realise why he was refusing to help.

'I am sorry I didn't help you out at Katpadi. But please don't hold that against me. I have to be aboard this train. Pull me up, *please.*'

Yadu listened to what she said, then turned to look in front deliberately. He was *loving* this. The girl had to be taught a lesson so that the next time somebody sought her help she wouldn't refuse.

The train continued to gather speed. Vandana was finding it difficult keeping pace with the coach. She was already exhausted and completely out of breath.

Getting desperate, she decided to grab hold of his attention with the only ace she held. '*Yadu*...please help me,' she screamed.

Nothing else could have got his attention any faster. He jerked swiftly to his left to look at her. Vandana knew that her gamble had paid off.

'Hey! How do you know my name?' Yadu demanded. As far as he could remember he hadn't told his name to anyone since he had boarded the train.

'Pull me up and I'll tell you,' she shouted.

Yadu was intrigued. He had to find out how this girl had learnt his name. The bandits! Yes, she must have overheard bits of their conversation. That could be the only explanation.

He decided to pull the girl up. There could be some very useful information in this for him. Besides, it was just not fair to let the girl languish in this place alone.

'Please Yadu...*please*,' Vandana cried. She was now falling back swiftly, unable to keep up with the speed of the train.

He turned around, got down the steps and then urged the girl to run faster. For a moment her eyes lit up when she realised that he was going to help her after all.

Yadu cursed himself for having reacted so late. The girl was panting so hard that there was no way she could run up and get close to him. Since the train had been travelling faster now, she had fallen behind drastically.

Then, suddenly, he had an idea.

He quickly got up the steps, cupped his hands around his mouth and shouted, 'I'll get you by the back door.'

The girl heard this and put up a fresh burst of speed.

Yadu slammed the door shut, turned into the walking aisle and then started thundering down its length. The aisle was empty. He reached the end of the coach in twelve seconds flat. He turned right, got to the door and then pulled it open.

He couldn't have timed it any better, because just then Vandana reached the door.

Yadu got down quickly to the last step, and then urged Vandana to catch hold of the handrail. This she did immediately. Then Yadu reached out for her free hand. He caught hold of it and then he screamed, 'Leap!' Even as he screamed he yanked hard on the girl's hand, and Vandana had no choice other than to leap up onto the step. Her leg landed near Yadu's. She placed her other foot quickly on the step above, and Yadu helped her the rest of the way.

Vandana reached the vestibule and collapsed in a heap.

17

Yadu closed the door shut and watched the girl sob like a child. He sensed that this had been a nerve-wracking experience for her, so he let her cry. He made no attempts to console her. He just stood there with his arms folded and watched silently.

For a couple of minutes the girl was absorbed in her crying. Then, she sensed Yadu's eyes on her. She quickly rubbed her cheeks with the back of her hand and then got up on to her feet. Avoiding eye contact with him, she went into the toilet and splashed water on her tear-streaked face. She then pulled out a half-damp handkerchief that she had tucked into her skirt and started to wipe her face with it. She reset her hair lightly with her fingers, and only when she was reasonably satisfied with her appearance did she return to face Yadu.

'Thank you *so much* for pulling me up,' she said, wiping a tear off her eye. She seemed genuinely grateful for the help. 'I mean, I didn't help you in your moment of crisis, but you still...'

'How can I forget that?' Yadu interjected sarcastically. 'I almost missed the train in Katpadi because you refused to help me. I shouldn't have pulled you aboard, really. I should have let you languish there all night in that ghastly looking station.'

'I probably deserve it too,' she agreed meekly. 'But in spite of what I did you were kind enough to help me out. You are a first class gentleman.'

Yadu snorted. 'I am no such thing, Miss. I pulled you up for purely selfish reasons. I was just curious about how you ended up under this train, that's all.'

Vandana looked up at him.

'You mean, you saw me roll out from under the train?' she asked, in a surprised tone of voice.

'I did,' he said. 'And I thought it was the most foolish, most audacious stunt anybody ever pulled off.'

This brought a weak smile on Vandana's lips. 'I didn't do it for fun, you know. My circumstances were such,' she said defensively.

'And what were these circumstances, Miss, if I may ask?'

'Please stop calling me 'Miss'. I have told you already, my name is Vandana,' she said. There was a pause. 'And you are Yadu, right?'

He nodded. 'That's another thing I want to know. How did you find out my name?'

So far both of them had been standing opposite each other. But now Yadu decided that this conversation was going to take a while, so he sat down on the coach floor. The girl looked at the floor distastefully for a second, then decided that there was no other option other than to squat opposite him.

She sat down, stretched both her legs, then said, 'Just before I rolled out from under the train I overheard a conversation the bandits were having. *You* were the topic of their discussion.'

Yadu shook his head in amazement. 'How did you know it was me they were talking about?'

'From what you told me on C5. You told me you had got aboard to stop a robbery. And these men were talking about a boy who was trying to foil their plans. Who else could they have been talking about? They mentioned your name a couple of times, and I just put two and two together.'

'I see,' he said nodding his head. 'These men who were talking about me, were there a couple of foreigners amongst them?' Yadu then asked, wanting to make sure.

'Yes,' said Vandana. 'I happen to know their names in case you are interested.'

'I know who they are,' Yadu said.

Vandana nodded. 'So my hunch was right then. These were the men you were after when I saw you on C5.'

Yadu smiled ironically. 'The situation has changed slightly. It's *they* who are after me now. I was eavesdropping on their conversation outside their coupe, and I almost got caught doing it,' he explained. 'And now *they* are after me.' Yadu then explained how he had got involved in all this. He told her about his father's job in the RBI, about the blackmail and how his father had been kidnapped.

When he was done Yadu crawled to the aisle and peeped. It was empty. He crawled back and sat opposite to the girl. 'Just making sure the TTE is not around,' he whispered.

'Even if he comes I'll bail you out this time. I promise,' Vandana said.

Yadu grinned when he heard this.

There was a pause in their conversation as Yadu tried to remember what he had wanted to ask her just before he had crawled to the aisle. He now remembered.

'So these bandits were talking about me, eh? What did they say?'

Vandana hesitated. 'They were actually devising ways to eliminate you.'

Yadu shrugged. 'No surprises there. How are they planning to get rid of me?'

'They expect you to go to the station master's cabin in Jolarpet. They will be there waiting for you. If they see you within fifty metres of the cabin they will shoot you down.'

This was bad news. If they stood guard outside the cabin it was going to be very difficult for him to get inside and warn the station master.

'If I were you I would stay away from the station master's cabin in Jolarpet,' Vandana said.

'I can't do that,' Yadu said categorically. 'I have to get in touch with the station master so *he* can get in touch with the police. These men have to be stopped.'

'You have to think of some other way.'

He bit his nail and remained silent for a while, thinking things over.

'There is another thing you need to know,' Vandana said, remembering something else. 'Just before they went their separate ways they split the coaches amongst themselves. They are conducting a search for you on all the coaches even as we speak. It won't be long before one of them ends up here,' she said.

'Thanks for bolstering my spirits,' said Yadu dryly.

'I am just telling you what I overheard.'

'I am sorry,' Yadu said, raising his hands up in apology.

Vandana pushed back a strand of hair from her face. 'You don't have to apologise.'

Yadu fell silent. His fingers were interlocked and he was looking at the ground in front of him. He felt this sudden urge to get away from it all – the responsibility that hung around his head, the tension, the anxiety. But then he thought of his father languishing somewhere in

Madras, expecting death and dishonour, and suddenly he felt revitalised again. He had to try his best to stop this robbery from happening. He owed at least that much to his father. This was not the time to feel down and depressed. There would be plenty of time for that if he didn't succeed in stopping these criminals.

Vandana broke the silence. 'Why don't you try telling one of the ticket examiners? I am sure they'll do whatever is necessary to prevent the robbery.'

Yadu smirked. 'They'll ask to see my ticket first. And when they learn I don't have one, that'll colour their judgement. They won't be willing to listen to what I've got to say.'

Vandana thought this over. 'You shouldn't judge them before you have tried them,' she said.

'I *have* tried them. I tried talking to the ticket examiner on C5, and I failed miserably. Personally, I think it would be much easier to convince a station master.'

'But how are you going to get past these men?'

'I don't have to get past them is what I am saying.' An idea had already started to form in his head.

'What do you mean?'

'I'll get down at Jolarpet and wait till the train leaves. *Then* I'll go meet the station master.'

Vandana stared at him.

'Don't you get it? ' Yadu asked. 'No matter what happens these men have to be on this train when it leaves Jolarpet. Well, *I don't.* I can stay back at the station. After the train has left the platform I can go to the station master and inform him about the impending robbery. Hopefully the police at the next station would be ready to pick these criminals up.'

Vandana gave this idea some thought. It sounded good to her.

'I just hope they don't rob the coach by then,' Yadu said.

'You don't have to worry about that. They intend to strike only after Erode.'

Yadu sat upright at once. 'You heard them say that?' he asked.

'Yes,' she said. 'They mentioned it during the course of their talk.'

Yadu felt a surge of excitement. 'Great! Tell me, what else did they say? What time are they going to strike? What's their modus operandi?'

'Hey! Hold on,' said a startled Vandana. 'They didn't discuss all that. They have obviously done that beforehand. All I heard was Hardaker instructing his men to get atop the RBI coach by Erode. They'll attack as soon as the train leaves Erode station.'

'That's good enough for me,' Yadu said. He was delirious. 'Vandana, I am so glad I pulled you up.'

Vandana chortled when she heard this. 'I am happy that I have been of *some* use to you,' she said good-naturedly.

Yadu went quiet once again. He was happy that he had got this vital piece of information. He now knew where they intended to strike. Using this information he could somehow find out how much time he had before they struck.

So far, working out a game plan had been difficult for him because he had no clue as to when or where they were going to strike. Now that he knew this detail, things seemed a little easier than before. It would make such a vast difference if he went to the station master with all the information. It would be far easier to convince him.

'Have you travelled on this line before?' he now asked Vandana.

'Around eighteen times!' she replied.

'Great! So you ought to know how far away we are from Erode.'

'We are quite far away, actually. We are at least four hours away.'

'Are you sure?'

'Of course. I know this route like the back of my hand. The next station we reach will be Jolarpet. After Jolarpet there is Salem, and the station after that is Erode.'

Yadu probed his molars with his tongue as he listened to this.

'An hour's journey separates each station from the next one, roughly speaking of course.'

Yadu leaned back in relief. 'Thank God,' he exclaimed. 'I have a little time then to plan out a strategy.'

'Yes, you do,' Vandana agreed. 'But don't get complacent. Just remember that this very minute they are busy searching the coaches for you. They might reach this coach any minute now.'

From the expression on his face she realised that he didn't want to be reminded about that. 'I was just putting things in perspective,' she said apologetically.

'I appreciate that.'

Both of them fell into a deep silence after that. Yadu got busy; he had lots of thinking to do. The girl was right of course. First of all he had to think of a place where he could hide until Hardaker's men left this coach. Since this happened to be the last coach he expected that it would be a while before they reached here. He had been atop the train, and he knew how difficult it was to climb up and down each coach. And now that Dorai had had a 'near death experience' he expected that all of them would be extra careful, meaning they would take more time than they normally would have. Just what the doctor ordered as far as he was concerned.

Another thing he understood quite clearly: if he somehow made it up to Jolarpet without getting into their hands, then he would have things back in his control. He could get down at Jolarpet, head to the station master's cabin and tell him about the impending robbery.

or...

Yadu had another idea. *The armed escorts.* What if he warned them about the impending robbery? At the end of the day the RBI coach was their responsibility, so they would do the needful to prevent the robbery, whether it was informing the station master or informing the police, or whatever else it entailed. All he had to do was to approach the armed escorts at Jolarpet. He knew they were travelling on C1. So, all that was required of him at Jolarpet was a walk up to the front of the train, and a nice long chat with the armed escorts.

Yadu told Vandana about his plan. She too agreed that it was best that he go to the armed escorts first.

'I would have come with you. Only, my sister will go berserk wondering where I have gone,' Vandana said.

'That's okay,' he said. 'I can manage on my own.'

Yadu decided that once the train stopped at Jolarpet he would accompany Vandana to her coach. After dropping her off he would check the station master's cabin to see if Hardaker's men were there. If they were there then he would head straight for C1, and inform the two escorts. Hopefully, it would all work out well.

In the silence that followed, Vandana happened to look at a portion of her skirt that was streaked with grease marks. She hadn't seen these marks before, so she started rubbing at it. But it wouldn't go that easily.

She excused herself and got to her feet. She went to the toilet and tried washing away the marks.

'If I were you I wouldn't bother,' Yadu said from where he was seated. 'It might take you all night.' He gestured with his eyes to the back of her skirt where there were more such marks.

'Uhhh!' she grunted when she saw the back of her skirt. 'I probably look like a beggar.'

'You won't feel so bad about it after the first couple of hours. Trust me,' he said grinning.

She gave up on the washing and came back and sat down opposite him. 'I'll probably change into a new set once I am back on my coach.'

'At least you have that option,' he commented wryly.

'So do you,' she said, her eyes twinkling with mischief. 'I can lend you a skirt and blouse – if you don't mind wearing them.'

Yadu laughed. 'I would have taken up on that offer on some other day. I can't do that today. *Surely* not today.'

'Why not?'

'I'll only be making it easy for Hardaker's men to spot me. It'll be the equivalent of carrying a huge board that says: "This is Yadu, in case anybody's looking for me".'

Vandana laughed. 'You have a point,' she said.

Some time after this Yadu opened the door and looked outside. He spotted twinkling lights far away.

'Jolarpet,' he announced.

'Good,' Vandana said. 'I am desperate to get back to my coach and see my sister. How I wish she were still fast asleep. It'll save me all the explaining.'

18

As the train started to curve in into Jolarpet station, Yadu and Vandana had a minor difference of opinion. While Yadu thought it would be a good idea to get down and walk on the platform, Vandana thought otherwise. She was of the opinion that it would be safer for them to walk on the other side of the train. Yadu thought she was crazy, and told her so, because it was not only extremely dark on the other side, but it was also pouring down heavily. But Vandana stuck to her guns. She maintained that she would rather see him wet than dead. Since it was apparent that Hardaker's men would be on the platform looking for him, what was the point in risking being seen by them, she asked. Yadu tried telling her that it was possible for them to use the platform and still not be seen by Hardaker's men. But Vandana wasn't willing to believe this.

In the end Vandana's argument prevailed. It was decided that they would get off on the wrong side of the train and they would walk together up to C5. From there Yadu would split and carry on towards C1.

The train took the final bend into Jolarpet station. They stood by the door on the right side of the train not sure which side the platform was going to come up. They waited patiently for the train to slow down. Yadu looked at his watch: it was just past midnight.

Outside, the rain showed no signs of abating. It was pouring so heavily now that the drumming that the rain pellets made on the coach roof overwhelmed even the sound of the coaches' metal wheels. Every couple of minutes flashes of brilliant lightning cracked up the northern sky into sharp jigsaw fragments. And as they branched from one end of the horizon to the other they outlined the shapes of the rain-heavy clouds that they streaked past.

Yadu looked up at the sky and then at Vandana wondering what impact the heavenly fireworks were having on her mind. He wondered if she would change her decision at the very last minute and decide to use the platform after all. His thoughts were cut short by the arrival of the platform beneath their feet.

Jolarpet was quite an important junction on this line. In keeping with this status the station had been sanctioned a very long, concrete platform. Also, it had a roof for almost its entire length.

The significance of this was not lost on Yadu. If they got down on this side they could surely save themselves the hardship of trudging through the pouring rain.

He turned to look at Vandana to see what she thought of it, now that she had seen the covered platform. But Vandana simply turned away and walked over to the door behind them. So that's that, Yadu thought. No points for guessing that she still preferred to get down on the other side. He shrugged his shoulders and continued to look out.

The first thing that struck Yadu, as the train glided in, was the huge turnout of passengers who were waiting for the train. Some of them were squatting, and some were standing and chatting amongst themselves. Quite a few were fast asleep, oblivious of the train's arrival. Most of them were dressed in crumpled half-sleeved shirts and off-white dhotis. Almost all of them carried sickles and baskets and other farm tools. Yadu guessed that they were vagabond farm-labourers travelling in search of work. Only, they had chosen the wrong day to travel.

He remembered something that Vandana had mentioned in passing sometime back. He had asked her if Jolarpet was a big station. She had said that this was one of the most important stations on this line. Because of its unique geographical positioning, almost all the trains that left Madras for the west (Bangalore and beyond) and for the south-west (Coimbatore, Salem, etc.) had to pass through this station. In fact, it was at this station that the western and the south-western lines met (or diverged, depending on which direction you approached from).

By now the train had slowed down considerably. It rolled past a snack stall. About a dozen people stood opposite the stall drinking coffee. It glided past a water fountain, and then past a restaurant that was closed. Yadu caught sight of the station master as he waved his red flag. In the distance he saw a couple of mobile fruit trolleys being pushed towards the coaches.

The train jerked a couple of times, and then it ground to a halt.

Vandana called Yadu over from the other door. 'Come on, let's go.'

Yadu cast one final glance at the platform, then heeded her call and walked over to the other side.

'You go first. I'll follow you down,' he said to her.

For a moment Vandana looked tentatively at the slanting rain that lashed at her feet. She then started her descent down the steps. Yadu caught hold of the handrail and followed her down onto the gravel stone track bed.

Such was the force of the wind and the rain that greeted them that they were soaked to their skin within seconds of stepping down. They could barely keep their eyes open for more than a few seconds at a stretch. The fat drops stung them with an intensity they believed impossible.

'Come on, let's go,' Yadu shouted over the din of the falling rain. It sounded as if they were standing next to a giant waterfall.

Yadu started walking forward, and Vandana caught up with him. Visibility was extremely poor on this side of the track. There were practically no lights on this side, just like it had been in Arakkonam. At least in Arakkonam Yadu had the benefit of the light pouring out from the coaches. But here, even those lights were unavailable. Since it was past midnight now, most of the lights in the coaches had already been put off. The only lights that still remained were the ones by the exit doors. The two of them could barely see anything that was more than six feet away from them.

They walked in silence for some time.

Yadu allowed Vandana to walk beside the train, and he himself walked on the edge of the gravel stone bed. He advised her to use the coach sides for support, in case she tripped on the stones. Vandana nodded to this.

Until they reached the first coupling gap Vandana walked very slowly. She was wary of every step she took. Time and again Yadu had to wait for her to catch up with him. But slowly she got used to the place and the darkness, and then her speed increased.

They went past two coaches swiftly. Yadu ignored these two coupling gaps. But when they reached the third coupling gap he stopped and leaned over to check the platform for the station master's cabin.

'It's further up the platform,' Vandana shouted out to him. He realised soon that she was right. So he got back next to her and they continued to walk.

By now the hair on their heads looked as if it had been plastered to their skulls. The two of them had started to shiver. The heavy downpour and the blast of cold wind blowing this way ensured that their teeth were chattering relentlessly. But as they moved further up the track, things got a bit better. The wind eased a little, and the rains subsided to a certain extent. Most important of all, Yadu learnt the knack of using the lightning flashes to see. He learnt to keep his eyes open every time the lightning flashed. Though the flash lit up the place only for a split second it was enough to give him a sense of place, an idea of where they were, and how far they had to go. Using these occasional flashes to good advantage they reached C5 uneventfully.

Vandana went up the steps and then waved to Yadu. 'Thank you so much for your help,' she said in all sincerity.

Yadu smiled.

'Keep me posted. I don't want to get down at Palghat not knowing whether Hardaker has been caught or not.'

'I'll keep you posted, don't worry,' Yadu assured her.

'My seat number is sixty-four, in case you need to find me.'

'Sixty-four,' Yadu repeated.

'Yes. Good luck to you, Yadu.'

Yadu waved to her once more, and then started walking towards the front.

~

He found the station master's cabin opposite the F1-C4 coupling gap, not long after he had seen Vandana off. On spotting the cabin he got onto F1, went over to the door that opened out onto the platform and then looked out.

Just a scan over the area in front of the cabin, and he had caught sight of two of the three men he expected to find there. Icy was hiding behind a pile of wooden crates opposite the parcels office, which was adjacent to the cabin. And Sethu was standing behind a cast iron support beam, smoking a cigarette and watching the station entrance.

Yadu remained behind the door for a few seconds to see if he could spot the third member of the gang: Dorai. He was sure that he too was around. His eyes scanned the area in front of the cabin once again, this time more carefully; but he couldn't spot Dorai anywhere. He decided that it was in his best interest to get down from this coach as soon as possible. This was the coach Hardaker was travelling on. He didn't want to get caught like the last time. So he got back down onto the ground and into the rain, and he walked briskly towards C1.

He felt a bit dejected with the way things had gone here. But at the same time he felt grateful that his life had been spared. If he hadn't had the sense to pull Vandana up he would never have heard about Hardaker's plans. He would not have known that a trap had been laid out for him opposite the station master's office. In all likelihood, he would have walked unawares into the trap, and then – *Pow* – they would have finished him off.

Wrapped up as he was in such thoughts, Yadu continued to walk on the gravel stone bed towards C1, completely unaware of the silhouette on the roof that was following him.

19

In C5, meanwhile, Vandana had finished receiving a verbal pasting, the likes of which she was unlikely to receive again in her lifetime. Kanchana, her sister, had been standing by the exit doors, anxiously looking out, when Vandana, rain-drenched, had got up the steps. She recognised her elder sister's silhouette against the platform's harsh light and had called out to her. Kanchana had whirled around with a look that was partly relief, but mostly anger. For the next five minutes Kanchana gave vent to all her fury, cursing her sister and scolding her for being so reckless, for having gone away somewhere without even telling her, that too in the middle of a thunderstorm.

All of Vandana's attempts at calming her sister were wasted during the first few minutes. It was obvious that Kanchana had been deeply disturbed to see her sister missing. Bravely fighting back her tears, Kanchana continued her tirade. Finally, in exasperation, Vandana had to cup her sister's mouth with both hands to stop her outburst.

Having spent most of her wound up energy in this short burst, Kanchana finally relaxed. She shut her eyes, made no attempt to resist, stopped screaming, and just stood there like a stone Buddha.

'Akka, bear with me for *two* minutes. I'll explain everything,' Vandana begged.

Still cupping her sister's mouth she looked out onto the platform towards the front, where she expected the station master's cabin to be. There she noticed Icy and Sethu guarding the cabin entrance.

In a low whisper Vandana spoke to her sister. 'Akka, I am going to take my hand off your mouth now. But you must promise to stop shouting at me.'

Vandana uncoiled her hand away from her sister's neck. Kanchana turned around and looked at her sister. 'You are soaking wet,' she said, in a far calmer voice. 'And look at the state of your clothes. I wonder what you have been up to.'

Vandana ignored this comment. She wiped her face, then said, 'I have something very important to show you.'

This last remark of hers caught Kanchana's full attention. She looked enquiringly at her sister.

For a moment Vandana stared deep into the eyes of her Kanchi, who she so dearly loved. She looked at her innocent looking eyes and felt a pang of guilt for having caused her so much anguish tonight. She knew her sister would have come pretty close to having a nervous breakdown. Kanchana was the type of person who got frightened quite easily. She was naïve in the ways of the world, and very sensitive. Also, she was extremely shy by nature. Though she was older by almost a decade she was not as street smart as Vandana. While Vandana was the gay type who mixed with everybody and didn't hesitate to make friends, even with strangers, Kanchana was the quiet and reserved one.

Most people who chanced upon the two girls would initially be strongly attracted to Kanchana, because of her dazzling good looks: she was dusky complexioned, had long flowing hair, and was blessed with a bharatanatyam dancer's eyes and effortless grace. But then, gradually, they would be put off by her reticence. They would find her younger sister far easier to talk to and joke with. Kanchana's reticence stemmed from her shy nature. But most people misinterpreted her reticence for arrogance, an arrogance they thought emanated from the self-knowledge that she was such a striking beauty. But that judgement was simply not fair to Kanchana, because she was neither vain, nor was she the arrogant sort. Luckily for her though, the people who mattered most to her knew her well.

Vandana now leaned out of the exit door and pointed out the two men outside the station master's cabin to her sister.

Kanchana too leaned out. Holding onto the handrail she had a good long look at them. She now looked back at her younger sister with a puzzled expression in her face.

'Anybody we know?' she asked innocently.

Vandana couldn't help smiling. She pulled Kanchana away from the door, closed it shut, and then propelled her towards their seats, which was in the middle of the coach. The two sisters made their way through the aisle guided by the blue-tinted night-lights that were still on.

'Who are those people?' Kanchana asked, even as she walked.

'Their pictures are going to be all over the papers tomorrow. Mark my words,' Vandana said, wanting to sound dramatic. She got the desired effect from her sister, who turned back and looked at her with questioning eyes. Vandana's face was expressionless. She wouldn't say a word though her sister tried enquiring what she meant by that statement of hers.

Once they arrived at the bay with their seats, Vandana pushed her sister onto her seat, and then she occupied the seat opposite her. The passengers who were to travel on the seats next to them had still not boarded the train, so the two sisters had the whole bay of six seats to themselves – at least for the time being.

Vandana's rather strange answer had aroused a good deal of curiosity in Kanchana. But she decided that her first priority was to do something about the wet condition of her sister. So, as soon as she was in her seat she bent down, pulled out a wire bag, rummaged through it, and finally pulled out a faded, checked towel. She now threw it across to Vandana.

'Wipe yourself first,' she ordered.

Vandana wiped her face and then undid her plait so she could wipe her hair properly.

'Those two men you saw by the station master's cabin – they are *bandits*,' Vandana said in a low whisper.

Kanchana was bent over her bag, setting her clothes right, when she heard this. Her first reaction was one of disbelief. She looked up at her sister, noticed the serious expression on her face and then slid to the window to have a better look at the men. She had to crane her neck; but she could see them alright, opposite the cabin.

Kanchana looked back at her sister, mouth slightly open, not knowing whether to believe her or not.

'It's no joke,' Vandana assured her. 'I am telling you the truth.'

'How do you know this?' she finally asked in a husky voice.

'I happened to overhear their conversation.'

Kanchana pushed her wire bag back to its original place and then sat up straight.

'By sheer fluke I ran into these men about an hour back. I overheard them discussing the details of the heist they were planning.' While she talked Vandana continued to wipe her head with the towel.

Opposite her, Kanchana's eyes had narrowed in suspicion on hearing Vandana's last comment. 'Where exactly did you come across these men?' she enquired.

Vandana had been thinking about how to answer this one from the moment she had stepped off C10. She knew this would be one of the first questions her sister would ask. And, it was quite a difficult one to answer. There was no way she could tell her sister about what she had done an hour back. Kanchana would blow her fuse if she was told that she had crawled under the train to eavesdrop on the conversation of the robbers. Her sister would not only scold her throughout the next part of their journey for this foolish act of hers, but she would also complain to her mother upon reaching Palghat. And then there would be hell to pay for.

So Vandana lied to her sister. She told her that she had overheard their conversation outside the C5 exit door. She said she had got down to hear their conversation better when the train suddenly started to move. She hadn't been able to get back on C5. She had managed to board C10 thanks to the help of a young boy called Yadu. She had stayed there, on C10, for the past hour, and the moment the train had stopped at Jolarpet she had made her way back here.

'I knew you would be worried about me, but there was nothing I could do about it. There was no way I could send a message across, or inform you of my whereabouts. I am *so* sorry Kanchi.'

Kanchana seemed to accept her sister's apology.

The train had started to move now. From the corner of her eye Vandana noticed Hardaker's men climb aboard the train. Further up the platform the station master was waving his lantern energetically. They sat there quietly for some time, the two sisters, looking out of the window, watching the train leave the platform behind, watching the train embrace the downpour.

Sometime later Kanchana said she wanted to know more about Yadu, so Vandana continued from where she had left, telling her sister about the teenage boy, and how he had got involved in this whole affair.

Kanchana asked her how the boy intended to stop the robbery, so Vandana then told her about their discussion on C10.

'He has gone to C1 to have a word with the armed escorts. I am sure he would have convinced them of the threat from the Hardaker gang by now. We are hoping the escorts will alert the Salem station master, and the station master will in turn alert the police at Salem or Erode. If all goes well, we expect the gang to be nabbed in the next couple of hours, before the train reaches Erode.'

'You better stop saying "we",' Kanchana said. 'As far as I am concerned, your involvement in all this nonsense has ended. I don't want to wake up and find you missing again. You have been warned.'

'Of course, akka. I am not involved in any of this any more. Believe me,' said Vandana. She actually believed this herself, not knowing what was in store for her in the next station.

Kanchana seemed satisfied hearing this. She said that she was tired and she was going to sleep. Vandana said she would hit her berth as soon as she had changed into some dry clothes. She wished her sister goodnight, picked a maroon and indigo paavadai-dhavani from the wire bag, and made for the toilet.

~

After boarding C1 Yadu did a quick check of the coach to see where the escorts were. He found them in the second bay from the front of the coach. He was surprised to find both of them fast asleep.

'That's all the sleep you are going to get tonight,' he murmured to himself. He started shaking the shoulder of one of the escorts. 'Excuse me...sir?'

There was no response from the man.

'Mr Constable...Hello...,' Yadu started shaking him more vigorously.

'Sir, I have something very important to tell you...Sir?' The man didn't budge. Did these people sleep tight or what?

Yadu paused. He looked up at the passengers on the top berths. They too were fast asleep. He started shaking the man again. The escort was breathing deeply, seemingly lost in a deeper realm where he couldn't hear Yadu's voice.

Exasperated Yadu turned his attention to the escort on the other berth.

'Sir...please wake up,' Yadu pleaded.

Not a muscle moved. There was no acknowledgement on the escort's face that he could even hear anything.

Yadu couldn't believe any of this. These men were supposed to be awake, guarding the RBI coach, and here they were, fast asleep. Just then his eyes fell on the half-eaten banana lying on the floor, skin and all. It looked as if it had fallen off the escort's. He suspiciously removed the banana from the floor and examined it for a few seconds. And then instinctively, he took it to his nose for a sniff.

A medicin-ish whiff emanated from the banana. Yadu's stomach muscles started coiling up as the realisation started to hit home.

Hardaker's men had paid these escorts a visit...

20

A quarter of an hour had passed since Dorai had sighted Yadu boarding C1. By this time the train had left Jolarpet far behind. They were now travelling through an area of such flatness that it could well have been the Great Indian Plain that they were crossing. The landscape was featureless in any direction you looked. No trees, no mountains. Just wild bushes and shrubs everywhere.

For the first ten minutes of their journey out of Jolarpet the downpour had still been heavy, beating down onto the roof with a ferocity that overwhelmed Dorai. But over the past five minutes the rainfall had died down to a drizzle and visibility had improved. But the headwind remained as strong as ever, threatening to rip him off the coach and discard him to the wayside bushes.

Dorai held on doggedly and waited with growing impatience for either one of his colleagues to show up. He couldn't understand what the problem was. They ought to have been here by now. He had seen them running towards the back end of the train at Jolarpet. In all likelihood one of them would have boarded C9 and the other one C10. They would have searched the last two coaches simultaneously and should have finished their job in five minutes. Even if it took them about ten minutes to travel the length of the train, still, they ought to have been here by now. Before they had split up they had decided that whatever be the outcome at Jolarpet they would all meet up on the roof before they went to brief Hardaker of the situation. So they knew he would be waiting for them.

He looked back once more, strained his eyes to see as far as he could, was disappointed yet again to find nobody on the roof.

Dorai was beginning to get restless now. If he had gone after the boy as soon as he had seen him, by this time he would have finished him off. Instead, he had decided to be patient and wait for his friends. He had thought it would be a better idea if the three of them went after the boy rather than just one. But all this waiting was now playing on his nerves. He was losing his patience. He told himself that if Sethu and Icy didn't turn up in the next two minutes then he would go after the boy, all alone.

Yadu was quite clever, Dorai acknowledged that fact. But he knew he was more than capable of handling the boy. If at all there was a slight hesitation on his part, it was because he had discovered some time back, that the safety catch in his gun had jammed on account of getting wet. But it didn't worry him much. He was confident that there would be no need to use a gun. He knew he was powerful enough to grab hold of the boy and throw him off the speeding train, all in one single motion. It would be over in a matter of seconds if he so wished, and the boy wouldn't even know what happened.

Dorai's fingers twitched as he thought in anticipation of that moment. He was yearning to wring Yadu's neck. The boy had caused them so much trouble in the past couple of hours that they hadn't had the time to think about their strike, which was less than three hours away. He knew that when he finally got his hands on the boy he would make him pay for all the suffering he had brought on them. For two hours he had made them run. Time and again he had outwitted them. They had assumed he would walk into the trap they had laid out for him at Jolarpet, but he hadn't. The boy had somehow anticipated the trap and had kept himself away. In fact, when he had finally caught sight of Yadu, it was more by chance than by his endeavour.

Dorai had got aboard the roof at Jolarpet so he could get a bird's eye view of the platform, so he could spot the boy the moment he stepped onto it. But Yadu had not made an appearance there, to their collective disappointment.

Luckily for him, he got an unexpected break when he had heard the soft crunching of a pair of shoes on the other side of the train. He had caught sight of a figure, had followed it out of curiosity and had been rewarded when he recognised it as none other than Yadu.

Dorai had immediately made a dash towards the station master's cabin to see if he could catch the attention of Sethu and Icy. But by the time he had reached C4, opposite which the cabin stood, the train had started to pull away. Sethu and Icy had already left their positions and were running towards the back coaches. So he had come back to C2 and had waited here for so long.

Now he was done waiting for them. He looked back one last time. Stared into the darkness: still no sign of his colleagues. He checked his watch and made a decision. It looked as if he was destined to finish this off all by himself.

He heaved a huge sigh, then started to descend.

~

Feeling tired, depressed and demoralised, Yadu wanted to sit down and rest for a while. He had not eaten anything substantial for the past seven hours and had been running like a mad man since early evening. He desperately wanted to put his feet up and rest.

He walked to the vestibule, chose the door on the left and collapsed beside it. For a moment he considered keeping the door open. If the door was open he could peep out of the train every now and then, to check the coach roof for Hardaker's men. He would know if they were headed this way.

It made a lot of sense to keep it open. But Yadu decided to keep it shut – to keep the winds out. He was feeling extremely cold, and his wet clothes weren't helping matters. He knew he would end up freezing himself numb if he kept the door open.

He was taking a huge risk of course, but he decided, what the hell.

The exit door beside Yadu thus remained closed around the time Dorai was descending down C1.

~

Even as the train screamed past the barren landscape in the direction of Salem, Yadu did everything in his might to stop himself from falling asleep. Every time his eyelids dropped shut he sprung up on his feet, splashed water on his face (from the sink inside the toilet), and then sat down again. He tried pacing up and down the vestibule. He even walked all the way down the aisle and back. But all of these acts only gave him temporary relief. Sometimes the cold water wash barely sustained him for a couple of minutes. His eyelids would start to droop again within no time at all. Before long he was at his wit's end. If he had a valid ticket he would have even walked up to the TTE and asked him to wake him up at Salem. That was how desperate he was.

Seeing the armed escorts in a drugged state had affected him badly. He doubted that he would have been this sleepy or tired had they been alert and awake. Seeing them in a drugged state had been like the proverbial last straw on the camel's back. It had broken his spirit so much that all he wanted to do now was go to sleep...

He opened his eyelids, sprang onto his feet and walked into the toilet yet again. No, he couldn't afford to sleep now, not with so much at stake.

For want of a better idea he finally decided to remain standing for the rest of the journey. That way, even if he dozed off without his knowledge he was bound to fall, which would wake him up. So he stood on his feet and leaned against the nearest bulkhead.

Yadu must have stood like that for two to three minutes maximum when he found his eyelids drooping again. He looked at the mirror in front of him, at the bloodshot eyes that were staring back. His eyes stung because of all the water he had splashed into it. Even as he kept looking at his eyes, his attention was drawn to a point on the mirror where a figure had appeared all of a sudden. A man was standing at the far end of the aisle stubbing his cigarette, and it was his reflection that Yadu saw in the mirror. The place where the man stood while stubbing his cigarette was dark, so he couldn't make out his features. But the moment he started walking up the aisle Yadu recognised his gait.

And his heart leapt up into his throat.

The man passed an overhead light, and at that instant he looked into the mirror. Their eyes locked for a second, both realising at that same instant who the other one was.

Dorai's reaction was instantaneous. He pulled out a gun from behind his back and started running up the aisle towards him.

Yadu's legs felt wobbly all of a sudden – as if they had turned to jelly. He looked around desperately, like a cornered wildcat. Then his eyes fell on the toilet door. Not bothering to think whether the idea was sound or not he made a dash for it. He leapt across the vestibule, slammed against the door, unlatched it and then threw it open.

'Stop!' Dorai screamed as he came skidding into the vestibule.

Yadu got into the toilet and banged the door shut. He had barely slid the latch into place when he heard a thud as Dorai threw himself onto the door. Yadu hurriedly slid the other bolt into place.

'Alright Yadu,' Dorai bellowed in triumph from the other side of the door. 'Game's over. Raise your hands and come outside now.'

Yadu remained silent. He took a few long breaths in a bid to calm his frayed nerves. He had momentarily escaped from Dorai's clutches, but he didn't know how long he could hold out here. Dorai was sure to attempt something to get him outside. Perhaps he would go to bring his other two colleagues, who he was sure were in the vicinity. The question was, would Dorai dare leave the door unguarded? He would only know too well that the moment such an opportunity was presented Yadu would take it gladly. He decided that no matter what happened Dorai wouldn't leave the door. No, he wasn't that foolish.

Alternatively, he might shoot his way in. Now this seemed entirely possible, and this Yadu was genuinely afraid of. All the man had to do was aim two bullets at the place where the bolts had been screwed in. The bullets would blow the whole bolt mechanism off the door. Dorai would have to just push the door open and walk in.

He prayed fervently that Dorai wouldn't dare use his gun here. It was possible that for fear of waking the passengers he might decide not to use the gun. But if he didn't give a damn one way or the other, then he wouldn't hesitate to shoot at the bolts.

Yadu moved away from the door, towards the farthest corner of the toilet, and stood there in silence. He was expecting Dorai to shoot any second now and he didn't want to be in the line of fire.

There was a loud knock on the door. 'I warn you, Yadu. Do not irritate me. Come out of there like a good boy and you'll be spared.'

'Get lost, Dorai,' Yadu called out from inside. 'I am not coming out.' To his own mild surprise Yadu's voice sounded even and assured. No crack in his voice. No sign of nervousness. And the sleep that had been troubling him just a couple of minutes ago – it was gone. He was wide awake now.

He heard the hoodlum's sinister laugh from the other side of the door. And then, without any warning, he heard a huge thud as Dorai launched himself onto the door. For a moment Yadu thought the door had crashed open. Such was the force with which Dorai had thrown himself upon the door. Luckily, the bolts held on.

Seconds later he heard another loud thud as Dorai threw himself on the door yet again. This had Yadu puzzled. He wondered why the goonda hadn't used his gun to rip open the bolts. Was he really afraid of waking the passengers?

A period of silence followed when it appeared as if Dorai was collecting himself. Yadu sensed a drop in the train's speed. It was not travelling as fast as it had been travelling five minutes back. He looked at his watch; it was a quarter to one. Salem was still at least thirty minutes away.

The door shuddered as Dorai threw himself onto it one more time.

Yadu had broken into a sweat by now. He knew that the door might not withstand many more assaults. The bolt and the latch would surely give way to the intense pressure. At the same time he couldn't help wondering why Dorai was taking the hard route. Why wasn't he using his gun? Surely there had to be a reason. Perhaps it was not working. It surely couldn't be because Dorai was afraid of waking the passengers, because he was making a much louder racket right now trying to break open this door. 'His gun's not working,' Yadu decided. 'That's the only explanation.'

He decided to work on this premise. If Dorai's gun was not working, then surely, there was no risk in standing by the door. He immediately crossed over to the door, and then stood with his back pressing against it. This was so that even if the bolts gave way, he could block Dorai's entry using his body weight.

From outside he heard Dorai's voice again. 'You are beginning to annoy me, Yadu. Open the door NOW. Or else...'

'Or else, what Dorai?' he asked, taunting him. 'Are you planning to shoot me down? Come on, shoot me Dorai. Let's see if you are man enough to do that.'

He could sense Dorai seething with rage on the other side. If he was going to use the gun it would be now. He would know in a few seconds whether his theory was right. He quietly moved away from the door and stood by its side.

Still more silence. The train continued to drop speed.

A few seconds later the silence was broken by a resounding crash as Dorai threw himself onto the door yet again. It looked as if he was venting all his anger and frustration at the door.

Now he was certain that Dorai's gun was not working. This gave him some hope.

Yadu had closed his eyes instinctively when he heard the thud. When he opened his eyes he noticed that one of the screws holding the bolt mechanism had splintered. The door latch too had been bent by the force of impact.

He realised that the door was not going to withstand Dorai's next charge

What was he going to do now?

His eyes moved to the windows to see if there was a way out through there. No. Not unless he had a fitter's equipment. Or at least a screwdriver. He then looked at the ceiling. Even that was a no-no. There was no way he was going to get out through there: the roof had been welded onto the coach body.

There seemed no way out. He was stuck here, like a lamb about to be slaughtered.

He prepared himself mentally for the slaughter, for Dorai's imminent assault.

At that desperate moment his mind threw up an idea. A very simple idea, really, but one that might work. He gave it a moment's thought.

Maybe there was a way...

21

On the other side of the door Dorai was fuming with rage, angry with himself and with the rest of the world. He was angry with himself for having placed his gun in his back in such a fashion that rainwater had got into it. He was angry with the boy for frustrating his efforts. And most of all, he was angry with Sethu and Icy for not turning up when he needed them most. If his two colleagues had turned up on the roof on time then he wouldn't be standing here helpless.

He kicked at the door in frustration and then started walking towards the exit door. He had expected the toilet door to give in to the weight of his body, but in spite of lunging at it so many times he hadn't done any damage to it at all.

He reached the exit door and then pulled it open. He too had sensed that the train had slowed down for some reason. They hadn't reached Salem yet; that much he was sure of. But he wanted to know why exactly they had slowed down in the middle of nowhere.

A blast of cold wind blew in through the open door. The rain had stopped momentarily, which was a big relief. He hoped it would stay that way until after Coimbatore. Carrying out their job would be a lot easier without the rain.

He looked in front to see if he could spot any signal. He didn't see any signal; he did however see the silhouette of a bridge against the flashing horizon. They had slowed down to cross the bridge. Yes, that was it. He should have remembered. They had travelled on this route last week on a trial run. They had come across this bridge, but the train hadn't stopped here the last time. It just slowed down to about twenty kilometres per hour – until the last coach had crossed the bridge. Then the engine increased speed. He didn't think it would be any different this time.

He now shifted his gaze to the back of the train. He strained his eyes to see if he could spot either Sethu or Icy on the roof above. He watched for a few seconds, then gave up. There was still no sign of them.

He then turned back to look towards the toilet door. The boy was still inside, not making any noise. He decided he was going to throw himself at the door one last time, with all the force he could muster. If that didn't open the door then he had no choice but to wait for his colleagues.

He held the handrail and leaned over to look at the roof one last time before he went in again. This time he was finally rewarded. He caught sight of somebody walking on top of C6 (or was it C7?). From the way the distant figure walked he guessed it to be Sethu.

Dorai was thrilled, ecstatic. He leaned further out of the coach and started waving wildly at the figure on the roof. Not sure whether Sethu had seen him, he placed his thumb and forefinger in his mouth and let out a shrill whistle.

'Sethu! Over here,' he shouted at the top of his voice, still waving wildly with his free hand. He could now see Icy too.

Sethu instantly caught sight of Dorai. At least his body language suggested that he had. He cocked his head, raised a hand and then turned behind to say something to Icy. He then started running towards the front.

Standing by the exit door Dorai felt a surge of confidence. Now that he was sure Sethu knew where he was, he went in towards the toilet.

'Now you are finished, Yadu,' he guffawed. 'My friends are here now. Start saying your prayers.'

Dorai lunged at the door one last time, this time with all the force he could muster. He had decided that he would try one last time to finish this job all by himself. It was a matter of pride. After all, the boy was just sixteen.

~

Yadu watched it happen from the side. He had deliberately stepped away from the door. He had undone the bolt, had removed the latch and had been holding the door closed using a single finger.

The moment he heard Dorai's grunt as he lunged at the door he let go of his finger. Dorai slammed against the door, expecting powerful resistance. But there was zero resistance from the door, which was something he had not expected. As a result he lost his balance and went crashing onto the floor. He had been taken *completely* by surprise. Not until he hit the floor did he realise that Yadu had kept the door deliberately unbolted. But by then it was too late.

The moment Dorai's body hit the ground Yadu leaped over his legs and ran out of the toilet. He glanced back for just a split second to assess the damage. Dorai had hit himself on the forehead and blood was dripping from his temple. He had surely hurt himself pretty badly, because he seemed in no great hurry to leap up and grab him.

Happy with the way his idea had worked Yadu arrived by the vestibule and then skidded to a halt in front of the door. He knew he probably had about a ten-second lead on Dorai, that's all. He had to make the most of it.

He opened the door and looked in front to see why the train had dropped speed. He saw what Dorai had seen just a couple of minutes back – the bridge. It was still about three hundred metres away. But that was not the only thing that Yadu saw. He saw something that Dorai had missed. Stretching all the way from where C4 was up to the bridge there were huge piles of gravel stones alongside the track. They had been made into flat heaps of three feet height. Each of these heaps was nearly half the length of a coach. It looked as if they were about to start track repair work in this area. That could be the only explanation for so much of the pebble-sized gravel stones in this place.

Yadu looked at these gravel stone heaps in an altogether different perspective. This was a godsend as far as he was concerned. Instead of getting onto the roof he now considered leaping off the coach onto one of these heaps. At twenty kilometres per hour if he leapt onto the ground there was a very real possibility that he would break his leg. But if he leapt onto one of the heaps and rolled over he might escape with minor bruises.

Behind him he could hear Dorai picking himself up inside the toilet. Yadu had very little time till he came rushing out at him.

Dorai wobbled out of the toilet, cursing and screaming expletives at him. He now prepared to lunge straight at Yadu who was standing by the handrail, still waiting for the heap.

The moment the heap passed by, Yadu leapt off the coach, to Dorai's immense surprise. He could obviously not see the gravel stone heap from where he stood. He came rushing towards the door with a look of amazement in his face. And that look of amazement turned into one of fury as he saw Yadu land on the heap, roll over a couple of times and then get up on his feet.

The moment Yadu was up he shot a glance at Dorai, and then started running towards the back of the train. Not looking back once he continued to run, wanting to put as much distance as possible between him and Dorai. He knew it would only be a matter of seconds before the goon too decided to leap off the coach.

Intent as he was in getting out of Dorai's reach there was one thing that slipped Yadu's mind completely. He had heard Dorai say that his colleagues were on their way. At the time he heard it he wasn't sure whether it was a psychological ploy Dorai was playing on him, or whether he was indeed telling the truth.

But now, as he looked up at the roof, his heart skipped a beat. Because he saw both Sethu and Icy up there. Both of them had seen him leap out of the coach.

Yadu ran down the slope of the stone heap he was on and then got up the slope of the next one. He was still hesitant about looking back. He was sure Dorai had leapt out of the train by now.

But more than Dorai he was suddenly more afraid of the two men on the roof. They were on what he thought was C4. C3 was just passing him by. He was eager to find out what they would do next. Would they dare to leap from the coach onto the gravel stone heap? Leaping onto the stones from a distance of about four feet was one thing. But leaping onto the heap from the roof of a moving train was an altogether different ball game. They would end up breaking all their bones if they didn't time it properly.

What worried Yadu was that, if at all the two men on the roof took the leap, then he was in deep trouble. Dorai was pursuing him from behind. On his left was the train. Onto his right were row upon row of thorny bushes. If the two men cut him off from the front then he would find himself cornered. Three against one.

He prayed that Sethu and Icy would chicken out from taking the leap.

He found out seconds later that this time his prayers didn't work. Yadu watched open-mouthed as Sethu leapt from the roof of C4. One moment he was flying in the air, the next moment he had landed in the middle of the very gravel stone heap that he was on. He landed on his feet, rolled a couple of times giving in to the inertia, and then got up on his feet, all in one swift motion. Seconds after he landed, Icy too leapt. He landed about ten feet behind Sethu.

The very thing that Yadu had feared had happened. He found Sethu and Icy blocking his path about twenty feet away. He looked back and confirmed for himself that Dorai too was pursuing him. He wondered whether he had a chance at all if he tried boarding one of the coaches. It looked extremely unlikely.

Yadu did not know whether it would work but he took a split-second decision not to break his run. He would continue running and would try to floor Sethu and Icy. If he got past them then he could board one of the back coaches. Of course, he still had to get rid of Dorai, but that he would think of later.

So he continued to run, as if nothing had happened.

He ran straight at Sethu bracing himself for a painful collision. Sethu swerved away at the last moment and went for Yadu's legs, hoping to bring him down. But Yadu was quick to spot his change of strategy. He leapt out of Sethu's reach and continued to run.

Sethu immediately got to his feet and started running after him. He signalled Icy to block him.

Half the train had gone past them already.

Icy had seen how Yadu had avoided Sethu. So, he stood in a sumo-wrestler-like stance waiting to pounce on him. As Yadu closed in towards him, two things happened all at once. Sethu, who had caught up with him, gave him a sudden push forward, and at the same time Icy threw himself forward. Yadu found himself losing his balance. Even as he struggled to remain on his feet, Icy brought him down in a tackle, grabbing him by his legs. Before he even knew what happened he was on the heap struggling to get out of Icy's grasp. He managed to get his right leg out of Icy's grasp, and then he kicked him hard on his chin. Icy immediately let go of his other leg. But before Yadu could get up Sethu leapt on top of him, landing squarely on his chest, knocking the wind out of him. For a few seconds both Sethu and Yadu exchanged blows. Yadu knocked him back with a powerful right fist on his cheek.

Dorai had reached them by this time. He too launched into the attack. Yadu suddenly found himself fending off blows from six fists. Power-packed blows were directed at his chin, at his cheeks, his solar plexus. He was able to deflect a few blows, but most of them found their mark. All three of Yadu's assailants were very strong men, and together they were an extremely potent force. Like a pack of wolves they attacked Yadu with no let up. And exactly the way the wolves in a pack behaved, each one of them took upon themselves a specific task. Icy had caught hold of Yadu by his neck so he couldn't move his head. Sethu was now sitting on his feet so that his legs were rendered immobile. As for Dorai, he was seated on his chest and was inflicting the most damage. He was punching at Yadu's face so hard that blood had started to drip from his nose. He already had a cut lip from a blow Sethu had inflicted a while back. It was a job the three of them carried out in a most professional manner.

Beside them C6 passed. And a short while later C7.

Sethu now murmured something into Dorai's ears and then went looking for something. Dorai too got up from his chest. But Icy still held onto his neck tightly. Yadu decided to try one last bid to escape. With all the energy he could muster he twisted out of Icy's control. He got on his knees and socked the Englishman just below his eye. But that was as far as he got. Before he could get onto his feet Dorai kicked him so hard on his chest that he thought he had died. For a number of seconds he couldn't even take in any air. Just so that he wouldn't dare try something like that one more time Dorai kicked him again, this time on his stomach. Yadu doubled over in agony

C8 had already passed them by. Now it was C9 that was gliding past them. Every one of them was aware of how important it was for them to get back onto the train, Yadu more than anybody else.

Sethu now returned, carrying a wooden log the size of Icy's arm. Icy caught hold of his neck one more time. Yadu had seen the log in his hand. He knew what was coming, but was in no position to do anything about it. He tried a token attempt at freeing himself from Icy's grasp, but he really was in too much pain to put any heart into it.

The wooden log came crashing onto his head now. He saw a blinding flash for an instant. And then he heard a scream well up from somewhere deep inside him. White-hot pain shot through his body.

He was vaguely aware of Sethu dropping the log and running after the last coach. He was soon joined by Dorai and Icy. In some deep recess in his mind he was registering all this. He could see them catch the handrail and get up. Alarm bells started ringing in his head as he realised that they had got aboard the train, whereas he hadn't. He struggled to his feet and stumbled forward forcing himself to get to the train. He moved four paces, then collapsed.

In a half daze, lying flat on the ground, he watched as the red taillight of the Mangalore Express disappeared from view.

22

Fifteen minutes after the trio had beaten and abandoned Yadu they entered Hardaker's coupe wearing broad smiles. Hardaker saw the grins on their faces, and instantly he knew that his men had succeeded in disposing off Yadu. For the first time in hours he allowed himself a smile.

'Well done boys,' he said, making way for his men to enter the tiny coupe. He plopped down heavily onto the seat to his left, then let out a huge sigh.

'We are not going to have any more trouble with that brat now, are we?' he said.

'No more trouble, Brian. Smooth sailing from this moment on,' said Icy, settling into the seat opposite him.

After beating the daylights out of Yadu, the three of them had boarded C10. They had been so exhausted with the effort that they had sat atop the coach for ten minutes. Then they had leapt all the way up to F1, and had got down. One by one they had been into the toilet to make themselves presentable to Hardaker. Finally they had walked into the Englishman's coupe.

Now, they all looked worn from the mental and physical strain of the past hour. Icy was eyeing the decanter of single malt whiskey that stood on the tiny table in front of his boss. Hardaker took the hint. He opened the bottle and then poured out a large measure for Icy. Dorai and

Sethu had settled opposite each other, Dorai sitting next to the spiky-haired Englishman.

Icy downed the measure of whiskey in one gulp, and then passed the glass back to Hardaker, who filled it for Dorai next. He poured a measure out for himself too – into the other glass that was in front of him.

'Yadu is lying unconscious, miles from civilisation,' Dorai said accepting the glass of whiskey.

Hardaker nodded his approval. 'You should have finished him off,' he said, smarting from the burn the drink caused as it ran down his throat.

'We could have,' Icy agreed. 'Only, we had a train to catch.'

Hardaker had a good long look at his drink. The coupe went silent for the next two minutes. Dorai finished his drink and then returned the glass. Hardaker motioned for Sethu to help himself.

The Englishman then leaned back and looked at the fan in the ceiling. 'That boy nearly ruined all my plans,' he said, to no one in particular.

'We'll make sure he pays for it, Brian, once we are done with all this.' It was Sethu who said this, as he poured himself a large measure. The bottle was down to its last one-third.

Hardaker turned away from the ceiling, and then asked Icy a question: 'Did the boy try getting into the station master's cabin at Jolarpet?'

'He didn't dare,' Icy replied.

Sethu said, 'I am sure our presence scared him away.'

Dorai took over at this point and explained how he had caught sight of the boy from the roof. He told him about how Yadu got trapped inside the toilet, how the boy gave him the slip and how he was eventually trapped by the three of them near the bridge.

Hardaker listened to it all with a stone-faced expression.

'So,' Hardaker said, when Dorai had finished, 'I can safely assume that the police and the railway authorities do not know of our intentions yet?'

'Yes, you can,' Dorai said confidently.

Hardaker didn't seem satisfied though. 'Is there any chance he could have got a message across to the station master *indirectly* – through a third party, that is. He could have told a TTE or a fellow passenger about us, you know.'

'I am worried about that too,' Dorai admitted. 'It would not augur well for us if this person or persons made it to the authorities.'

'The good news is,' Icy said, 'no passenger or TTE entered the station master's cabin at Jolarpet. Even if Yadu told somebody about us, they haven't passed the information to the Jolarpet station master. That I can vouch for.'

Hardaker said, 'My point is, they might make the effort at the next station, at Salem or at Erode.'

'Can't allow that to happen,' Icy stated categorically. 'There will be far too many complications if that happens.'

'Let's continue our vigil in the next two stations then,' Sethu suggested. 'Anybody tries approaching the station master, we deal with him right away, right there. It's the only way we can be certain that our intentions remain a secret.'

'Good idea,' Hardaker remarked.

Dorai marvelled at how Hardaker had manipulated this 'suggestion' out of their mouths. The way he had worked the conversation it seemed as if *they* had come up with the idea of maintaining vigil outside the cabins. In actuality, Hardaker had cleverly led the conversation in the direction he had wanted. This was how Hardaker got all his dirty work done for him. It was not the first time Dorai had noticed Hardaker's subtle man-management skills.

'The slightest suspicion you have that a passenger or TTE or the guide is talking about us, just barge in and do what's got to be done.'

'Understood,' Sethu said. The other two nodded their heads obediently.

There was a lull in the conversation for a few minutes. Icy kept eyeing the whiskey decanter, but this time his boss ignored him.

Hardaker interrupted the silence some minutes later. 'What about the escorts? Have they been taken care of?' he asked Dorai.

'Absolutely,' Dorai said. 'They'll sleep till kingdom come.'

23

Twenty minutes past one. An earthshaking round of thunderclaps was heard as the Mangalore Express rolled into Salem station.

As soon as the train came to a standstill, the twenty-odd passengers waiting to board the train got onboard, the passengers getting off at Salem disembarked and the train was ready to go in less than three minutes. However, it would be another fifteen minutes before the Mangalore Express actually left the station. While the train itself was ready to leave, and the passengers ready to leave, the engines of the time usually weren't ready to leave in three minutes. These were steam locomotives, after all. It took the drivers at least a quarter of an hour to get the engine ready for the next part of its journey. For fuel and water intake.

Most of the steam engines used coal as their primary fuel. They carried the coal at the back of the engine in what was called a coal tender. These tenders had a limited capacity, and the coal lasted at the most two to three hours. The tenders had to be replenished with more coal at every other stop. Also, the water in the engine tank had to be changed frequently. The purpose of the tank water was to cool down the engine. But in the process of cooling the engine down the water itself would turn hot. This water had to be disposed off and fresh water taken in at every stop so that there was sufficient water to cool the engine constantly. The coal lugging and the water changing usually took a quarter of an hour. So, even if the passengers needed only five minutes at a station, the engine itself would need at least fifteen minutes at each stop.

In some stations it took even longer than this. A steam engine and the crew that drove it had to be changed every four to six hours. It was impossible for one driver and one fireman to drive the entire distance from say, Madras to Mangalore. Even if the weather conditions were favourable that journey would take not less than twenty hours. For one set of drivers to drive that entire distance was an impossible task. The locomotive too would simply not have the power to haul a train for such a distance. The railways, therefore, had designated crew and loco changing stations. While the train remained in the station, the loco alone would be detached and driven to the shed. Another loco driven by a fresh set of drivers would be attached to the train for the next part of the trip.

For a journey like the one the Mangalore Express undertook, crew and loco changes would happen at least thrice, and sometimes even four times. After four and a half hours of journey there would be a change at Jolarpet junction. The next batch of drivers would drive the train up to Erode, or sometimes all the way up to Shoranur. From Shoranur the third batch of drivers would drive the rest of the distance up to Mangalore.

The delays from the water, crew and loco changing were all usually factored into the journey time. There were however other delays that could just not be factored in at all. There would always be the odd nut who would pull the alarm chain so he could get off at his village. What was meant as an aid for emergencies was usually used as a tool of convenience by a few passengers. This practice was quite common those days and there was very little the authorities could do to stop it. In such cases, one man's selfishness would disrupt not just the schedule of one train, but several trains. An unscheduled stop of one train would mean that that section would be blocked off temporarily. It would be a 'no entry zone' for all other trains. The guard of the affected train would have to make a thorough check to make sure there was no real emergency, and only then could he give the drivers the go ahead to continue. The train would have to reach the end of the section (usually a railway station) before the section could be considered 'safe' and unblocked for further traffic.

Probably the biggest problem of them all during the steam engine era was that of communication: between the engine drivers and the station master of the approaching station. There was *no* means of communication between the two. How, for example, was an engine driver to know that there wasn't a train approaching on the same track from the other side? If it was during daytime, and if the track was along a straight line they could sight the train. But what would they do on a night like this when it was pouring cats and dogs? Laying dedicated rail tracks for each train was out of the question because of the high costs involved.

They worked around this problem by resorting to signalling, and by splitting the railway track into sections. On the Madras-Mangalore route for example, Arakkonam to Katpadi would be one section, Katpadi to Jolarpet another, and so on. The station master of Salem would be responsible for the section from Jolarpet up to Salem. When the Mangalore Express approached Jolarpet, the station master would have called the Salem station master on a telephone and asked him if he was ready to receive the train. The Salem station master would say yes if he didn't have any other train on his section. The Jolarpet station master would give the Mangalore Express the green signal and the train would enter the Jolarpet-Salem section. The Salem station master would have 'received' the train and the Jolarpet station master would have 'dispatched' the train. The information that the track ahead was safe was conveyed to the engine driver by means of a green signal for that section. The engine driver of the train, having got the green signal would know that no other train is on the section, so he would raise his speed accordingly.

Most times this system worked like clockwork. But in just a few hours that system was going to fall apart on this line because of one un-thought of eventuality. One unexpected incident was going to throw the entire system out of gear for hours.

~

Three minutes after the train had stopped at Salem, Vandana, after making sure that her sister was fast asleep, walked to the exit door. She was now wearing the maroon and indigo half-saree that she had changed into. Most of the train's passengers were still fast asleep. The platform too was quiet. Except for a porter and a gum-candy seller, there was no one else about in the big wide platform. The red shirted porter was seated on a stone bench with a pile of groundnuts beside him. Vandana watched on as he cracked the shells and popped the nuts into his mouth. Then her head roved to the ceiling and she realised that she wasn't the only witness to the porter's midnight snack. A couple of monkeys were eyeing the pile of groundnuts, no doubt debating with themselves whether it was worth the risk of getting caught. Further up the platform, the gum-candy seller, with his gum-candy pole resting on his shoulder, had fallen asleep on his feet. He seemed oblivious to the flies buzzing around his pole. It didn't look as if he had even noticed the train's arrival.

Vandana got down onto the platform and looked around for the station master's cabin. She found it to her right, opposite C7. Then she turned in front to see if she could spot either Yadu or the armed escorts. There was nobody there opposite C1.

That's strange, she thought. She had expected Yadu and the armed escorts to be out on the platform by now, on their way to see the station master. So why hadn't they got down from C1 yet? Had Yadu failed to convince the armed escorts of the imminent robbery? Were the escorts overconfident that they could take care of Hardaker and his men at the time of the strike? She stood there silently and stared ahead, hoping to catch sight of them as soon as they stepped onto the platform. A couple of minutes passed. One of the monkeys had got down from the ceiling. It now ventured bravely towards the stone bench where the porter sat.

She sensed a movement to her left. She whipped her head around and noticed three men get off from F1, one after another. *It was the bandit gang.* Sethu got down first, then Icy and finally Dorai. Vandana sucked in her breath and looked away. She pretended as if she was keenly interested in what the monkey was going to do next, but all her attention was on the bandits. She was aware of them splitting and going away in two directions. Sethu and Dorai started walking towards the station master's cabin, while Icy seemed headed for the signalling cabin that was bang opposite to where she now stood.

She watched on as Sethu and Dorai went right past her. It looked as if they were continuing their vigil outside the station master's cabin, to make sure Yadu didn't go to the authorities with what he knew.

She looked in front again, but she still didn't catch sight of Yadu or the escorts. She was beginning to get worried now. Why were the escorts not out here yet? She was beginning to suspect that something had gone drastically wrong. She decided there was only one way to find out. She would run to C1 and see what was happening. She would find Yadu, talk to the escorts and find out why they hadn't got out to inform the station master. She hadn't forgotten her sister's warning to her yet, that she shouldn't get herself involved in any of this. But she was worried for Yadu now. She had to go and make sure everything was going as per plan.

Casting one last look at the backs of Sethu and Dorai she started walking briskly towards C1. She half-jogged and half-walked, hoping all the time that her sister wouldn't get up suddenly from her sleep. She definitely wasn't in the mood for another pasting from Kanchana. Arriving beside C1, she boarded the steps. She walked the length of the coach looking desperately for Yadu. For an instant she wondered if he had fallen asleep out of sheer fatigue. It was improbable he would do that considering what was at stake, but then one never knew.

With each bay she passed her anxiety grew. And when she reached the front of the coach and had still not caught sight of him she began to fear the worst. She remembered what Hardaker's men had told the Englishman a few hours back: that they would find and dispose off Yadu one way or the other. Had Yadu's luck finally run out? Had he run into the goons on C1? She shuddered to think of what they might have done to him. Poor boy! She hoped that he was alive and well.

Some moments later she found the escorts lying on their berths. A sense of relief swept through her when she caught sight of their reassuring uniforms. But that relief didn't last long. It gave way to anger when she realised that they were both fast asleep. Just like Yadu had felt less than an hour back. And just like Yadu had found out Vandana too realised, seconds later, that the armed escorts were not asleep. They were *unconscious*. She saw the half-eaten banana on the floor and realised instantly what had happened here.

Vandana's head started to swim the next instant as the ramifications of all this began to dawn on her. Yadu had gone missing; the escorts had been rendered useless. She was the only person on the train now who knew about Hardaker's plans. The responsibility of stopping the RBI coach robbery was in her hands now.

She cast a quick glance at her watch. In less than five minutes the train would leave the station. She had to find the station master and warn him about the robbery before that. There was no time to lose. She sprang to her feet and started running towards the nearest vestibule. Arriving by the exit door she leapt onto the platform and then started sprinting towards the station master's cabin. She passed C2, C3, F1, C4 and then her own coach C5.

When she arrived beside C6 she finally slowed down. She didn't want to draw any undue attention upon herself, especially from the two thugs standing outside the station master's cabin. She just hoped now that she would be able to get into the cabin without getting into a confrontation with these two men. She was reasonably confident that she could manage this. After all, Dorai and Sethu were on the look-out for Yadu, not for her.

She was roughly sixty paces away from the cabin when Dorai and Sethu caught sight of her. It didn't take them long to figure out that she was headed for the office they were guarding. Even as Vandana watched, both men started walking towards her in an intimidatory swagger. Her heart started to thump wildly. What was she to do now if they refused to allow her to pass? She whipped her head this way and that to see if she had company on the platform, somebody who could come to her rescue if she called for help. She couldn't see anybody nearby. A couple of railway employees were headed in this direction but they were still quite a distance away.

Vandana kept her head straight and walked on towards the booth. She locked eyeballs with the men and refused to be intimidated. For a moment she contemplated breaking into a sprint, dodging the men and getting into the cabin. But she knew that the idea was impossible to execute.

By this time the two men were within ten paces of her. 'Get back onto the coach,' Sethu barked, gesturing with his finger. 'The train's about to leave.'

'I am aware of that,' Vandana countered in a level voice. 'I need to see the station master first.'

'What for?' Dorai asked.

Vandana had an urge to tell him it was none of his business. But she held her tongue. A quick temper was not going to take her anywhere with these men.

'Somebody's stolen my handbag,' she improvised. 'I have to file a report.'

Sethu and Dorai looked at each other. Then they both looked carefully at Vandana, sizing her up.

'Nobody's in there,' Dorai said, coming within two paces of her. He looked around to make sure nobody was looking, caught hold of Vandana's shoulders and then he pushed her back roughly.

Vandana stumbled backwards, furious at Dorai for manhandling her.

'How *dare* you?' she screamed. 'I demand to see the station master. Who are you people to...'

Vandana stopped, looking at the knife Sethu had just pulled out. He walked to within inches of her and then he pressed the tip of his knife to her neck.

Whatever doubts Vandana had, about how serious these two men were, evaporated now. These two meant business. They had made the office out of bounds not just for Yadu but for *all* passengers, maybe as a precaution. No doubt they suspected Yadu of having told his fellow passengers about the impending robbery.

She cast a glance in the direction of the signalling cabin and noticed that that too was out of bounds for her, with Icy standing guard outside. Vandana's blood boiled at being pushed and treated thus. But she realised that there was nothing she could do about it. She quietly backed off from the two, her face flush with humiliation.

'I get the message,' she said, throwing her arms up. 'I am going back.'

Sethu gave her an oily smile, glad at having got his way. Dorai now gestured for him to put his knife away.

Vandana turned around and started walking back to her coach not knowing what to do next. She had just started to think on the lines of approaching her coach TTE when suddenly she noticed a movement to her right. It was the station master, dressed in white trouser, white full-sleeved shirt and a black tie. He was coming out of the booking office, no doubt to send the Mangalore Express on its way. She realised that Dorai had inadvertently told her the truth! The station master had not been in his cabin after all.

Sensing an opportunity Vandana slowed her steps. She changed her course ever so slightly to the right and continued walking, albeit slowly. If the station master continued to walk in the same pace, then their paths would intersect in about thirty seconds. Vandana checked to see what Icy was up to. The Englishman was still standing by the signalling cabin for some reason. But it was obvious his eyes were on the station master. She decided that she couldn't care less if Icy noticed her talking to the station master. She was going to do what she had to do.

The departure bell started to ring. The station master took his signal lantern, and even as he walked towards the train he started waving it. Vandana decided that it was now or never. She broke into a sudden sprint and headed for the station master. From the corner of her eye she noticed Icy watch this sudden development with interest. She reached the station master and grabbed hold of the arm that was swinging the signal lantern. In as forceful a voice as she could muster, she said, 'Stop this train! Stop waving the lantern.'

The station master spun around to face her. 'What?'

'There are bandits onboard. *Stop this train.*'

By this time two things started to happen simultaneously. One: the train started to move slowly. Two: Icy realised that whatever was happening near the train needed his intervention. So he had broken into a run.

Vandana, aware of both, joined both her hands in a pleading gesture and implored the station master once again to stop the train. He had stopped waving the lantern. But his hand still held it suspended at an angle over his head.

'What are you talking about?' the station master demanded. He was a silver-haired, puffy-faced man, aged fifty-five or thereabouts. He seemed to be shaken by this sudden assault on his arm.

'I overheard a conversation aboard the train. Some men intend to rob a coach belonging to the RBI.'

'Who are these people? Where are they?' His voice cracked as he spoke.

Vandana cast a glance behind to see where Dorai and Sethu were. Her line of vision to the station master's cabin was blocked by a pile of crates, which proved to be a blessing in disguise. If she couldn't see them then neither could they see her talking to the station master. As for Icy, he was closing in on her rapidly.

'There, that's one of them,' Vandana said, pointing to Icy. 'They are a gang of four and they intend to rob the coach after Erode. You *must* stop the train and call the police immediately.'

The station master's hand came down now. 'This is not a prank, I hope?' he asked tentatively.

'I *swear* on my mother,' Vandana almost shouted. 'Stop this train and I'll explain everything to you.'

That's as far as she got, because Icy had by this time come thundering down from the cabin. He seemed to instinctively realise from Vandana's animated gestures and the way she kept looking in his direction that she was talking about them. In the last few metres of his dash, it was confirmed as he overheard bits of the conversation. Realising that the station master had brought down the lantern to stop the train, he flew at Vandana. He brought her down and slapped her across her face.

If the station master needed confirmation that the girl was telling the truth, then he got it now seeing the man attack Vandana. Dazed by this sudden turn of events he shouted out to his staff for help.

The train now stopped, since the driver couldn't see the signal lantern. Icy, still on the ground, sensed this immediately. He now sprung to his feet. Forgetting Vandana for the moment he went after the station master. He pulled the lantern from his hand and thwacked the man on his neck. The station master collapsed onto the floor. Icy then started running towards the engine, swinging the lantern above him. On no account could he allow the train to stay here any longer.

The train – that had stopped momentarily – now started moving again.

Vandana, with great difficulty, got to her feet. She looked behind and noticed that Dorai and Sethu had already boarded one of the coaches, unaware of what had happened here. She sauntered over to the station master and checked with him if he was alright. The man groaned loudly. He was lying flat on the floor holding onto his neck with both hands. She looked around and noticed a couple of railway employees running towards them. They had seen the assault on the station master from far away; they were now rushing to his aid.

Vandana decided she couldn't remain on the platform any longer. If she didn't board one of the coaches now she would be left behind.

She now placed a hand on the station master's shoulder. 'Sir, I have to get back aboard now. But please, *please* call up the police and get them to stop this robbery somehow.'

She was aware of the train picking up speed now.

The station master nodded faintly, still groaning. 'I'll see what I can do,' he croaked.

Vandana thanked the man, and then she started running behind a handrail. She realised that she was beside C6. Not wanting to repeat the mistake she'd done at Ambur, she impulsively leapt.

24

Luckily for Vandana, the Salem station master took her words seriously. Almost as soon as the Mangalore Express was on its way he went into his cabin to make some calls. His first call was to the station master at Madras Central. He wanted to find out first if there really was a coach belonging to the Reserve Bank on this train. The station master at Madras took some time to pore over his record books. When he came back on the line he informed his counterpart that there was indeed a RBI coach on that train. So it was confirmed that the girl had been telling the truth.

The silver-haired station master, whose name was Gangadharan, then burnt the telephone lines with a blaze of calls. His next call was to the station master at Erode. He repeated verbatim what the girl had told him a few minutes ago: that there were bandits onboard the train who were out to rob the RBI coach.

'...so do the needful,' he finished.

'What do you mean do the needful? What exactly am I supposed to do?' the flustered station master asked, not having handled such a situation before.

Gangadharan was silent for a beat. Then he said, 'Call up the police in your town and ask them to send you some armed men. When the train stops at Erode, get these men on top of the RBI Coach, or on top of the engine. Let them escort the coach up to Coimbatore.'

'Is that where the coach gets dropped off?'

'Yes,' said Gangadharan.

'How many policemen do I ask for?'

'I don't know...ten...twenty...the more the better.'

'Anything else I need to do?'

'The section controller has to be informed, but I'll do that for you. You get on the phone to the police first.'

'Okay,' said the Erode station master.

'And don't forget to inform them that they have less than forty minutes to make it to the railway station.'

'I'll do that,' the station master said, and dropped the receiver.

Gangadharan's next phone call was to his section controller at Palghat. While the station masters were responsible for their individual sections, the overall responsibility for all the sections in a region was always vested with a controller. Erode, Tiruppur and Coimbatore came under the jurisdiction of the district controller in Palghat.

The Salem station master informed the section controller in Palghat of the girl's warning, and the robbery she thought was imminent on the Mangalore Express.

'Did you get in touch with the Erode station master?' the section controller asked.

'I did,' Gangadharan said. 'He is in the process of arranging additional police escorts for the coach.'

'I can stop the train in Erode and block off the section, if there is any chance of catching the bandits,' the controller suggested.

Gangadharan thought about this for a few seconds. 'They see the police searching the train, they are going to slip away. Nothing will come of that exercise. It will only cause a major delay in the section.'

'What else to do then?' the controller asked.

'I think the police escorts that the Erode station master is arranging should suffice. After all the coach is on the train only up to Coimbatore.'

'That makes sense,' the controller said. 'I'll tell you what I'll do: I'll prioritise the entire section from Erode to Coimbatore for this train, so they will make it to Coimbatore at the earliest. What do you think?'

'Good idea,' Gangadharan said. 'A couple of minutes stop in Erode is more than sufficient to get the police escorts on board. I am sure the coal and the water they loaded up in Salem is sufficient to last them up to Coimbatore.'

The two of them then split the calls they had to make between themselves.

Gangadharan called up the Erode station master and told him he was getting a 'line clear' for the Mangalore Express. The moment the escorts boarded he was to green flag the train. No coal hauling and no water changing.

The controller, on his part, made two calls. The first one was to the station master at Madras. The station master was told to inform somebody at the Reserve Bank in Madras about the imminent robbery. The second call was to the Coimbatore station master to keep him informed of the situation. Also, the Coimbatore station master was asked to get in touch with the bank's receivers in the city so they could be informed as well.

By this time, the Erode station master had already made contact with the police. He had spoken to the duty officer at Erode Police HQ, a gentleman by the name of Kripakaran. After briefing him of the situation, the station master asked for twenty policemen. Inspector Kripakaran reminded him that it was half past one in the morning, where was he to go for twenty policemen? The inspector said he'd muster as many men as he could find and would be there in the railway station in twenty minutes.

Inspector Kripakaran dropped the receiver on the cradle and yelled out to his two duty constables. He sent one of them to the police residential quarters nearby to muster all the policemen there and bring them here. The other constable he sent to load up their van with rifles.

He then waited impatiently for his men to arrive.

~

On the train, Hardaker had by this time convened an emergency meeting with his men. Icy had told him about what had happened at Salem, and that's what prompted the sudden meeting. Hardaker, understandably, was quite upset.

'Who was that girl?' Dorai asked, fiddling restlessly with the amulet tied to his arm.

'Who knows, and who cares? Yadu has told her about us, and that's all that matters,' Hardaker said.

Dorai couldn't help but marvel at the Englishman's foresight. He had anticipated that Yadu would tell somebody about their plans, and also that this somebody would go to the station master. There was definitely a lot to learn from this man.

Opposite him, Icy was having a tough time defending his actions. 'It all happened in a flash. I had only a split second to react. What was I supposed to do?' he asked.

'You should have shot both of them first. Only then should you have signalled the train's departure,' Dorai said.

Icy sneered. 'Are you crazy? If I had shot the station master the entire police force would be waiting for us at Erode.'

'That's going to happen anyway, you have just ensured that,' Sethu rejoined. The bearded man with the long flowing locks was glaring harshly at Icy.

'By now the station master would have alerted the next station. By the time this train reaches Erode they would have a huge reception party ready for us,' said Dorai cynically.

Icy looked helplessly at Hardaker. 'What do we do now?'

The bushy eye-browed Englishman didn't answer immediately. He was lost in thought, staring intensely at the ceiling. The train was thundering at top speed, something they could tell by the dangerous manner in which the coach was swaying.

After a few minutes Hardaker looked calmly at his watch. 'The train is running fifteen minutes late,' he informed them.

'So?' Sethu asked.

'So, we are going to be late arriving at our rendezvous point,' Hardaker said.

Dorai was furious when he heard this. 'Brian, frankly, who gives a damn about the rendezvous point now? We have to deal with the police in Erode first. How are we going to get past them?'

Hardaker's gaze moved slowly from Icy to Dorai. 'We'll have to *jump* Erode station.'

Sethu looked at the other two, not sure if he had heard the Englishman right.

Hardaker now looked at Sethu and explained. 'A slight change of plan: instead of hijacking the coach and the engine after Erode we are going to hijack it fifteen minutes *before* we reach Erode. That way even if there are policemen standing on the platform – waiting for us – they can't do anything. What do you all say?'

Silence.

Icy was the first to lend his acceptance to the idea. 'I like the idea,' he said buoyantly.

Dorai mulled over it for some time. 'Can't find fault with it,' he said eventually.

Icy was relieved that there was a way out of the mess he had created for them at Salem. He couldn't stop praising Hardaker. 'Stellar idea, captain,' he said, with a tinge of admiration in his voice. 'That way, not only will we be on time for stage two, but also, we'll take the police by surprise.'

'Two birds with one stone,' Hardaker said, grinning like Satan himself.

~

The authorities now knew of the impending robbery, and Vandana was sure plans were afoot to foil Hardaker's ambitions. She must have therefore felt upbeat with the way things had gone. However, she was not feeling very happy. On the contrary, she was in a state of high anxiety. She could almost picture what must have happened after the train left Salem. She was certain Icy had informed his colleagues about her warning to the station master. They would be aware that the police would be waiting for them at Erode. The question was, what would they do about it? Would they abandon their attempt and jump off the train as it approached Erode? That way they wouldn't fall into the hands of the police. Vandana couldn't get herself to believe that this was what Hardaker would do. She had a hunch that the bushy eye-browed Englishman would go for the other option, which was to rob the coach *before* the train arrived at Erode. The journey from Salem to Erode was roughly one hour. One hour was more than sufficient for these four men to rob the RBI coach. If Hardaker preponed his strike what could she do? What could anybody do to stop them?

Standing by the C6 exit door, watching the incessant rain, she realised some five minutes later that, yes, there was one thing she could do: she could tell the ticket examiner on this coach and find out if he could do anything to stop the bandits; this seemed her only option at the moment.

Closing the door Vandana walked in search of the TTE. She found him lying on his berth, fast asleep. She woke him up and asked him to sit down, saying she had something important to tell him. Two things worked in Vandana's favour: the late hour, and the anxiety on her face. The TTE, a short, wiry man, realised even before she opened her mouth that the matter was serious, whatever it was. As a result he was receptive to what she had to say.

Vandana briefed him of the situation and asked him to do something to stop the robbery.

'What do you want me to do?' he asked, once she had finished.

'I don't know,' Vandana conceded.

'There is nothing we can do until we reach Erode,' the TTE stated categorically.

'But that will be too late,' Vandana said, panicking. 'Is there nothing at all you can do in the meantime?'

'I can stop the train. But tell me what good will come of it? It will only delay our arrival at Erode.'

Vandana clenched and unclenched her hands in frustration. Hardaker and his men, at this very moment, could be mounting an attack on the RBI coach, and it seemed as if there was nothing she could do to stop it.

❧

25

Yadu had no idea how long he had been lying unconscious. And he had no clue as to what had brought him back to consciousness. Was it the rain? Or the pain?

Yadu got up slowly and squatted on his knees, holding his head in both hands. He remained in that position for some time, praying that the skull-cracking pain would go away. Only after the pain had subsided did he open his eyes and look around. Darkness greeted him everywhere. His eyes vainly swept the area for an electric lamp or some other vestige of civilisation, but none met his eye. The steel girders of the bridge reminded him of where he was. That, and the gravel stone heap were reminders of the fight he had lost some time back. He felt depressed thinking about it, so he forced the memory out of his head.

There was a deep gash in his forehead from where blood oozed out in tiny trickles. It marked the spot where the club had made impact. Yadu pulled out his handkerchief and pressed it to the wound in an attempt to stem the flow. It took some five minutes for the trickle to finally stop.

He then tried to stand up, but a wave of intense nausea forced him back on his knees. For a while he just sat there and mulled over the utter hopelessness of his situation. He was stuck in the middle of nowhere, with apparently no human being around for miles; he had no means of transportation, and he was hungry, wet and tired.

He had, by now, resigned to the fact that stopping Hardaker was beyond him now. He had tried his best, but his best had not been good enough.

He now started to wonder how he was going to get out of this godforsaken place. He thought for a while about the options available to him. The top of the head option that presented itself was a tedious one: that of walking alongside the track until he came across a house. He had no idea how far the nearest house was in any direction. What if he walked for the next two hours without finding a house? He decided walking could only be his last option.

The other option was to wait for the next train to arrive by the bridge. If he caught the attention of the driver he may slow down. Perhaps the driver could be persuaded to drop him off at the nearest station.

While he thought on these lines his eyes fell on the bridge's steel girders. All of a sudden it occurred to him that he needn't even wave the train down. The train would slow down on its own. He remembered that the Mangalore Express had slowed down on approaching the bridge. It was probably mandatory for every train to slow down on approaching this bridge. If those restrictions were in place then his transportation problem had just solved itself. All he had to do was simply wait patiently for the next train to arrive by the bridge. As and when it slowed down he would board the train and hop a free ride to the next station. Even if the train didn't slow down, he could still get the attention of the engine driver and get onboard.

The only trouble with this plan of action was that he had no idea when the next train would come along. It could be in ten minutes time or it could take ten hours.

But there was one part of him that argued, what does it matter, how long? Now that there was very little chance of stopping the robbery, time really didn't matter all that much.

~

When hardly thirty minutes remained for the train to arrive at Erode, at a quarter to two in the morning, Hardaker and his men swung into action. All four of them clambered onto the roof of F1, and from there they leapfrogged their way upto C1. Dorai, Icy and Sethu had by now become experts at this. Hardaker, not that experienced at this, was a tad slow to begin with, but he soon caught up with them. The rain that had stopped briefly had started yet again. Left to their devices, Dorai, Sethu and Icy would have abandoned the job, or would have postponed it for a day with better weather. Not the bald Englishman though. He was determined to go ahead with the strike come what may. In fact, he considered the rain a blessing in disguise.

From C1 they leapt onto the RBI coach, and from there onto the steam locomotive. Hardaker slid down the coal pile, followed closely by Dorai. The other two just sat on top of the coal pile waiting for these two to finish their job inside the cabin.

To reach the driver's cabin one had to pass through a narrow passageway. Going through it had an effect similar to the experience of walking through a revolving door. If there were winds that froze you to the bones on one side, there was a blast of extremely hot air on the other. On one side was the sound of rainfall, on the other, the deafening roar of the engine. Two different worlds.

Hardaker led the way holding a gun in each hand, with Dorai following close behind.

The engine driver – a middle aged man with salt and pepper hair – was leaning out on the left and staring at the track ahead, while the fireman was busy shovelling coal into the fire box.

Neither of them noticed Hardaker's entry for the first few seconds, and this gave the Englishman time to have a quick look around the cabin. The place was poorly lit. A naked bulb that hung from the ceiling was all there was to light the place. That, and the light pouring out of the fire box. This much light however was enough for anyone to make out that virtually everything in the cabin was covered in a layer of soot. The myriad dials, the instrument panel, the levers, the pressure gauges, the roof – everything was black. While it was pitch dark outside it was rather fittingly soot black inside.

The fireman was the first to sense their presence. All of a sudden he whirled around, shovel in hand. One look at Hardaker and he let out a sharp cry.

'Devraj!'

The engine driver turned to his right and stared at the intruders. 'Hey! Who are you people? What business have you...?'

The engine driver didn't finish the sentence, as his assistant had struck at Hardaker's hands with his shovel, sending both his guns flying out into the jungle. The Englishman was momentarily stunned at the speed of the boy's reaction. Then, recovering, fuming at having lost both his guns, he launched on the boy smashing his face with a right upper cut. The boy crashed onto the floor and rolled dangerously close to the open fire box.

'Stop,' the engine driver cried, running towards his assistant. Hardaker swung his powerful right arm with considerable force and slammed it onto the engine driver's chest. It knocked the breath out of Devraj. He slumped onto the floor right next to his assistant.

Dorai meanwhile had knocked the shovel to the other corner of the cabin. He now leaned over and placed the muzzle of his gun on the fireman's temple. The boy had fashioned a cap out of his handkerchief by knotting its ends, and this he was wearing on his head. Dorai removed it and threw it into the blazing fire. 'You try any more tricks and you'll follow that kerchief into the fire,' he warned the boy.

'What do you people want?' the engine driver croaked.

Hardaker stared at the two drivers until he had got his anger back in check, until his breathing was back to normal. He then pulled Devraj onto his feet catching hold of his cut banian. 'We are here for the RBI coach. We are hijacking it and you are going to help us do it.'

All trace of colour disappeared from the engine driver's face. He looked at his assistant disbelievingly. The fireman just gaped at Hardaker.

'Slow down the train first,' Dorai demanded.

'You must be out of your mind,' the fireman shouted.

'Mani, shut up for your own sake,' the engine driver said. Dorai had already shut him up with a kick on his chest.

The engine driver was trembling slightly now. He realised that these men meant business.

'Get on with it,' Hardaker barked, getting ready to take one more swing at the driver.

Devraj got to work immediately. He pulled the brake handle all the way back.

'Reduce the speed to twenty and keep it at that until my boys have uncoupled the coach from the rest of the train. Purinjutha?'

'The train has to be brought to a standstill if you want to uncouple the coach,' the engine driver said, mopping his brow.

'That won't be necessary. Just slow it to a crawl' Hardaker snarled.

'Don't do it, *Anne*. You could be jailed for this.' Mani said from down on the floor.

The engine driver ignored him. He went ahead and applied the brakes.

'It's not going to be easy, uncoupling the coaches on the run,' Devraj tried again. 'The train *has* to be stopped.'

'We'll see about that,' said Dorai.

At the back, Sethu and Icy had leapt back onto the RBI coach from the coal tender. It was still raining heavily so they were very careful. Neither of them wanted an accident at this stage of the hijack. As the train's speed continued to fall, they ran to the far end of the coach. Then they slid down the side and landed on the track. The train had slowed down to a crawl by this time. The two of them then tried uncoupling the coach. After just two minutes they realised that it couldn't be done until the train had come to a complete standstill. So Icy whistled in the direction of the engine. Hardaker peeped out of the cabin and understood what Icy was telling him in sign language. The engine driver had been right.

'Bring the train to a halt,' Hardaker ordered.

The engine driver did as he was told.

~

Vandana and the TTE (whose name she learned was Koshy) were powerless spectators to the drama unfolding at the front. Standing by the exit door they had seen the silhouettes of the four men as they dashed towards the RBI coach.

'There they are,' Vandana had said desperately. '*Do something.*'

The TTE had said, wait a minute, let's see what they do next. Biting her nails Vandana watched on as all four jumped onto the coal tender. She was taken aback when she saw this. What were they getting into the engine for?

Five minutes later they found out as the train started to slow down.

'Looks like they are stopping the train,' the TTE said. He thought for a moment. 'Okay, here is what we are going to do. As soon as the train stops I'll run to C9 to inform the guard. I suggest you go to C1 and wake the escorts somehow. Throw a bucket of water on them if you have to. Wake them up *somehow* and tell them what is happening.'

Vandana said okay, though she had no idea at the moment how she was going to do it. The two of them waited for the train to further reduce speed. The sheets of rain, the blanket of darkness and the gravel stone bed reminded her that it was well past her bedtime. Not that she felt sleepy. She was actually busy thinking about the next few minutes. How was she going to run in such conditions? How was she going to wake the escorts?

The train had slowed down considerably now. Vandana leapt off the train; the portly TTE followed after her. She started running towards the engine, and the TTE started running towards the back. It was pouring so heavily now that it felt like she was running through a waterfall – a never-ending waterfall. She had passed F1 and was running past C3 when the train finally ground to a halt. Her heart pounding wildly, she started running faster. She hoped that this stop had nothing to do with the silhouettes she had seen minutes ago.

They seemed to have stopped on an isolated stretch. She couldn't see any houses or lights anywhere in the vicinity.

Then, when just about a hundred metres separated her from C1, the train started to move. At least that's what she thought initially. She saw the engine moving, belching smoke into the air. *But the coaches by her side were not moving.* For the first few seconds she didn't know what was happening. Then it slowly dawned on her: Hardaker and his men had uncoupled the engine and the RBI coach from the rest of the train.

They were *hijacking* the coach.

26

Vandana stood there, transfixed, watching the track long after the RBI coach had disappeared. It was still raining heavily. She was thoroughly drenched by now, but she was beyond caring.

Then she turned and looked all around her. The scene was so surreal that she couldn't believe she was part of it. The train had stopped on a stretch the locals called the 'palm tree mile'. It was an apt name, considering that it was a long stretch of track with palm trees planted on either side. Beyond the palm trees it was just shrub and wilderness. There was no civilisation for miles, no matter which direction you looked in.

With the rain and all, the landscape looked bleak. The only place that was emanating some warmth was the belly of the train. And it seemed to be getting warmer by the minute, because people were switching on the lights to see why the train had halted here.

Vandana wanted to get inside the train pronto. She wanted to change into warm clothes, she wanted to get onto her berth and go to sleep. She wanted to tune out of this nightmare unfolding in front of her.

Just as she was about to start for C5, Koshy, the portly TTE from C6, came running to her. There was a uniformed man along with him who he introduced as the guide of the train.

'It's all over,' Vandana told them. 'The bandits have hijacked the RBI coach and the engine.'

'*Oh my God!*' said Koshy, his hands going up involuntarily to his head.

The guide looked dumbstruck.

Vandana told them what had just happened, something she would be repeating over a hundred times over the next twenty-four hours. No sooner had she finished, than Kanchana came running. Vandana thought her sister would start screaming at her again. But Kanchana seemed to understand the gravity of the situation, and more importantly, her sister's foul mood, so she didn't say much. She just listened to Vandana tell her about the hijack.

Then the other TTEs started arriving, one by one. The guide called two of the TTEs aside and he told them that he kept flares in his cabinet on C9, for emergencies such as this. Could they please go fetch the flares, so one of them could stand in front of the train and one behind the train?

'If either of you see or hear a train approaching, send the flares up into the air. We have plenty to keep us occupied as it is. The last thing we need now is a head-on collision.'

The two TTEs went away taking the cabinet key with them. For some time after that they all stood there in the rain, staring at each other, not knowing what was to be done. Nobody had a clue how to proceed in such a situation, so they all stayed put. After a few minutes the downpour fizzled down in intensity. And that was all that was needed for the exodus to begin – the exodus from the train onto the ground. The passengers, who had woken up and had been hearing rumours about why the train had stopped, started getting off the train to see what was happening. Men, women, children, anybody who was awake, and was curious enough, got down from the train. The only thing that had kept them inside the train so far was the foul weather. Now that the rain had stopped they were getting down to sate their curiosity.

There was, however, a select batch of passengers who didn't get off the train. These were the passengers who would think twice before getting off the train even if there was an earthquake. This exclusive bunch of travellers were the ones who travelled in the third class unreserved coach. The reason why they never got off the coach was because, if they did, they would lose their seats for the rest of their journey. That said, on this train it was debatable whether there was going to be a 'rest of the journey'. Those passengers on this coach without a seat tried hard to tempt other people with seats to step out of the train – so that they could take their seats. But these were men of such exemplary character that they wouldn't let a full bladder tempt them. How effective a temptation could curiosity be then?

Vandana thought that all the passengers would be raving mad at what had happened. She thought that they would be angry and upset. But it turned out that she was the only one who was upset and in a bad mood. The passengers were all cracking jokes about the efficiency of the Indian railways, about how 'it was never like this during the British rule'. The TTEs good-humouredly bore the brunt of the jokes. In fact, they themselves were laughing at this predicament they found themselves in. This kind of an incident had never happened with the Indian railways, so they didn't have a precedent. They didn't have a clue as to what had to be done. What were they supposed to do? Get the passengers to push the train till the next station?

None of them knew how far they were from Erode; so there were no volunteers for the long walk to the nearest telephone, wherever *that* was.

The guide and the TTEs were certain of one thing though: the Erode station master would be sending a relief engine here soon. Until its arrival all they could do was grin and bear the jokes that the passengers were cracking at their expense.

~

Erode Station, 2 am

The two civil servants greeted each other in the middle of the platform. Both men were tall, and both were in their early thirties. Inspector Kripakaran was the trim looking one of the two. He had a flat stomach, a lean frame and a thin moustache. Nandakumar, the Erode station master, was barrel-chested and over-weight. He was very ordinary looking. If at all he could be picked from a crowd it would be because of his moustache. It was so fertile, it formed a perfect canopy over his upper lip. Surely, it had not seen a pair of clippers in a long while.

'I am expecting the train any minute now,' Nandakumar said. His bulbous nose had gone red for some reason. 'Thanks for coming at such short notice.'

'No problem,' Kripakaran said.

'How many men did you bring?' the station master asked, looking beyond the inspector's shoulder. The constables were all standing some distance away. Some of them were seated on a couple of stone benches, and the rest of them hung around the area watching the downpour.

'Twelve is all I could manage,' the inspector said.

'That should do,' the station master said, sniffing. 'We need them only for a couple of hours, to frighten the bandits away. A show of strength, so to speak.'

For a few moments the two of them stood there next to each other watching the rain.

'The coach belongs to the Reserve Bank?' asked the inspector.

'Yes. The Salem station master got that confirmed from Madras. The girl was not lying.'

'And you said the coach is headed for Coimbatore?'

'That's right. Your job is done the moment the coach is uncoupled and handed over in Coimbatore. You and your men are free to come back as soon as it is done. Three hours is all it will take, at the most.'

The station master then went on to give a lay of the coaches to the inspector. He suggested that the inspector post four men atop the RBI coach, four atop the coal tender and four men on C1.

'These bandits, they should see these men with rifles atop the coach, and they should abandon all their plans. That's the idea.'

The station master then told them how the next section had been priority-line-cleared so that the train could reach Coimbatore at the earliest.

'The train's going to stop here only for a minute. As soon as you get your men onboard, I'll green flag it.'

The inspector was okay with this. 'I only wish it wasn't raining so heavily,' he said. 'It's not going to be easy for my boys atop the coach.' He looked in the direction of his constables. Some of them were doing a last minute check of their rifles. The others were chatting nervously. Besides the fourteen of them there was nobody else on the platform. Not a single passenger.

'Do you know how many bandits there are onboard?' the inspector asked.

Nandakumar sneezed loudly. 'Excuse me,' he said, and then went into a prolonged bout of sneezing. The inspector looked on, amused.

'The weather...I have got this...atchoo.' The station master thrust his hand into his pocket and pulled out his snuff box. He helped himself to a generous pinch of the powder, took it to his nostrils and took a deep sniff. He started to sneeze again.

'Four, I think,' the station master said, at length.

They could see the train's headlights in the distance now.

'Here we go. This is the train,' the station master said, unfurling his red flag. The engine announced itself with a sharp whistle. Inspector Kripakaran walked to where his men were standing and divided them into three groups of four. As discussed with the station master, he allotted one group to the coach roof, one to the tender and the third to C1.

The station master was already waving the flag now as the 'train' entered the platform. Until the engine was just four hundred metres away the station master didn't suspect anything. Then, all of a sudden, he let out a sharp cry. The inspector, the constables, everybody whipped their heads around. And they all saw what the station master had already noticed. What was thundering down the track was not a train but an engine towing a *solitary* coach. And it showed no signs of slowing down. The station master was waving his red flag furiously now.

'*Inspector, come here, quick.* This doesn't look right,' Nandakumar shouted.

Pulling out his gun from the holster the inspector ran towards the station master. The engine was now less than two hundred metres away but it was still clipping at top speed.

'What in the name of god is the engine driver up to?' Kripakaran screamed. 'Why isn't he reducing speed?'

The inspector spotted a man leaning out of the driver's cabin, a bald, white man. He didn't look like an engine driver at all.

Nandakumar continued to wave his red flag furiously. 'What happened to the rest of the train? *What is going on?*'

The inspector aimed his gun and tried to shoot the bald man, but the train was moving too fast, and the man ducked before he could even take proper aim.

The engine then shot past them, smothering them in a rolling mass of smoke. They both stepped back hastily, coughing and holding their noses. The dozen policemen watched on helplessly, not knowing what to do.

By the time the smoke lifted, the engine and the RBI coach were gone. The endwall of the RBI coach had become one with the surrounding darkness.

27

It took a few minutes for Inspector Kripakaran to comprehend what had just happened.

The moment it dawned on him that this was a hijack he started whipping out orders to his men. He called his head constable, Inder Singh, aside, asked him to take seven men and go after the engine.

'Use my jeep. Get onto the track and follow the engine as fast as you can. Try your best to keep up with the engine.' The inspector then lashed out to his men to get into the jeep immediately. He kept just four of them behind as standbys.

'What the hell just happened?' the station master asked, snapping out of his reverie.

'They changed their plans, that's what happened,' Inspector Kripakaran said, shaking his head in disbelief. 'They knew we were going to be here waiting for them, so they hijacked the coach. This is *so* unbelievable...'

Inder Singh took the jeep keys and made a run for the portico with the seven men following him. Kripakaran then sent one of his men running to the police station with orders to send a wire to all police stations informing them about the hijack.

Realising that he too had to do the same, Nandakumar got cracking. He ran into his cabin to send a wire to all nearby signal points. He issued an all-station alert for the runaway engine. If any of them saw the engine-coach they were to divert it to a catch siding, and sand trap it. The station master then telephoned the section controller's office at Palghat, and his colleague at Tiruppur, to brief them of the hijack. That done, he sat by the telephone and waited for further orders from his superiors. It was up to the section controller to decide what had to be done next.

Outside, Inspector Kripakaran was still busy barking orders to his men, sending them on various errands. He sent one constable to go wake all the policemen in town and get them here. He sent another one to make phone calls to all nearby police stations – for reinforcements. He sent a third one to get him all the maps: road maps, rail track maps, political maps...every single map he could get his hands on. While his men were busy doing his bidding he got busy making phone calls. He woke up his superior, the assistant commissioner of police, Erode region, and told him what had happened. He then telephoned the Tiruppur police station and asked them to send men to the Tiruppur railway station. Tiruppur was the next station on the line. If the engine was successfully sand-trapped there they would need men to nab the perpetrators. That done, he walked into the station master's cabin to cross-check something with Nandakumar.

The station master was dropping the receiver onto the cradle as he entered. He motioned the inspector to take a seat. Kripakaran said he would rather stand.

'Arrangements have been made at Tiruppur to sand-trap the engine,' the station master informed him.

'I don't think it's going to serve any purpose,' Kripakaran said, rather bluntly.

'What do you mean?' Nandakumar asked.

'What makes you think they are going up to Tiruppur?' the inspector asked.

'Where else can they go? This line leads to one town only and that is Tiruppur. There are no diverging tracks, so they can't go anywhere else.'

'That's not what I meant.'

'What did you mean then?'

'Why should they go to Tiruppur at all? In fact, why should they go anywhere at all? Ask yourself this – what is their purpose in hijacking the coach? To break in and rob it. I think they would do that and abandon the coach in the next ten-fifteen minutes. By the time Inder Singh reaches the coach it will be too late. He might find the coach, only it would be empty inside.'

Nandakumar sucked in his breath. 'Is that what you think is going to happen?'

'I am *certain* that's what is going to happen,' the inspector said. 'That engine is capable of sixty to seventy kilometres per hour. Considering that it is raining so heavily, and considering that Inder Singh is riding atop the track, he can't go at more than thirty kilometres per hour. What the bandits are going to do is, go a safe distance, stop the engine and then break into the RBI coach. By the time Inder Singh and my men arrive by the engine they would have disappeared into the wilderness with the loot.'

Nandakumar's face clouded up. 'Is there nothing you can do about it?'

This is what Kripakaran had come inside for, to cross-check if the grain of an idea running in his mind had any feasibility at all.

'Can you arrange an engine and a driving crew for me in the next five minutes?' Kripakaran asked.

Nandakumar looked taken aback by this sudden request. He thought about it for a moment, and then shook his head. 'That is impossible. It's two in the morning, where am I going to find a driving crew at this unearthly hour?'

'I thought as much,' the inspector said. 'We will have to resign ourselves to the inevitable then. Without an engine there is no way we can catch up with the runaway vehicle. If we can't catch up with them then we can't stop them. As simple as that.'

Nandakumar went into another bout of sneezing. When he was through with it he blew into his handkerchief. 'This is not going to affect the way things stand. But, just so you know, even if I had a spare engine with a crew ready I can't send it on the track. The weather being what it is, there might be a rear end collision if the runaway vehicle has stopped somewhere in the middle.'

Kripakaran nodded his head to say he understood. 'And if they sent an engine from Tiruppur there might be a *head on* collision. Either way we would be inviting more trouble than we are already into.'

'Right,' Nandakumar said, sneezing again.

28

The phone call they were expecting from Inder Singh came one and a half hours later.

'Sir, I am calling from Tiruppur railway station,' he told Kripakaran. 'I am afraid it's bad news.'

Inspector Kripakaran sighed into the phone. 'The bandits got away with the loot, didn't they?'

'They have, sir, though not in the way you think.'

'What do you mean?'

'I know this is going to sound ridiculous, but here it is anyway: the engine and the coach have *vanished*.'

'What nonsense!' Kripakaran fumed. 'Where could it have gone?'

'I have to admit, sir, I have no idea. The Tiruppur station master maintains that the runaway vehicle hasn't passed his station. And I am equally confident the 'RV' isn't on the track. So I really don't know.'

Kripakaran went silent. The look on his face was one of utter bafflement. The RV hadn't gone past the next station, it hadn't come back here, and Inder Singh was saying it was not on the track. What had happened to it then?

The inspector's voice was harsh when he got back on the phone. 'Inder, are you sure you didn't just miss the vehicle in the darkness?'

'With all due respect sir,' Inder replied, 'the RV is the size of six elephants. Do you seriously think that *all eight of us* in the jeep just *missed* it?'

Kripakaran had to admit, that didn't seem likely.

'Okay,' he said, 'here is what you do. Get back onto the jeep, get back onto the section and keep searching for the RV. As soon as I get more reinforcements I'll send them into the section to help you people. It must be in the section somewhere. Maybe they jumped it off the rails and took it into the woods. Keep looking.'

'Yes sir,' Inder Singh said, and cut the line.

'Looks like your men didn't find the RV in the section,' said Nandakumar, as the inspector dropped the receiver onto the cradle.

'You are damn right, they didn't,' Kripakaran said pacing the room. 'It's not gone past Tiruppur and it's not in the section. Inder says it's just vanished, all hundred tonnes of it.'

'Is this a night shift or a nightmare?' Nandakumar asked.

Kripakaran didn't say anything.

'The irony is that I opted for this night shift thinking I could sleep on duty.'

'Bad choice. Go back to the day shift after all this is over.'

'Thanks, I'll keep that in mind.' Then, getting serious the station master said, 'You know, you maybe right about what you just told Inder. Maybe they ran it off the rails and took it into the woods.'

'Yes, I maybe right. But my point is, why would they have done such a thing? They knew that they had taken us by surprise; they knew they had a head start; they had all the time in the world to raid the coach and get away with the loot. So why should they even risk jumping off the rails?'

'Fair point,' Nandakumar admitted.

Just then, one of the station employees happened to walk past the door. Nandakumar yelled out to him asking him to come inside. He ordered the man to run to the loco shed and inform the foreman that a relief engine was required at the earliest to go in the direction of Salem. The Mangalore Express had been left stranded, god knew where, in the Salem-Erode section. The relief engine had to find the train and then haul it here.

'Did you get that?' Nandakumar asked.

The employee nodded and then shot out of the cabin.

Kripakaran was still pacing up and down the small room. While the inspector was occupied, Nandakumar got back on the phone to intimate the section controller of the situation. He told him, that they were no longer dealing with a runaway vehicle. What they were dealing with now was a *vanished* vehicle.

Nandakumar had just dropped the phone down when Kripakaran said, 'You better get the Erode-Tiruppur section blocked. Talk to your section controller, get him to reroute all trains, because I don't think this section is going to be used for the next few hours.'

'Are you planning something?' the station master asked.

'Yes. A physical search of the entire line, all fifty kilometres of it. I am going to call Coimbatore for more men and vehicles. I suggest you do the same. Get as many railway handcars as you can get your hands on, and as many men as you can mobilise. We are going to need all the manpower we can get. Let them get here as early as they can.'

'Okay. Anything else?'

'See if you can find out if there are any abandoned lines in the area that we don't know about. Also, tracks leading into industrial units, petrol depots and such. Any line that the bandits could have used to vanish. Will you do it?'

'Sure,' Nandakumar said.

'Also, I am going to call in the air force. I am going to request them for a couple of helicopters. An aerial survey will take a lot less time, and will be more effective.'

'That's a good idea,' the station master said.

The inspector nodded, then started making the necessary calls.

~

SUNDAY, 7 DECEMBER 1947

At daybreak, nearly four hours after the hijack, the search operation finally started to fall in place. An engine towing two flat cars arrived on the main platform at Erode. The Coimbatore station master had sent forty gangmen, four railway handcars, two motorbikes and a jeep for the search operations. The rain had finally stopped a couple of hours back, which was a good thing; now the search operation could be conducted with one worry less.

It was not yet six in the morning. The skies were yet to light up – what with the dark clouds and all. And yet, the main platform wore a crowded look. Policemen, soldiers, the railway top brass who had descended here to organise the search for the missing coach, people from the Reserve Bank, officers from the Intelligence Bureau, officials from the ministry of railways – they were all here. Word was out on the street about what had happened just a few hours ago, and curious townspeople had got out of their beds, and had come straight to the railway station (even without brushing their teeth) to hear the gossip, and contribute their bit to the rumours. Inspector Kripakaran, anticipating the trouble these people would cause to the operation, had ensured that none of them would enter the station grounds. He had placed his men outside the gates to ensure that only people who had business inside would be let in. Since all trains on this route had been temporarily cancelled, even passengers with valid tickets weren't allowed inside.

On the main platform Nandakumar had set up a 'command centre'. He had put out two huge wooden tables, a few chairs and two telephones. The table was strewn with maps: from present day rail track maps to maps dating back fifty years. A couple of railway officers who were seated at the desk were slicing up the sections into two-kilometre stretches and allotting the area to different search parties. Nandakumar was doing the actual allotting. As soon as the flat cars had ground to a stop he walked over to the gangmen and split the forty of them into eight teams. He assigned a team leader, and told them which stretch they would be searching, and what they were searching for. They were to look for places where the engine could have jumped off the track, and they were to search the woods and the wilderness on both sides of the track for any clues to the RV's whereabouts.

Inspector Kripakaran, meanwhile, was giving the same set of instructions to the battalion of soldiers and to the thirty-odd policemen. They had been assigned their sections already. Some of them would be searching the old abandoned lines, others, the tracks that led to a couple of industrial units. Anybody who caught sight of the engine or the coach was to telephone the command desk immediately.

Overhead, the two helicopters were already on their third round over the section. The choppers had been the first to arrive here. Kripakaran had briefed the pilots on their arrival, and had asked them to particularly check the woods by the track. The pilots had said, don't expect results at least until daybreak, because it would be difficult sighting the RV in the dark.

Above them the choppers banked sharply to the left, made a wide turn and returned towards Tiruppur.

While Nandakumar was giving instructions to the gangmen, two more flat cars were attached to the train, so that the soldiers and the policemen too could be dropped off at their points. Once the coupling operation was complete, the men were told to get onboard. The train would leave shortly.

For three and a half hours the inactivity in the Erode railway station had been total. But when things started to fall into place, everything fell into place at once. Just as the search operation began in full swing, the Mangalore Express too arrived at the station, on platform number two. The relief engine had taken some time getting to palm tree mile. A loco had been readily available, but it had taken two hours to get the driving crew. And then the drivers were told by Nandakumar to deliberately drive very slowly. It had still been raining at that time and nobody knew where the train had got stranded, so they had been extra careful. But once the relief engine reached the train, things had moved pretty quickly. The coupling took just a few minutes, the passengers got inside in double quick time and they had set off for Erode.

Now they were here, on platform two, and Vandana and Kanchana took in all the action standing by the C5 exit door. They saw the choppers in the sky and the train of flat cars with the police and the railway personnel. Coming in, they had seen the crowds thronging the gates of the railway station, not to mention the crowd on platform one. They had been through this station several times before but never had they seen the main platform as crowded as it was today.

'Hardaker has made a major blunder hijacking the coach,' Vandana said to her sister.

Kanchana stared at her sister with a peculiar expression. 'What's the matter with you this morning? It's not like you to state the obvious in such a dramatic fashion.'

Vandana couldn't help smiling at her sister. 'What I meant was, Hardaker could have robbed the RBI coach, while in transit, and could have escaped with the loot, and it wouldn't have caused so much commotion. But the idiot decided all of a sudden to hijack the coach. Now see what he has brought upon himself. This is going to be front-page news in tomorrow's papers. The hijack is going to be the topic on everybody's lips for the next few weeks.'

'I agree,' Kanchana said. 'Robbing a coach is one thing. But hijacking a coach – now that is something else. The police and the railways are not going to take this lying down.'

'It's like he has insulted them, like he has thrown the gauntlet, daring them to catch him.'

'I haven't seen this man, but I can tell that he is arrogant and overconfident. It'll be the cause of his downfall, you can take it from me.'

Vandana nodded her head. She continued to look out onto the main platform.

'One thing does bother me though,' Kanchana said, at length.

'What's that?'

'It's been, what, four hours since the hijack. Why have they still not found them? If what the engine driver told us back there was true, the hijacked coach hasn't gone past Tiruppur. The helicopters ought to have spotted the coach by now, don't you think?'

'It is a worrying thought, yes,' said Vandana. The thought had occurred to her the moment she had seen the helicopters.

What she had wanted to do, what she still wanted to do was to go meet the people in charge of the operation and tell them what she had seen. She was the only one on the train to have seen the hijack. Now that there was no sign of Yadu, she was the only one who could identify the bandits to the police. She was certain she could be of use to the police in helping them nab the perpetrators. But she was afraid of bringing it up with her sister. Kanchana would deny her permission to go see the police. She would say if they went to the police now they would be stuck here all day. As it is they were late. Their parents would be wondering why they hadn't come home yet.

Vandana was busy thinking along these lines when suddenly the tannoy on the platform outside came alive with a burst of static. It was the station master, a man who introduced himself as Nandakumar. He said the announcement was meant for the passengers of the Mangalore Express. He started by apologising for the delay caused to their journey. Then he sneezed into the mike, and apologised again, this time for almost tearing their eardrums. He then went off the air suddenly and everybody could hear the muffled sound of him blowing into his handkerchief. When he finally returned, he said that the Mangalore Express would be leaving in another five minutes. The section had been closed to all other trains, but in the case of the Mangalore Express they were making an exception so there would be no further delays for the passengers. There was loud cheering when the passengers heard this.

Finally he said something that brought a smile on Vandana's lips and a scowl on her sister's. He said the train however wouldn't leave until the girl who had warned the Salem station master about the bandits stepped down from the train and identified herself to the police. She was needed for questioning.

29

To Yadu's chagrin, not a single train passed the bridge that night. The trains that were to pass that section had all been rerouted or cancelled because of the coach hijack further up the line. But he had no way of knowing this.

Good fortune however smiled on him the next morning. Just after seven, a truck carrying labourers and equipment arrived by the bridge. After dropping the workers it was just about to head back when Yadu ran in front and stopped the vehicle. He explained his situation to the driver and requested him for a drop to the nearest town. Yadu was hoping for a free ride. But the driver, a scoundrel, said it would cost him money. Was he willing to pay five rupees? If he did, then he could hop in for the ride. Yadu had no choice but to agree. He would pawn his gold chain when he got into town. What else was he to do? He hopped onto the seat next to the driver, and the truck headed off in the direction of Salem.

Along the way he could see the destruction the rain had wrought the previous night: fallen electricity poles, broken tree branches, flash floods. Even the road in some places had caved in. Still, they managed to get into Salem at a quarter to eight. The driver asked where he wanted to get off and Yadu asked him to take him to a pawnshop.

So, early in the morning, they started driving around Salem, trying to find a pawnshop that was open. It proved to be a tough task because most of the roads in the town were inundated with water. It was difficult driving in such conditions. The truck driver could have taken the easy way out by just asking Yadu to get off and forget about the five rupees he owed him, but for some strange reason that thought never crossed his mind. The truck driver, he knew, would look for the pawnshop; he was just going to sit here and enjoy the ride.

This was the first time Yadu had set foot in Salem. He observed that compared to Madras all the streets here were narrow. And the previous night's rain had not been kind to the town. There was debris floating all over the place: flower garlands, banana leaves, tree branches, waste paper and bamboo baskets. Floodwater had gotten into quite a lot of the shops, and the merchants were trying to salvage their goods by putting it atop their tin roofs. It was not easy because most of the shops were packed tightly together, and there was only that much space on top. Merchants of perishable items were selling their goods at throwaway prices to cut their losses. There were a lot of grumpy looking men on the streets today. However, there were some happy faces too: school children returning home. A holiday had been declared in a nearby school because the classrooms were flooded. The school meant for children was fit today only for schools of fish. People were wading through knee-deep water trying to get to their workplaces. In several places he noticed street urchins playing in the water gleefully. Yadu thought these kids must have awfully short memories because they were playing in the same streets where they normally defecated.

The truck driver finally spotted a pawnshop that was open and pulled over next to it. Yadu got down, went inside and handed over his gold chain to the seth. In five minutes he was out with eighty rupees. He paid the truck driver the five rupees he owed him and sent him on his way. Yadu already had expenses lined up for the rest of the money. He was going to buy himself a fresh set of clothes; he would then rent a room in a lodge and have a bath. With the money he had left he would then buy himself a ticket to Madras.

He now started walking towards the nearby market in search of a clothes store. There was not much water-logging on the street leading up to the market. However, this didn't mean that the walking was any easier. He stepped aside to allow a handcart laden with vegetable crates to go by. A couple of hefty looking women were loading up their baskets onto a cycle rickshaw, so they could go sell elsewhere. The smell of pudina and coriander leaves wafted in the air. Further ahead were the garland sellers who were spinning zari on to finished flower garlands. A donkey standing behind them was ripping a cinema poster off the wall and making a meal off it. The poster was for a film called *Mariamman* that was going to be released next month.

Yadu found the clothes store not very far from where the garland makers had set up shop. He went inside, picked out the cheapest pair of clothes he could find and came out. Then he went looking for accommodation.

It was while he was looking for a lodge that he heard the news broadcast. The radio inside a thatched-roof tea shop was tuned to the All India Radio morning news. As he passed he heard the words 'Reserve Bank coach', and he went stiff instantly. He walked into the tea shop, ordered a special tea and sat down on a wooden stool. There were four other men inside, all listening raptly to the broadcast.

Though Yadu had resigned to the fact that Hardaker would succeed in his attempt, his heart still sank when he heard the news. The newsreader said the bandits had hijacked the coach. *That* came as a major surprise to him. An even bigger surprise was the fact that the police and the railways were yet to find the runaway vehicle. The tea arrived but Yadu was in no mood to drink it. He sat there, wide-eyed, as the newsreader continued. All other news had been cast aside and full coverage had been given to the hijack because this was sensational news. There was nothing about Nehru, nothing about Gandhi or Jinnah, nothing about the Indian cricket team's defeat against Australia a couple of days back. It was the RBI coach story all the way.

Then the newsreader said something that made Yadu sit up. She said that it was a girl called Vandana who had identified the bandits to the police. It was because of her that the police at least knew who they were looking for. According to the newsreader, the girl had been detained at Erode and was being interrogated by the Intelligence Bureau officials.

This piece of information put Yadu in a sudden dilemma. He had been thinking of heading back to Madras this morning. But now he wondered whether it would be a better idea to go to Erode first. If he left in a couple of hours he could be in Erode by one in the afternoon. Hopefully, Vandana would still be there. From her he could find out firsthand what exactly happened on the train after he got left behind. There were questions in his mind that he needed answers for. At the moment only Vandana was capable of giving him those answers.

On the other hand he had to think of his grandmother. It had been nearly fourteen hours since he left home. Paati would be a wreck by now not knowing where he had gone, or what had happened to him. As far as she knew he had just gone to the railway station. She didn't know he had boarded a train and was miles away from home.

He got up from the stool, paid for his tea and stepped out. He decided the best thing to do under the circumstances was to call his uncle and brief him of the situation. His uncle could then send a message across to his paati about his whereabouts so that she wouldn't worry unnecessarily. This way he could buy himself a little more time. He could go meet Vandana, find out what had happened, and maybe tonight he could catch a train for Madras.

But before all that he had to find a lodge and freshen up first. There was so much mud in his clothes that he felt ten times heavier.

30

The crowds outside the railway station had dwindled considerably. There were just a handful of onlookers now. A few of them were seated under a neem tree, still gossiping about the daring hijack. The number of vehicles in the vehicle stand however gave a hint of how much activity was going on inside the station and in the section. Yadu walked up the steps and entered platform one.

Any doubts that he might have harboured on how well mounted the search operation was disappeared that first instant his eyes roved the platform. Never had he seen so many uniformed men grouped together in one place. There were policemen, soldiers and railway personnel all waiting patiently, for a train no doubt, to take them into the section. A couple of officers were giving them instructions, showing them parts of a map. At the command desk a couple of railway staff were busy answering phone calls. Intelligence officers were grilling a couple of cabin control attendants.

Yadu walked on towards the front of the platform looking out for Vandana. He didn't find her at first, so he thought she had probably gone home. But as he walked past the station master's cabin something made him look inside, and there she was seated inside, being interrogated by two Intelligence Bureau officers. He thought for a moment that he would wait outside the cabin until they were finished with her but then he decided that didn't have the patience right now for such niceties. He knocked lightly on the wooden frame of the window and then waved. Vandana whipped her head this side, saw him and her jaw dropped in disbelief. She excused herself and then was out of the room in a flash.

'*Yadu!*' she cried, her face aglow. 'Thank God you are alive!'

Yadu smiled as he shook hands with her. 'You thought I was dead?'

'You go disappearing all of a sudden, what else am I to think? I thought Hardaker's men had got you.'

'Well, they did get me.'

'You have no idea how relieved I am to see you,' she said. She caught hold of his hand and dragged him towards an area of the platform that was less crowded. They found an empty stone bench and both sat down.

'You heard what happened?' she asked, sitting down facing him.

'Yes, I did,' Yadu said. 'I heard it on the radio. Did he really hijack the coach?'

'Yes,' Vandana said. 'It took all of us by surprise.' She told him what had happened since she had last seen him. She told him of how she had found the escorts in a drugged state, and how she had warned the Salem station master. She then told him of the hijack, of how they had been stranded for hours at palm tree mile and how they had eventually got here.

'It looks like they still have not caught the bandits.'

'They haven't. They are all trying hard, but so far there's been no success,' Vandana said.

Yadu then suggested she had better go and get the interrogation out of the way. Then they could continue talking. Vandana said: to hell with the interrogation. They had been at her since six this morning and they had been asking her the same questions again and again. They could wait. Yadu then wanted to know what had happened here since the hunt for the coach began. And she obliged again, telling him in glorious detail the efforts of the police, the railway staff and the helicopter pilots.

'...yet all their efforts have come to nought so far,' she finished.

Yadu had gathered that much from the mood on the platform. The policemen wore tired looks, the railway top brass walked around with droopy shoulders. Their body language said it all: they'd had *no* success whatsoever in finding the vehicle.

Yadu then said, 'I thought you were travelling with your sister. Where is she?'

'She left for Palghat an hour back. The Intelligence Bureau officers told me I might be required here all day. One of us had to go back so our parents wouldn't get worried.'

'I see,' Yadu said.

They sat in silence for some time watching the activity on the platform. Then Yadu told her about his fight with Hardaker's men and how he got left behind.

'If I had somehow got back onboard maybe the hijack could have been prevented. Now it's too late. It's going to be all downhill from now on,' he said. 'In all likelihood, my father's name will be in the papers tomorrow.'

Vandana patted his shoulder lightly. 'They'll catch Hardaker, Yadu. They are *sure* to catch him. I mean, where can he go when there are so many people searching every inch of the section?'

'I do hope so,' Yadu said.

Vandana then said she was hungry, she was going to grab some lunch, did he want to come along? Yadu said he'd had something to eat on the way here.

'In that case, stay right here. I'll see if those officers are finished with me. I'll grab something to eat and I'll be here as soon as I can.'

'Okay,' said Yadu, and watched her go.

~

When Yadu had heard on the radio that Hardaker had hijacked the coach he had immediately labelled the Englishman a stupid ass. How far could he go before he got caught? But now Yadu wasn't so sure. He counted the hours. It was twelve hours since the hijack and the police were yet to find the bandits. Let alone the bandits, they were yet to find the engine and the coach. Hardaker wasn't stupid at all. No sir, he wasn't.

He started to think about where the police could have gone wrong. From what Vandana had said they had done everything by the book: they had checked the tracks and the abandoned lines; they had sent for helicopters immediately *and* had put them to good use; they had mobilised a huge force within a short span of time, and had used them well. In spite of doing everything, they hadn't found the coach.

What really stumped him was how Hardaker had so ingeniously concealed the engine-coach inspite of changing his plans at the last minute. Hardaker and his men were supposed to have *robbed* the coach, not hijacked it. The hijacking was actually a last minute change of plan after Vandana had warned the Salem station master.

Or was it?

Yadu was gripped by a sudden doubt. If Hardaker had never meant to hijack the coach then how was it that he had so effectively hidden eighty tonnes of metal from a hundred men and two helicopters for nearly twelve hours? It couldn't be. It looked as if Hardaker had intended to hijack the coach all along. Only if he had intended to hijack the coach would he have thought of finding a spot to hide it.

Now, he wondered, had Vandana misinterpreted their bandit-slang? When they talked of their 'strike', their 'job', had they actually meant the hijack? And why had he assumed right from the beginning that they would rob the coach? It occurred to him now that they only had themselves to blame for the false assumptions they had made. It now looked like Hardaker had intended to hijack the coach all along. His only change of plan, after Vandana warned the station master, was the *timing* of the hijack. Previously he had intended to hijack the coach after Erode. With the warning and all, he would have preponed the hijack, to before Erode, so as not to get caught by the police at the station.

The more Yadu thought about this, the more certain he was that he was thinking along the right lines. He was certain that with a last minute change of plan Hardaker and his men could not have achieved such success.

Now that he was certain about this, other equally intriguing aspects of Hardaker's decision occurred to him. If Hardaker had decided right at the beginning that he would hijack the RBI coach, not just rob it, what was the reasoning behind this decision? Why did he choose to hijack the coach as opposed to robbing it? Robbing the coach was one thing, but hijacking a coach was something else. The police wouldn't take lightly to a hijack case because of the sheer audacity involved. Hardaker would have anticipated the media frenzy it would create – the hourly news bulletins, the newspaper headlines. So why did he do it? Surely Hardaker would have known that he would attract far more attention for the same amount of money inside the coach? Why did he do it then? Why did he go deliberately seeking all this attention and notoriety? Is that what he wanted from this whole exercise? Did Hardaker do it as a self-serving stunt? Was he just a vain man wanting the nation's attention?

The theory that this was an attention-grabbing stunt somehow failed to hold any water with him. Yadu had seen the coldness in the man's eyes from close quarters. If his reading of the Englishman's character was correct, then Hardaker was a professional to the core. For him, the emotional high of flummoxing the nations' police would hold little interest. He seemed the kind who would take such huge efforts only if some material dividends were in it for him.

So why had Hardaker hijacked the coach? And where had he hidden it? Had he found a spot between Erode and Tiruppur that nobody else knew about?

Or...

A most interesting thought occurred to Yadu just then. Sweeping away all the clutter out of his mind, he gave this thought the singular attention it deserved.

31

When Vandana returned Yadu told her of his theory that Hardaker had never intended to rob the coach. All along his intention had only been to hijack it. He told her how they both had misunderstood their bandit slang.

'What difference does it make to us whether Hardaker intended to rob the coach or hijack it?' Vandana asked. 'To me it means the same thing.'

'It's not the same thing,' Yadu said. 'You are making the same mistake the police are making.'

'And what's that?'

'The police think Hardaker's decision to hijack the coach was a last minute one.'

'It *was* a last minute decision, Yadu. The warning I gave the Salem station master is what pushed Hardaker to hijack the coach. If it wasn't for that warning he wouldn't have hijacked it.'

Yadu shook his head. 'I believe Hardaker had planned to hijack the coach all along. Your warning to the station master *did* have an impact but only on the timing of the hijack. Instead of after Erode the bandits hijacked the coach *before* Erode.'

There was a confused look on Vandana's face. 'What's your point?'

Yadu smiled. 'My point is: the police must stop thinking that the hijack was a last minute change of plan.'

'Okay, so what's wrong with this thinking?'

Yadu sighed. 'Everything. Because they are thinking on these lines, they are concentrating all their efforts in the fifty kilometre stretch between Erode and Tiruppur only. They believe the coach has been hidden somewhere in this section. They think if they search long enough they are bound to find the coach and the engine.'

'You don't agree with this method of search?'

'I think the police are wasting their time. I think the coach and the engine have already gone a few hundred kilometres away from Tiruppur, if not more.'

'None of the signalmen or the station masters have seen the engine go past. Did I fail to mention that, or have you just plain forgotten?'

Yadu had been expecting this question. 'Just because they haven't seen it, it doesn't mean the engine hasn't gone past them.'

'What are you saying?'

'I am saying that the engine and the coach *have* gone past all these signal men and the station masters. Only they haven't realised it yet.'

'I am afraid you have lost me,' said Vandana.

'You know what people are usually like, Vandana. You ask them to look for an engine towing a coach, they are going to look for an engine towing a coach.'

'What's wrong with that?'

'Everything. Sometimes just following instructions can be dangerous. I believe that's what happened here with the RBI coach.'

Vandana started to realise where Yadu was going with all this.

'Hardaker knew the signalmen would be looking for an engine towing a solitary coach. So he attached the coach and the engine to another train.'

'*What*? Come again?'

'I am saying the RBI coach and engine have piggybacked on another train. That's why none of the signalmen or the station masters have seen it.'

'I don't believe I am hearing this.'

'Hardaker knew how the signalmen would respond to the wire from Erode. He knew how everybody would be looking for an engine towing a coach. So he tailored a plan to take advantage of the way they responded.'

'But...but how is that possible? How could Hardaker have known there would be a train in the vicinity that was willing to piggyback the coach?'

'It's called planning, Vandana. Hardaker must have travelled on this line several times. He must have done his homework. He would have decided well in advance the right place, the right train, the right engine driver to bribe...'

'The hijack couldn't have been a last minute change of plan. I am beginning to see what you mean.'

'If it was a last minute change of plan, Hardaker couldn't have organised any of this. Even if he's hidden the coach between Erode and Tiruppur he couldn't have found a good enough hiding place so quickly.'

Vandana went quiet for some time. She started mulling over their exchange. A while later she said, 'You are saying this engine driver of the other train was bribed?'

'Yes,' said Yadu. 'He must have been paid a hefty sum. He would have been asked to be at a certain point at a certain time on a certain day. Hardaker and his men would have driven the engine and the coach to that place. They would have then coupled the coach to this other train. And they would have set off after that.'

'I am with you now,' Vandana said. 'The train would have passed a few stations, the engine driver would have given a friendly wave to every colleague he passed. They would have waved back not suspecting one instant that the coach they are searching for was going right past them.'

'That's the only way it could have happened,' Yadu said.

'What about the passengers and the TTEs on this train? Wouldn't they have suspected anything on seeing this extra engine and coach being attached?'

'Who said anything about a passenger train?'

'You mean...'

'Hardaker would have wanted as few eye witnesses as possible to this incident. He would have chosen a tanker rail or a goods train. That way he needs to bribe only three individuals: the driver, the fireman and the guide.'

'What about the signalmen? Wouldn't they have suspected anything seeing a train with two engines?'

'I doubt if they even noticed that there were two engines on this train, the weather being what it was yesterday. Even if they did, why would they suspect anything? Engines are being shunted from one place to another all the time. It's quite a commonplace occurrence.'

'And the RBI coach?'

'That coach doesn't look any different from the hundreds of coaches I have seen. How is the signalman going to know that a certain coach passing that way is the RBI coach?'

Vandana fell silent as she thought things through. 'I don't understand one thing though,' she said, after a considerable duration of time. 'Did you not tell me that Hardaker got the details from your father only yesterday, on the day of the train's departure? How could he have arranged all this with the engine driver then?'

'I believe the arrangement with the driver and his crew was made a long time back.'

'That sounds ridiculous.'

'No, it doesn't. We are dealing with two bits of information here. Through his source in the RBI Hardaker knew there was a coachload of reissuables and banknotes being sent to Coimbatore in the next few days. Based on this information he would have sent his men to identify a suitable corrupt goods train driver who plied this route on a daily basis. After tempting this driver and his team with a suitable reward they would have laid out their plans, and would have told them what they had to do for their share of the money. At that point of time they didn't have the second bit of information. They didn't know what train the coach was being sent on and when it was being sent. The driver would have been told to wait for further instructions. Yesterday, as soon as they got this second bit of information from my father, they would have called the driver and told him today was the day.'

'And if that particular driver was not plying on this route today? What would they have done then?'

'They would have cancelled their plans, or maybe postponed it for next month. Who knows? He might have even had two or three teams on his payroll. I wouldn't put that beyond Hardaker.'

Vandana fell quiet again as she thought things over. She was obviously trying to find holes in Yadu's theory.

'So, you are saying the coach is not where the police are searching.'

'Yes. I believe the coach is in some far off place now. The police are just wasting their time.'

A few seconds later she continued her attack, this time from another angle. 'I can understand the bandits taking the RBI coach. But why did they take the engine along?'

Yadu had a ready answer for this one too. 'What would have happened if they had left the engine behind? The police would have immediately jumped to the conclusion I had jumped to: that the coach piggybacked on another train. The coach cannot go anywhere on its own, can it? It has to be pulled. If the engine was left behind, naturally the police would have blocked all trains and would have checked each and every coach. Hardaker obviously understood the importance of retaining the engine.'

'Somehow it all sounds too farfetched to me.'

'I admit it does. But in the light of the search operations taking such an unprecedented amount of time, this has to be the only explanation.'

Vandana still had reservations about the whole thing, so Yadu continued to work on her, clearing her doubts, clarifying some points. Finally, after going through everything in her mind she was convinced he was right. She said they had to tell this theory to the officers manning the command desk, to see what they thought of it.

The police inspector and the station master on duty heard them out. And then they started laughing. They thought it was so hilarious that they called out to their colleagues and asked them to hear out this theory that these 'kids' had come up with. Vandana and Yadu were so humiliated they bolted from the place.

32

After he had learnt that the IB officers would require Vandana for almost the whole day, Inspector Kripakaran had arranged accommodation for the girl at Hotel Brindavan, which was just half a kilometre away from the railway station. Vandana didn't have an opportunity to use the room at all. She hadn't had the time. In the morning she had gone there by jeep, she'd had a quick shower, left her bag there and had returned to the railway station without even having breakfast. But she had seen enough of the hotel and her room to recommend it to Yadu.

'I think you ought to stay the night in Erode,' she said, when they were back at their bench. 'Those men who are manning the desk right now are buffoons. The ones that I met this morning, Inspector Kripakaran and the station master Nandakumar, now they are more likely to listen to your theory and act on it.'

'You are saying I have to wait here until they get back on duty tonight.'

'That's what I am saying, Yes. If they think your theory has merit they'll act on it, I promise. If they find no merit, then tomorrow morning you go back to Madras and I'll be on my way to Palghat. It's just a matter of staying over for one night.'

Yadu said okay. So she recommended Hotel Brindavan to him. He said he'd go immediately and get himself a room. Vandana wanted to go along too, but the IB officers and the police wouldn't let her. They said she might be needed any minute, so she had to hang around the railway station. So Yadu went on his own. Vandana said she'd meet him at the hotel when these people were done with her for the day.

~

It turned out that Vandana had been right about the hotel. It was quite good, definitely one of the better hotels in Erode. Like its namesake, the Brindavan had a well-tended garden in front, a huge lawn, plenty of trees, and a lotus-shaped water fountain. It had a portico, the likes of which one saw in palaces and luxury hotels.

Yadu and Vandana had been given rooms on the first floor, on either side of the central staircase. The staircase opened out into a hallway, to the left and right, of which were the rooms, and in front of which was a balcony. Since the balcony had been built atop the portico it was quite huge in size. There was a big wooden swing in the centre and knee-high redoxide thinnais on three sides. If one sat on the swing, or on the thinnai, one had a good view of the gardens and the greenery below.

When Vandana reached the hotel that night, at a quarter to nine, she was out of breath and shivering with excitement. She burst into the lobby, found out what room Yadu was staying in, and then ran up the stairs. The IB officials had been done with her two hours back, but she had stayed back in the railway station because she had heard rumours of a major breakthrough in the case. She had wanted to find out all she could before she left for the hotel. In this, however, she had been unsuccessful because the morons at the desk had gone secretive on her. They didn't want to tell her what they knew, and were throwing airs. Luckily, she had got a note from Inspector Kripakaran around this time, and the note confirmed the rumours. She couldn't wait to show the contents of the note to Yadu.

She reached the upper hallway and found Yadu reclining on the balcony swing.

'Get up you lazy ass, I have some news for you, hot off the press.'

He heard the lilt in her voice, saw the spring in her step, and instantly, he knew that there had been a breakthrough. He sprang to his feet immediately. 'They have nabbed the bandits, haven't they?' he asked eagerly.

'Scale down your expectations,' she said, as she sat down on the thinnai opposite him. Yadu sat back on the swing.

She took the note Kripakaran had sent her out of her pocket and waved it in front of him in a teasing manner. 'They have found the coach.'

Yadu fell out clean of the swing when he heard this. 'They found the coach? Really?'

Vandana now thrust the note into his hand. 'It's from Inspector Kripakaran. It turns out he didn't break off duty today. He had been summoned to Shoranur late in the afternoon. That's where he sent me this note from.'

Yadu got to his feet, opened the note and read it.

Vandana,

No sign of the engine or the bandits yet. There is some good news, though: we have found the RBI coach. The bandits had abandoned the coach near Shoranur. Intriguingly, its seal is intact, and our preliminary inspections have revealed that nothing's been taken. We have no clue what's happening. Will talk to you tomorrow. Have a good night.

(signed)
Inspector Kripakaran.

Vandana sat down on the empty swing now, and Yadu sat opposite her in the balcony thinnai, with his back against the pillar.

Yadu's face had erupted into a broad smile. 'This is fantastic,' he said. 'This is *such* a great piece of news.' It was like a livewire of current had just left his body. So intense was his feeling of relief as it flooded his veins.

'It's taken a while coming, but this is a genuine breakthrough, isn't it?' Vandana asked, barely able to suppress her joy.

Yadu nodded. 'God bless Kripakaran for sending this note promptly. I think I'll sleep well tonight.'

'I had almost started to fear that there was no chance of finding the coach or the bandits,' Vandana said, as she pushed the floor with her legs. The swing started to move forwards and back.

Yadu nodded, because he too had experienced the same feeling some time back.

'It would have been a real catch if one of Hardaker's men were caught too. But this will do for the time being, so long as there are more such breakthroughs to come,' she continued.

Yadu said nothing. He was basking in this mini-victory. For him what mattered most was that his father was off the hook now. Since nothing was stolen he couldn't be slapped with any serious charges. Of course, it remained to be seen if he could get out of Hardaker's clutches alive. He wanted to believe – for the time being at least – that the outcome of all this was going to be positive.

'Where is Shoranur? Do you have any idea?' Yadu asked Vandana.

'It's two hours west of Coimbatore. It's not very far from Palghat, my hometown.'

'I see,' said Yadu, breaking into a laugh. 'This is a double treat for me then.'

'What do you mean?' Vandana asked.

Yadu flapped the note in the air. 'This is not just a piece of good news. It's a vindication of my theory as well. Don't you see?'

Vandana didn't catch his drift immediately.

'To reach Shoranur the RBI coach must have passed through Tiruppur and Coimbatore, right? How come the railway personnel didn't report seeing it? Was it because they didn't see it as an engine towing a coach?'

The look of ignorance left Vandana's face.

'The piggyback theory. I see what you mean,' she said, tapping her toes on the red oxide floor.

'The RBI coach *must* have been attached onto a larger train. That is the only explanation,' Yadu maintained. His spirits had suddenly lifted with these twin successes.

'You were right after all, Yadu. I can't see how else the coach could have reached Shoranur. Good thinking.'

Yadu smiled, accepting the compliment. His mind though had already jumped to another matter.

'I wonder what's happened to the engine?' he asked.

Vandana thought for a bit. 'It's too early to say,' she said. 'Maybe the engine too is parked in the vicinity of the coach, only the police haven't spotted it yet.'

'That's possible,' Yadu agreed. 'Tomorrow morning, when the darkness lifts, maybe they'll find it.'

'Let's hope so.'

For about ten minutes after that neither of them spoke. Yadu looked out into the dark garden and the road beyond. There was zero traffic on the road because of the late hour. In the distance a gurkha walked, tapping his baton on the road every two minutes, sending out a warning to would-be burglars.

Vandana was looking at the silhouette of the trees in the garden. She too seemed to be immersed in deep thought.

Shortly, she plucked the note out of Yadu's hand and read it again. 'You know,' she said, 'I would like to know what is going on inside that Englishman's mind.'

'Why do you say that?' Yadu asked.

Vandana shook her head in bewilderment. 'We both know the lengths to which Hardaker went to hijack the coach, right?'

'I suppose we do.'

'Now, why did he not steal anything from the coach after successfully hijacking it? Why did he abandon the coach like this?'

'That is something I have been thinking about too,' Yadu admitted. 'I can't understand why he left all those banknotes behind.'

'Something smells fishy,' Vandana said. 'How can anybody pull off such a daring hijack and then leave *all* the spoils behind? If you had been in his position wouldn't you have taken at least part of the spoils with you?'

Yadu agreed that he would have surely taken at least part of the spoils with him.

'So why didn't they clean up the coach?'

'I haven't a clue,' Yadu admitted.

She went through the note again, this time very slowly. 'Maybe Inspector Kripakaran can tell us tomorrow,' she said.

Yadu agreed.

Vandana then suggested that he better explain to Kripakaran his 'piggyback' theory tomorrow morning.

'I'll do that. First thing tomorrow morning we'll pay the inspector a visit.'

Not long after this conversation Vandana said she was retiring since she was tired. Yadu escorted her to her room and came back to the balcony after wishing her a good night.

For a long time after that he lay on the swing thinking about the case till he ended up falling asleep, right there, on the swing.

33

The Hindu

In a daring attempt last night, unprecedented so far in Indian history, four bandits hijacked a coach belonging to the Reserve Bank of India. The coach, part of the Mangalore Express, was hijacked at 2 am early yesterday morning just before the train was to reach Erode station. It's reported that the bandits jumped onto the engine and threatened the drivers at gunpoint. Taking over the engine in this fashion, they uncoupled the rest of the train and made off with the RBI coach. The Mangalore Express, as a result, was left stranded for over three hours in a place called palm tree mile.

Later, a relief engine was sent to the place from Erode so that the train could continue on its onward journey.

It's learnt that as soon as the railways heard about the hijack they issued an all-station alert to block the runaway engine. They had expected to cut off the engine's flight within an hour, but they were in for a surprise. The engine and the coach simply vanished from their radar screens. No station in the vicinity reported seeing it. The station masters and the signalmen swore that the runaway vehicle hadn't passed their respective stations.

Early this morning, the Coimbatore police and the southern railways combined to mount a massive search operation. Reserve police units and even battalions of soldiers were pulled in to aid the search.

Since no railway personnel had seen the engine pass Tiruppur, it was initially believed that the coach was kept hidden in some place between Erode and Tiruppur. So the search for most of the day was confined to this area.

It indeed came as a surprise this evening when a station master wired in saying he had found the coach a hundred kilometres away – outside Shoranur, to be precise. The police and the railways fail to understand how the coach reached Shoranur without falling into the sight of so many railway personnel.

When asked about this the general manager of southern railways, Mr Babu Rao, blamed the heavy rains. He said because of poor visibility his staff hadn't seen the 'RV' go past. The GM also said that they were looking into the possibility that some railway employees had been bribed to bypass the coach. An enquiry committee was to be set up to get to the bottom of this.

The mystery of how the coach reached Shoranur was not the only question to puzzle the police. The *state* of the RBI coach when they found it gave rise to a bigger puzzle that nobody had a proper answer for. The police had expected the coach to have been vandalised, robbed of every last rupee it carried. There was well over 40 lakh rupees of currency in the coach. Bizarrely, nothing had been taken. The RBI wax seal seems not to have been tampered with. Officials of the Reserve Bank have checked the currency notes and have certified its authenticity.

If the Shoranur station master is to be believed, no attempt was made to even conceal the coach properly. It was left out in the open, on an abandoned line, very near the main track. The police are baffled as to the intent of the hijackers. Having taken such pains to hijack the coach the question arises as to why everything was left behind.

When asked why nothing was taken from the coach, the police commissioner for Coimbatore said, offhand he could think of two reasons. He said, either the whole hijack was an attention grabbing exercise devised by an egomaniac. Or, the hijackers must have realised that they had bitten off more than they could chew. They must have left the coach untouched so as not to earn the wrath of the police.

'We'll know shortly,' the commissioner said, when asked about this.

He then released the names of the hijackers to the press. It was believed that an Englishman called Brian Hardaker was the ringleader. Another Englishman called Icy, and two local men, Dorai and Sethu, were the other gang members. Policemen all over the state have been asked to be on the lookout for these four men.

Intelligence Bureau officers in Madras, meanwhile, are trying to find out how the bandits came to learn about the consignment. The details of the consignment was supposedly known in advance to only one Reserve bank employee, Ranganathan by name. In a related development, Mr Ranganathan has been reported to be missing for the past three days. At the moment police strongly suspect his involvement in this conspiracy at some level. IB officers are in the process of digging out more information.

Search operations are still on in full swing to find the missing engine. It is believed that the bandits would have used the engine as a getaway vehicle upto a predetermined point. From there they would use more conventional means – a car perhaps – to escape to wherever their hideout was.

The police are confident about finding the engine in a few hours. As for nabbing the bandits, they are just keeping their fingers crossed, hoping for a break.

~

The next morning, at twenty minutes past eight, Yadu and Vandana found themselves seated in front of the Coimbatore station master.

It had been a hectic morning for both of them so far. At six in the morning they had gone to the Erode railway station, where the IB officers said that they didn't need Vandana for questioning anymore. She was free to go home. The two of them had then asked the officers where they could find Inspector Kripakaran. One of the officers said he might be found in the Coimbatore railway station.

Hearing this the two of them had set forth for Coimbatore. They took a tonga upto the bus stand, and from there caught a bus to Coimbatore.

They found Kripakaran on platform five, standing opposite the RBI coach, in deep discussion with some RBI officers. They waited until he was done with them, then they caught his eye and walked over to him.

After he had been properly introduced Yadu told the inspector of his theory. To their delight they found the inspector quite receptive to the whole idea. They learnt from him that the Coimbatore station master, Mr Sukumar too had come up with a similar theory the previous evening. It had gladdened Yadu's heart to hear that somebody else had thought on the same lines – a railway man at that.

The inspector then asked the two of them if they wanted to discuss their idea further with the station master. 'I'll send a constable with you for introductions, if you like,' he had said. 'Something might come out of your discussion, you never know.'

Yadu and Vandana grabbed this opportunity with both hands. They wanted Kripakaran too to accompany them, but the inspector told them he couldn't, because he was getting off duty in a few minutes. This was his first break in thirty hours. The two of them understood; they didn't press him further. So, Yadu and Vandana, in the company of the constable the inspector had provided, made their way to the station master's cabin on platform one.

Arriving at the office, the constable introduced the two to the man saying Inspector Kripakaran had wanted the station master to discuss the case with these two youngsters. The constable made the introductions, then made himself scarce.

'How did you two get involved in all this?' Sukumar asked, once they had taken their seats.

The station master was not more than twenty-five years of age – too young to be a station master, really. He was of average height and build, and had a boyish face. Though already in his mid twenties it appeared as if the man shaved very rarely – not because he wasn't required to, but because there was nothing in his face to shave. Except for a tinge of green stubble on his chin, the rest of his face looked smooth as a baby's bottom.

A pair of wire-rimmed spectacles lay in front of him. Yadu guessed the spectacles served no purpose other than to make him look older. It looked like he wore them to render an intellectual aspect to his boyish personality.

Vandana explained how they came to be involved with the case. Yadu then repeated what he had told Kripakaran just a while back; his theory of how the hijackers had escaped with the coach.

'Is that what you think happened?' the station master asked.

'Yes sir.'

The station master nodded solemnly. 'I don't know if you are aware of it, but I told the Intelligence Bureau officers almost the same thing yesterday. But they didn't listen. Their whole investigation hinges on one point: they believe the hijack wasn't planned in advance.'

Vandana shook her head in disgust. 'I don't see the police or the bureau making any headway in the case until they stop being stubborn about that point.'

'What do *you* think?' Yadu asked. 'Do you believe this is what must have happened?'

There was not a hint of hesitation on the station master's part. 'I do,' he said, like an eager bride.

Sukumar got up from his chair and then walked to the file drawer to his left. He rummaged through the files until he found the log he was searching for. 'I've been doing a bit of detective work around here since last evening,' he said, dropping a heavy, bound logbook onto his desk.

'I found something very interesting last night.'

Yadu and Vandana both stared at him, wanting to hear more.

'This is the train register, my bible,' Sukumar said, sitting down. He now started to flip through the pages. When he came to the page dedicated for 7 December he stopped.

'Here, have a look,' the station master said, stabbing his finger at the 3-5 am time window.

Yadu and Vandana leaned forward in their chairs to have a better look.

'As you can see,' Sukumar said, 'there is only one entry here in the 3-5 am time slot. A goods train that originated at Madras passed through Coimbatore station at 4 am.'

'Did this train stop here?' Yadu asked.

'For ten minutes, just to take in water.'

'Where was it headed?' Vandana asked.

'Calicut.'

'If it passed Coimbatore at 4 am then it ought to have been near Erode at 2 am or thereabouts,' Vandana surmised.

The station master nodded.

'That was around the time the hijack took place,' Yadu said excitedly.

The station master nodded again. 'I called up the Erode station master last night and enquired about the time this train passed his station. Guess what I found?'

'What?' asked Yadu and Vandana in unison.

'This train had passed Erode at a quarter past one in the morning.'

'What?' Vandana asked, her tone of voice a testimony to the astonishment she felt.

The station master smiled. 'But this log says that the train arrived here at 4 am. In other words, this train had taken two hours and forty-five minutes for a journey that routinely takes just two hours.'

'That is rather suspicious,' Yadu said.

There was still more to come from the look on the station master's face. 'Just to be sure I checked with the signal inspectors, with the linemen *and* in the defect log book. No defect was reported on the line or in the engine that night, or since then. As far as I can see there was no reason why it should have taken this train so long to arrive here.'

'Except the most obvious one,' Vandana said. 'The goods train was waiting for the engine and the RBI coach.'

Yadu rapped the desk in delight.

Sukumar smiled. 'That's the conclusion I had reached too. Normally, when there is already a train in the section a second train is not green signalled, because it might end in a collision. But that night what seems to have happened is this: the section controller at Palghat, on hearing about the bandits, green-lit the Mangalore Express all the way upto Coimbatore so the train could reach here as fast as it could. The sooner the RBI coach reached its destination, the better for them. He would have known about the goods train on the line of course, but I suppose he thought it was forty-five minutes ahead of the Mangalore Express, so there wouldn't be any problem.'

'It would have never occurred to the section controller, even in a thousand years, that the goods train drivers were hand in glove with the bandits. The bandits hijacked the coach, jumped Erode station, brought it to a place they had mutually decided on, they coupled the engine and the coach to the goods train, and they were on their way. The funny thing is, that train was standing right here in this station when the search was on in the section. Only, nobody suspected the goods train at all because everybody thought the engine and the RBI coach were still in the Erode-Tiruppur section.'

The station master paused for a few seconds, then continued. 'Last night I tried telling the IB officers all this, only they would hear nothing of it.' He now shut the log book and leaned back.

'Horses with blinds,' Vandana said. 'Maybe Inspector Kripakaran can help us persuade the police brass. He seemed quite receptive to this idea.'

'Give it a shot,' the station master said. 'What have you got to lose?'

A young boy knocked and entered the cabin, carrying a tray with a few cups of coffee.

'Will you have coffee?' Sukumar asked.

Yadu nodded a 'yes', and Vandana said no.

After placing a cup opposite the station master, and another opposite Yadu, the boy left. The station master and Yadu sipped at their coffees quietly for a while.

'How long have you suspected this particular goods train?' Vandana asked some time later.

'It's been at the back of my mind ever since the day of the hijack. When I heard last night that the coach was found in Shoranur, then I was certain of it. This goods train, in my opinion, is the only means by which the coach could have reached Shoranur.'

'Exactly our thoughts!' said Vandana.

Yadu was quiet until he finished his coffee. Then he said, 'I am just curious. Let's say you were the station master that morning. Let's say you did notice this goods train with two engines. Would you have suspected any foul play?'

'I wouldn't have suspected anything at all,' came the prompt answer. 'Goods trains tugging along an additional engine are quite common.'

'Just what I thought.'

Vandana then wanted to know the name of the driver helming the goods train that night.

The station master said he had no idea. 'That is the domain of the freight division COM.'

'COM?' Vandana asked.

'Chief Operations Manager. He is the one who maintains records of goods-driver deployments. If you ask him nicely he might look up the 'power plan' and tell you who had been deployed that night'.

'What if we ask you nicely to ask him and get that information for us?' Yadu asked cheekily. 'If we go to him we'll have to answer a thousand questions before we get to the point.'

The station master thought for a moment or two. 'What exactly do you want to know from him? Just the name of the driver?'

'The name of the driver, the fireman and the guard,' Vandana said. 'Also information about where exactly they are at the moment. Are they still in Calicut, or have they been deployed elsewhere? We want to know what their next assignment is, which town or city they are headed for...everything.'

'What do you want all this information for?' Sukumar asked.

'If we go to the police top brass with all this information, there is a chance they might listen to us and act on it,' Yadu said.

'They might do it anyway, don't you think?' Sukumar countered.

'I doubt it,' said Yadu. 'As far as the police are concerned, they have got the RBI coach – with all its contents – back. So the case is closed for them. They'll only get more complacent from this point on. To me that is bad news, because I still have to find my father. They can afford to relax the search; I can't.'

The station master nodded. 'I see your point. I'll see what I can do to help.'

In a minute he was on the line talking to the COM. Sukumar pulled a notepad towards him and started scribbling the details. They talked for over fifteen minutes with both Yadu and Vandana watching him silently.

Finally, Sukumar dropped the receiver onto its cradle. He pushed the notepad towards Yadu.

'The engine driver's called Mathew. The COM believes he is in Calicut until 10 pm tonight. After that he leaves for Trivandrum.'

34

Coming out of the station master's cabin Yadu asked Vandana how far Calicut was from there.

'About four hours I think. It's not all that far.'

Turning right they walked along the platform. A train had just arrived next to them, and the scene was reassuringly chaotic. Canteen employees carrying trays piled up with idlies and vadais boarded the coaches. The passengers who were disembarking had to jostle with these men to get down from the train. Other passengers embarking in this station were running helter-skelter trying to find their respective coaches. One man, with a luggage in one hand and his son's hand firmly in the other, was rushing past them when a woman unwittingly stepped on his chappal. The chappal strap snapped and the man started to curse the woman in foul language. Not satisfied with abusing the woman he kept his luggage down for a moment, picked up his now useless chappal and then flung it at the woman. Then he resumed his running, luggage in hand, son in tow, this time faster than before.

As they walked Yadu told Vandana of his intention to leave for Calicut immediately. 'If it's just four hours from here I can go there and be back here by nightfall. What do you think?'

'You want to grab hold of the driver before he leaves Calicut,' Vandana guessed.

'Yes,' Yadu said. 'I want to find out the extent of this man's involvement in the hijack. Maybe I can wring out some information from him.'

'Like Hardaker's whereabouts?' Vandana asked.

Yadu nodded.

'I suppose there is no harm in trying,' Vandana said. Then, as an afterthought she added, 'Perhaps it's a better idea to inform the inspector about this. I am sure he can arrange for these men to be brought in for questioning. What do you think?'

'The inspector has to be informed, no doubt,' Yadu said. 'But I don't have the patience to wait for the police to bring these men in. By the time Kripakaran gets back on duty, and sends his men to Calicut, I could be back here after meeting Mathew.'

'You have a point,' Vandana conceded. 'The engine drivers might be in another town by the time the police reach Calicut.'

They continued walking through the crowded platform negotiating through piles of luggage. Here and there they had to squeeze their way past knots of people. The two were now headed for the booking office. To reach it they had to exit this platform through a wrought iron gate and then they had to go to the forward foyer.

'You want to come along to Calicut?' Yadu asked, as they exited through the wrought iron gates.

'I would love to, but...'

'What's the problem?'

'If I go to Calicut with you I can't make it home by nightfall.'

'Your mother will be worried, is that what you are thinking?'

'Yes.'

'You better not come then,' Yadu said.

Vandana nodded, then went quiet for a few seconds. Then, just like Yadu was hoping, she had a change of heart.

'It's only one night. I think I'll come with you,' she said, with a sheepish grin. 'I want to get to the bottom of this as much as you do.'

Yadu bowed his head slightly. 'I won't say no to good company.'

At the booking office Yadu found out that there was a train towards Calicut at ten to ten, which was in roughly forty minutes. Vandana insisted on buying the tickets, and Yadu didn't mind, since he wasn't sure he had enough money with him for two tickets. Tough to be chivalrous when your pockets are empty.

After buying their tickets they both went to platform five and left a note for Kripakaran with the police constable who had introduced them to Sukumar. In the note Vandana briefed him of what they had learnt at the station master's office. She mentioned as well that they both were going to Calicut to have a word with Mathew, the goods train driver.

Half an hour later they boarded the Cannanore Express. It was a dull and uneventful journey up to Calicut.

~

Stepping down at Calicut, having his first look at the platform, Yadu thought it wasn't going to be difficult finding the engine drivers here. It was a relatively small place, a one-platform station in railway parlance. The platform was less than ten inches high, perhaps in keeping with the small town status of the place. It did have the mandatory snack shop, the newspaper vendor's shop and the administrative offices.

Vandana caught sight of the station master first. She nudged Yadu's elbow, and soon they were walking towards him. They waited until the man had waved the Cannanore Express off the platform. Then they approached him and enquired about Mathew.

'Now which Mathew is this?' the station master asked. The nameplate on his coat lapel read 'Unnikrishnan'. He was a fair-skinned, rotund man in his late thirties. His hair was jet black and neatly trimmed. 'There are so many Mathews in this place.'

'His full name is K.P. Mathew. He is a goods train driver,' Vandana said.

'Ah, you are looking for KP,' Unnikrishnan said. 'He'll be in the running room, there in that building.' The station master pointed to a long row of houses across the tracks. Part of it was hidden behind a box-shaped tool room; but they could see it alright from where they stood.

Yadu thanked the man and then they walked down the platform onto the tracks. Crossing the tracks they then headed in the direction the station master had indicated.

It was overcast weather here in Calicut today, and oppressively humid. Yadu's shirt had dampened under his arms, and his back in the past hour or so. He thought to himself that this place was even more humid than his hometown Madras. Here and there as they walked he saw puddles of water. Surely the storms that had raged in the east had brought some rainfall to this area too. Fortunately, it didn't seem as if the skies were about to open up just now.

They passed the box-shaped tool room. Now they had a clear view of the building the station master had pointed at. There was a disused rail track, and next to it was the transient crew quarters. As was usually the case in government constructions the design was purely functional. It was a single storey structure with a tile-top built north to south, with five rooms on the ground floor and five on the first.

As they came nearer they caught sight of two scruffy men, dressed in lungis, seated just outside the gate. They were seated on small stools with a stone slab separating them. On coming nearer it became apparent that they were playing cards.

They reached the men. Vandana decided to do all the talking because she knew Malayalam. She enquired about Mathew with the two men.

'He is a goods train driver, and he must have arrived here yesterday morning.'

The man to Vandana's right was wearing a cut-banian above his lungi. Scratching his armpit lazily, he asked her what business she had with KP.

'I have a few questions to ask him, that's all,' Vandana said.

'He is not around,' the man to Vandana's left said. He was wearing a crumpled, light-blue shirt. His lungi was a riot of bright colours.

'They have gone off somewhere – the drivers and the guide.'

Yadu frowned on hearing this. He knew enough malayalam to make out what was being said.

'Where have they gone, do you know?' Vandana asked.

'I have no idea. They have taken their bags along, though. I suppose they have left town,' Cut-banian said.

'They have left town? But they have a train to drive tonight, don't they?'

'Actually they do. I really don't know what they are up to. Maybe there was an emergency; maybe they'll land up here a couple of hours before their trip.'

Vandana and Yadu exchanged a glance. Both of them knew this sounded very suspicious.

Vandana asked, 'What kind of emergency was it that all three of them left with their baggage?' Her tone said it all. She wasn't convinced with the emergency theory.

'If they don't arrive by 7 pm tonight they are going to be in a lot of trouble,' the man in the crumpled blue shirt said. 'The loco foreman has been looking for them since this morning.'

'Have they not told anyone where they were going?'

'If there is anybody they would have informed it would have been us. But they didn't tell us. So I reckon they haven't told anybody else,' Cut-banian said. 'This morning I went to their room and was surprised to see it empty. It didn't look as if the beds had been slept in last night.'

'You think they left last night itself?'

'It looks to me like that.'

The look of disappointment Yadu had on his face was enough to tell Vandana that Yadu didn't need much translation of their conversation. He had really been looking forward to this meeting with the drivers and the guide. But it looked like this was another setback in a long series of setbacks he'd had since it all began.

'Are you Mathew's relative or something?' the man in the crumpled shirt asked.

'No,' Vandana said. Then she fell silent not wanting to elaborate more. But the looks that the two were giving her suggested they were waiting to hear more.

'I...I am just...,' Vandana stammered to give them a valid reason.

Then suddenly an idea struck her.

'I am looking for a couple of Englishmen,' she improvised. 'They might have arrived here on Mathew's engine yesterday. Have you seen them around by any chance?'

Vandana was just shooting in the dark here. She had no idea if the two had really come to Calicut. For all she knew Hardaker and his men could still be in Shoranur. But it had struck her suddenly that this line of questioning was well worth pursuing. If Hardaker had come here on the engine there was a good chance these men would remember seeing him.

'Englishmen?' Cut-banian asked. 'In *this* place?'

'Yes,' Vandana said. 'One was middle aged, bald, with bushy eyebrows. The other one was young with blond, spiky hair. Both are tall men.'

'I haven't seen any Englishmen around here,' Crumpled shirt said.

Cut-banian couldn't help smiling. 'Surely you are joking, Miss.'

Then, still grinning, he selected and threw two cards from the deck he was playing with: a king and a jack. 'Are these the two you are looking for?' he asked, then started laughing at his idea of a joke. His friend too joined him.

'See, this one's even got bushy eyebrows,' Cut-banian continued, pointing to the Jack of Spades.

Vandana didn't take offence. Instead, she smiled sportingly, because she had a couple more questions to ask them. She waited until their laughter subsided, then she went on to her next question.

'Were you two around when Mathew drove his train here?'

'Why do you ask?' Crumpled shirt wanted to know.

'Did you see if the train he drove here had two engines?' she asked.

Both of them replied in the negative. They had not been around when Mathew had arrived with his train. The man in the crumpled blue shirt suggested they come back in an hour or so and see if Mathew had returned.

They nodded to this. She thanked them both and they were about to leave when she thought of something else.

'Can I ask you one last question before I leave?'

'What's it?' Cut-Banian asked.

'Have any of you seen or heard about an abandoned engine around this place?' Another shot in the dark. She didn't expect much, but this question she had to ask. What if these men had seen an engine on their journey here?

'An abandoned engine?' Crumpled shirt asked. 'Why would anybody abandon an engine?'

'I haven't come across any abandoned engine,' Cut-banian said.

'What's this all about?' the man to Vandana's left asked. 'Who abandoned this engine, and what for?'

'Why are you interested in all this?' Cut-banian asked.

Vandana had no intentions of telling these men about the RBI coach hijack. It was obvious they hadn't heard about it on the radio.

'I'll tell you what it's about as soon as I speak to Mathew,' Vandana said evasively.

'Very secretive aren't you?' the man to Vandana's right asked. But they didn't press her further, to her great relief.

Vandana thanked the men again for their help. She told them they'd be waiting for Mathew on the platform. If any of the three came any earlier could they please tell them to come to the platform? Receiving a nod from them Yadu and Vandana left them to their game of cards.

~

They decided to talk with the people who worked in the railway station next. They went into the station master's office first. The station master was not alone this time. He was having a chat with a line inspector named Elango who was seated opposite him.

After they had introduced themselves Vandana repeated the questions she had asked the two drivers. Unnikrishnan replied in the negative to every one of her questions: he hadn't seen any Englishmen around here; he hadn't been around when Mathew's train had arrived; and no, he hadn't heard anybody mention an abandoned engine to him.

The station master though was quick to see through Vandana's pointed questions. He demanded to know what all this was about. Unnikrishnan had no doubt heard about the coach hijack. So, Vandana was forced to tell him Yadu's theory. Yadu then took over at this point, telling him that he suspected Mathew of having helped the hijackers, and that was why they were here. He told them that now they were even more suspicious of the goods train crew, since they seemed to have fled with their baggage.

'So, nobody has mentioned seeing an abandoned engine around these parts?' Yadu asked again after he had briefed the man.

Unnikrishnan shook his head. 'If this engine was anywhere nearby, believe me, I would have heard of it by now. Neither my track repair men, nor the drivers driving along here have mentioned seeing such an engine.' Then turning to his colleague he asked, 'Have you heard anything, Elango?'

'No,' Elango said.

Yadu was disappointed to hear this. He thanked the men for their time and then they came out of the cabin.

The two of them next went and put the same questions to the snack shop owner and the newspaper vendor. The shopkeepers too replied in the negative to every one of their questions. The snack shop owner suggested they talk to the gang men (the track repair men) who were just returning from work.

Though the station master had already told them that none of these men had reported seeing an abandoned engine, still they wanted to find this out for themselves. So, they stepped down onto the track and walked to the group that was squatting just outside the tool room. To the group of eight Vandana put the same questions again. These men too replied in the negative.

The two of them were now beginning to feel frustrated.

~

After they got back onto the platform they went to the snack shop again, this time for some tea and biscuits. This was going to be their lunch for today. After a rather late 'lunch' they went to the stone bench at the centre of the platform and sat down on it. They sat there for some time wondering about their next course of action.

A train arrived and then departed after five minutes. Yadu sat swatting flies while Vandana was looking at the road beyond the tracks. It was beginning to dawn on them that their Calicut trip had been in vain.

'Let's take the next train to Coimbatore,' Yadu said.

'I was thinking along the same lines.'

They could go back to Coimbatore and inform Kripakaran that the two drivers had flown. Hopefully, Kripakaran would raise a state-wide alert and get them nabbed quickly. This is all they could hope for at the moment.

Yadu and Vandana were talking along these lines when both of them noticed somebody step out of the station master's office. They realised that it was Elango – the line inspector.

The man looked around as if looking for someone. Then their eyes met and Elango waved to them. Surprisingly, he started walking towards the bench they were occupying now.

Elango must have been in his late twenties. A man of average height and athletic build, he sported a thick black moustache. He was wearing a khaki trouser and a white shirt.

As Elango came nearer Yadu and Vandana rose from the bench.

'I am glad you two are still around,' he said, stretching his hand to Yadu. 'I wanted to speak with the two of you in private.'

Yadu asked Elango to sit down on the bench. Vandana sat facing him and Yadu stood opposite them.

'I have to confess something to both of you,' Elango said. 'What I told you back there wasn't the whole truth. I think I know something about this engine you are looking for.'

35

'You do?' Yadu asked, a jolt of current spreading up his spinal cord.

'What you told us back there has cleared a few things in my head,' Elango said.

Neither Yadu nor Vandana had any idea what this man was talking about. They waited patiently for him to elaborate. Yadu could hear the rhythmic pounding of his heart.

'Before I tell you what's on my mind I have to clarify a few things with you first,' said Elango. 'First of all, are you two sure Mathew aided these hijackers?'

'All the clues we have unearthed so far point to that,' Yadu said confidently. 'After coming here and finding that Mathew and his assistant have vanished I am even more certain of his involvement. I believe the man is absconding only because he knows he is guilty.'

'Okay,' Elango said. 'So Mathew helped these hijackers. But how certain are you that he brought this engine all the way to Calicut?'

Yadu folded his arms and then looked at Vandana. 'We are not certain of that at all,' he said, quite candidly. 'The engine could have been dropped off at any place between Shoranur and Calicut. In fact it was to find out *where* Mathew had dropped off the coach that we made this trip to Calicut.'

'I see,' said Elango.

There was a lull in the conversation as Elango engaged in some deep thinking.

Then he asked Yadu the date and the time the coach got hijacked. Yadu told him.

'Hmm,' said Elango. 'It all seems to fit in.'

Yadu and Vandana waited.

'You both are not from Calicut, are you?' the line inspector then asked. They replied in the negative.

'I guessed as much,' Elango said. 'So you wouldn't have heard of the Keyyurli railway bridge then?'

'I can't say I have,' Yadu admitted.

'Neither have I,' Vandana said.

Elango nodded solemnly. 'I wish you had seen this bridge. Then you would have understood what I am about to tell you a little better,' he continued. 'A few kilometres south of here there is a small river that flows into the Arabian Sea. It's called the Keyyurli. There is a railway bridge across this river. Once you cross this bridge you'll find a thick forest to your left. Locals call it the Keyyurli forest.' He paused. 'Now, what I am about to tell you happened near this spot, which is why I've had to describe the place to you. Yesterday, one of my crew mentioned hearing the whistle of an engine coming from inside this forest.'

Elango looked at the expression on Vandana's face and smiled. 'Yes, you heard right. The whistle came from *inside* the forest. This woman had been walking along the track. It must have been around eightish in the morning; she was headed out to work further along the track. Suddenly she heard this whistle. She heard it once, then there was silence, and then a couple of minutes later she heard it again, this time more muted, but again coming from somewhere inside this forest. The woman reported this to me almost as soon as she got on duty.'

This is interesting, Yadu thought.

'What did you do after you heard this?' Vandana asked. 'Did you go check the place?'

Elango grinned awkwardly. 'No, I didn't. Maybe I should have, but I didn't. I didn't think much of it at the time. I thought the woman had imagined the whole thing.'

He then elaborated in defence of his inaction. 'You would understand if you knew my crew: they are an illiterate lot. They are always telling me stuff like this, that they have seen a ghost, that they saw a hovering evil spirit, stuff like that, you know. I usually don't take what they say seriously. This time, maybe I should have.'

Yadu now understood why Elango had wanted to talk to them in private. If he had told them this back in the station master's office, the station master would have surely pulled him up for not reporting such a thing to him – especially at a time when the entire state was looking for this engine.'

'But you surely must have heard of the RBI coach hijack before we told you?' Vandana said.

'I'd heard about the hijack alright, but I had failed to make the connection. Only when I heard you in the station master's room did the possibility occur to me. I suddenly realised that the engine whistle the woman heard could have been from the hijacked engine.'

Standing in front of Elango, Yadu was thinking of the same thing. His spirits had sagged since his arrival here, but now it started to puff up again. He started to believe that they were really onto something now. Though it was still too premature to say for sure, he still wanted to believe that the engine the woman had heard was indeed the engine of the Mangalore Express, the one they were so desperately looking for.

'You think this could be the missing engine?' Vandana asked.

'I am certain that it is, especially in the light of what you have told me so far. You both are sure that Mathew's train hauled the engine here early yesterday morning. And now Mathew has suddenly vanished, which like you rightly said, it makes me think he is guilty of something. But forget about all that. For me, personally, the clincher is the time.'

Vandana and Yadu waited with bated breath.

'You said the engine got hijacked at around 2 am from Erode. This place is roughly six hours away from Erode, so it must have reached here around eight?' A dramatic pause, and then Elango finished with a flourish. 'That is around the time the woman heard the whistle.'

Yadu's heart did a somersault inside his ribcage.

Vandana pinched Yadu's arm in excitement. It took enormous resolve on her part to resist the impulse to jump up and down.

'Did this woman see the engine?' Yadu asked, keeping his excitement in check.

'No she didn't.'

Vandana was thinking that if the forest was as thick as Elango claimed then it was possible Hardaker and his men were holing out inside this forest. From what they had heard of the place she believed it would be the perfect hiding place for fugitives fleeing from the law.

Both Vandana and Yadu had this desperate urge now to go see this place immediately.

There was one thing however that Yadu wasn't clear about. 'But how did this engine get into the forest in the first place? Is there a railway line in there?'

One could see on Elango's face that he knew this question was coming. 'There is, and there isn't,' he said somewhat cryptically.

'What do you mean?' Vandana asked.

'An old railway line does exist in there, but it's not in use. It's an abandoned line, you see. It's been almost eight years since a train ran on this track. Most people – and that includes the locals – don't know of its existence.'

'This woman who heard the whistle, did she know about this line?'

'I doubt it. She wouldn't have told me about the whistle if she had known about the line. She would have just thought the railways were running trials in the area.'

'Maybe they were running trails,' Yadu said.

Elango smiled. 'Trials that *I* wasn't informed about? Not a chance.'

There was a further pause in the conversation at this point. Yadu was busy assimilating what he had just heard.

'You ought to see this place,' Elango said after some time. 'Keyyurli forest could be the perfect hiding place for criminals on the run.'

Elango had no idea how desperate the two of them were to see this place immediately. Yadu wanted to charge this very minute into the forest in search of the engine. Mustering up some courage he asked Elango for a favour.

'If it's not too much to ask, will you take us there?' Yadu asked.

'Sure, why not,' Elango said. 'Give me about fifteen minutes to clear up my desk. Then we'll go.'

~

Half an hour later Yadu and Vandana were riding on Elango's railway handcar. Since there were only two seats Vandana and Elango sat in them. Yadu squatted just in front of their feet. Two railway employees were pushing the handcar from behind.

It was just after four in the afternoon and the weather was quite pleasant. The humidity had dropped considerably because of the relentless sea breeze now coming in from the Arabian Sea.

For a little while they rode past paddy fields. Then these fields gave way to coconut groves, and still later these groves gave way to forests. It struck Yadu that he had seen this scenery before. It seemed like déjà vu, until Vandana told him that they had seen this landscape from the train, on their way to Calicut.

Elango didn't talk much during the ride.

Some time later they reached the rail bridge that the line inspector had talked about.

It was exactly the way he had described it: a river was flowing under the bridge and emptying into the Arabian Sea to their right, and there were forests on either side of the river. Both forests were packed tightly with trees. Quite expectedly there was not a house in sight.

The handcar pushers slowed down, negotiated the bridge carefully, and then they brought the handcar to a dead halt. The three of them jumped onto the ground and they started to scout the area. Elango told his men that they could go for a smoke if they wanted. The handcar pushers set off immediately towards the bridge.

Yadu and Vandana had a good look around. It was thick forests everywhere they turned. Elango then pointed to the forest to their left. 'That's the Keyyurli forest. That's where the whistle of the engine came from.'

Yadu looked in that direction. 'How big is this forest?' he asked.

'I don't know. Maybe fifty kilometres.'

'*Fifty* kilometres?' Yadu asked.

'It maybe even bigger than that.'

Yadu's gaze now went to the ground to look for the tracks of the abandoned line that Elango had told him about. The railway line was supposed to lead into the forest but Yadu couldn't find the rails at first glance. The line inspector watched as Yadu looked all over for the tracks. He obviously knew where the track was, but he seemed to be having fun watching Yadu hunt for it. Vandana, meanwhile, was gazing up at the tall trees and taking in the scenery. She found the place quite enchanting.

Finally, Yadu found the tracks, just a few feet away from where the handcar stood. It seemed to have sunk considerably into the soil. Also, the rails had been made invisible by the foliage covering it. If he hadn't been consciously looking for it he might not even have noticed it.

Yadu walked over and squatted between the rails. Moving his gaze up the tracks he noticed a tunnel-like entrance in the forest that the track seemed to be headed for. At first glance it just looked like a well-trodden forest path, and nothing more. But looking closer he realised that this was the path of the abandoned line that Elango had told him about. Perhaps years ago, at the time it was built, the rail path would have been quite wide. But now, with the passage of years, the forest seemed to have reclaimed part of the tracks. Except for the gravel stone bed on which the track had been laid, the rest of the area around the tracks seemed to be overgrown with shrub and bushes.

'You are probably wondering where this line leads to?' Elango said.

'I am.' Yadu said.

'It leads to nowhere, actually.'

'You are joking,' Vandana said, joining in.

'No, I am not. This line has an interesting history. Do you want to hear about it?'

'Sure, tell us,' Yadu said.

Elango took out a cigarette from his pack and lit it. 'Ten years ago, the British floated an ambitious project to link Calicut to Mysore – with a railway line. Both these

towns were growing at a rapid pace, and a need was felt
to connect them. It was supposed to be a 275-kilometre
line and was expected to cost many crores of rupees. A lot
of people were excited about the project, but as is usually
the case with any expensive undertaking, there was a lot
of opposition to it as well. There were many who believed
the project was unfeasible – because the line had to be
built across the Western Ghats, which as you probably
know is inhospitable terrain. Anyway, in spite of all the
opposition the project got sanctioned in 1936.

'Work on the line started two years later and it progressed
at great speed all through that year. About seventy
kilometres of the track had been laid by 1939, which was
something of a record, considering that the track wound
its way through dense forests and deep ravines.

'The track had been finished up to a point called
Keyyurli, when disaster struck, not here in Calicut, but
in far off Europe. The Second World War had just been
declared. The repercussions of that war were felt as far away
as this place. The British government instantly froze this
project along with a number of other expensive projects;
they wanted to preserve funds for their war effort, you see.
Thus, this project became a casualty of World War II. The
track-laying team was sent home, the engineers were asked
to pack up, and within weeks the line was abandoned. The
line was meant to lead to Mysore but like I said, right now
it leads to nowhere.'

'They abandoned the line just like that?' Vandana asked,
surprised. 'But they must have spent so much money on
the project.'

'Of course they had. But they still had another two
hundred kilometres to build. The government was not
willing to shell out that kind of money, so what could
the railways do? Of course everybody kept saying the

rest of the line would get built after the war ended. But after the war ended the British were not interested in the line because giving India her independence had become imminent at that point of time. They had no use for the project anymore.'

Yadu shook his head in disbelief. 'You mean this line has been lying in disuse all these years?'

'Yes,' said Elango. 'For the past seven to eight years not a single train has travelled on this line, at least to *my* knowledge. This hijacked engine might have been the first one from the looks of it.'

'Has nobody made an effort to restart the project at all?' Vandana asked.

'I doubt if anybody will,' Elango said. 'It's too expensive a project. Not just that. The engineering difficulties are far too many. It doesn't seem worth all that effort.'

'What a pity,' Yadu said.

'Indeed,' said Elango.

'You said the track was finished up to a place called Keyyurli. Why can't the railways introduce a Calicut-Keyyurli service or something, to at least keep the rails from disuse,' Vandana asked.

'What's the point? The train will run empty, because nobody lives in these forests anymore. Maybe a few tribals do, but I don't see them using the service.'

'It's forests all the way up to Keyyurli?' Yadu asked.

'Yes, mostly.'

'How big is this Keyyurli anyway? What is it...a village? A town?' asked Yadu.

Elango chuckled when he heard this. 'Keyyurli is nothing more than a clearing in the woods. That place was the base camp for the track laying operations. Who knows, it probably doesn't even exist anymore.'

'Why do you say that?' Vandana asked.

'The forest might have reclaimed the land. It's nearly eight years since the line was abandoned, after all.'

Vandana didn't catch the last portion of what Elango said, because her attention had suddenly been pulled away in another direction.

She had gone stiff, having caught sight of a glint of steel poking out from a thicket.

36

Vandana looked at Elango and gestured for him to continue talking to Yadu. Then she slithered down from the track onto lower ground. Elango, realising something was up continued to talk, though Yadu had stopped following what he was saying. His eyes now followed Vandana as she walked down stealthily towards the riverbank. She zigzagged her way past all the man-sized bushes, moving further and further away.

'What's the matter?' Elango asked in a whisper. 'Where is she going?'

'She's seen something,' Yadu said. 'Let's wait here until she calls us.'

A few seconds later she arrived by the thicket from which the steel was poking out. She looked at the steel more closely. She realised that she was looking at the handlebar of a cycle.

Somebody had hidden a cycle in the bush.

Who? She wondered. What for?

She walked around the bush only to find more bicycles. There was a cycle behind every bush here. Six cycles in all.

Vandana now came out from behind the bush and gestured for the other two to come here. She had to show them this. She was certain Yadu would find it interesting.

'Cycles,' Vandana said when they arrived. 'Half a dozen of them, all without locks.'

Yadu and Elango went behind the bushes and had a look at the cycles.

'Interesting,' Yadu said, coming out of the bushes a few seconds later. 'Who do you reckon these cycles belong to?' he asked Elango.

'I haven't the vaguest idea.'

'Maybe it belongs to your crew,' Yadu suggested.

'I don't think so,' Elango said. 'They wouldn't leave their cycles here like this.'

Over the next ten minutes they scouted the area to see if they could find anything else here. The best was of course yet to come. A few minutes later Yadu found a jeep, hidden behind a huge peepul tree.

He wasted no time, scrambling into the jeep to check for clues to ownership. He didn't find any though.

'Any idea who owns this jeep?' Yadu asked Elango once he had got out of the vehicle.

'I have no idea,' Elango admitted. 'I can't say I have seen this jeep before.'

'You don't think this is strange, people parking their vehicles behind bushes?' Vandana asked.

'It does look suspicious,' Elango admitted.

The three of them continued their search for some more time, but they didn't find any more vehicles.

An exhausted Vandana got into the jeep then and sat down on the driver's seat.

'What are we going to do now Yadu?' she asked, drumming the steering wheel with her fingers.

'If I were you I would rush back to Coimbatore to get the investigating team here,' Elango said.

Yadu didn't reply immediately. He stared at the jeep for some time.

'Mr Elango is right,' Yadu said a few seconds later. 'I think that's what you ought to do Vandana.'

Vandana looked up from the steering wheel thinking she hadn't heard this right. 'You are talking as if I am going to Coimbatore alone,' she said.

'That's how it looks to me at the moment. I don't think I can come back with you.'

'What do you mean by that?' Vandana asked.

Yadu gave her a smile. 'It means I am staying here to watch over these vehicles. Since it's a strong possibility that these vehicles belong to the hijackers, I intend to stay right here and keep watch. Who knows, I might get lucky and Hardaker's men might come for these vehicles tonight.'

'You are going to stay here all night? On the edge of this jungle? I think you are asking for trouble, Yadu,' Vandana said.

Even Elango didn't seem too pleased to hear this. 'I don't think that's a good idea, Yadu. What if nobody comes for these vehicles all night? What if the owners have just abandoned these vehicles?'

'All I would lose is one night's sleep. I can live with that.'

'What if the vehicles belong to some locals who have gone on a hunting trip or something?' Vandana said.

'Then it'll be confirmed that these vehicles don't belong to the hijackers.'

Elango continued to dissuade Yadu. 'This is not a safe place to be around at night Yadu. There are wild animals about...and poisonous snakes.'

'Forget it Yadu,' Vandana said, as soon as she heard the word 'snakes'. 'Let's just tell the police what we have found out so far. They'll take care of the rest.'

'It's just a matter of one night,' Yadu said stubbornly. 'I can feel it in my bones that these vehicles belong to

Hardaker. I have a feeling that somebody or the other will come out of the forest for one of these vehicles.'

Elango put his hands up in a gesture that said he was giving up advising Yadu.

'I'll tell you what's brewing in my head,' Yadu told Vandana. 'While I stay here tonight and watch these cycles, you will go back to Coimbatore. Find Inspector Kripakaran. Tell him that the drivers have disappeared. Tell him about this place and the whistle the woman heard. I am certain the inspector will arrive at the same conclusion that we have arrived at. Persuade him and bring him here tomorrow so he can see the place for himself. By that time, hopefully, I would have found out who these vehicles belong to. Then we can all go inside the forest in search of the missing engine.'

The idea was not a bad one, Vandana had to admit that. It was more than likely that these vehicles belonged to Hardaker and his men. If the engine had indeed been driven into the forest, then the men would need cycles to move about. They couldn't use the engine to get to town now, could they? Also, like Yadu had said, it was only for a night. She would go get the police while he stayed here and watched over the vehicles. It would be perfect.

'What if Inspector Kripakaran refuses to come with me?' she now asked. 'What if he is unable to leave the desk or something?'

'Beg him. Fall at his feet. Do anything, but get him here. You have to manage that somehow,' Yadu said. 'In spite of your efforts if he still doesn't come, then I guess I'll have to go check the forest all alone.'

'Don't you dare do anything like that,' Vandana warned. 'I'll get the inspector here somehow. Just promise me you'll stay right here.'

'You have my word,' Yadu said, grinning.

At this point Elango asked if Yadu wanted him to stay back here for company. Yadu sensed from his tone that Elango was just asking it as a formality. It was obvious he didn't want to stay the night here at the edge of this great forest.

'No, I'll be alright,' Yadu said, putting on his most confident tone of voice.

Vandana then asked Elango if he would be kind enough to take her back to Calicut.

'Of course, I will,' Elango said, stubbing his cigarette. 'I still think it's foolish of your friend to stay here all night.'

'He can be stubborn sometimes,' Vandana said.

They all started to climb back up towards the tracks. Elango now whistled to get the attention of his men.

'I don't blame him. I guess I might do the same if my father was held captive by a maniac like Hardaker.'

Five minutes later they were back on the main track. They had to wait a few minutes for the handcar pushers.

'Are you sure you are going to be okay here?' Vandana asked, as she got onto the seat.

'I'll be fine,' Yadu said.

The two men arrived by the handcar panting. Yadu thanked Elango once again for going out of the way to help them. He then waved to both of them as the railway handcar started on its journey back to Calicut.

~

Soon after Elango and Vandana left, Yadu started his nightlong vigil by the cycles. He got onto a low hanging branch of the peepul tree (under which the jeep stood). From up here he had a clear view of not only the jeep and the half a dozen bicycles, but he also could see the bridge clearly. If anybody was headed in this direction he would be able to spot them easily.

It was getting dark now. The jungle started to fall silent as if in homage to the dying sun. In a matter of twenty minutes the place went from twilight to total blackout. He couldn't see a thing. He then started to wonder if this had been a mistake – wanting to stay here all night. If he couldn't see a thing then what was the point? He wouldn't even know if somebody came and drove off with the cycles.

But as time passed Yadu realised his fears were unfounded. After an hour or so the moon rose in the sky, illuminating the area to a reasonable extent. Now he could at least make out the shapes of the cycles and the jeep. This would do, he told himself.

The next couple of hours Yadu spent were anxious ones. The eerie silence that prevailed was not at all to his liking. It made him feel lonely; he longed for companionship; he wished Vandana was here beside him, so the hours would pass away quickly. The night wore on slowly with nobody coming for the vehicles. Yadu tried not to think of a couple of things. One was food. All he'd had for lunch was tea and biscuits. He felt hungry now. He tried pushing these thoughts away since there was nothing he could do about it.

The other thought was that of the wild animals and the snakes that Elango had mentioned. At the time the line inspector had mentioned them it didn't seem all that frightful. But now, with all this darkness around him, and the silence that prevailed, he felt jittery at the very thought of lurking animals.

Yadu deliberately pulled his mind away and thought of other things. He thought of Mathew, the goods train driver, and his assistant. He thought, if only they had been in

Calicut there would have been no need for all this waiting here by the cycles. He could have met them, found out where they had dropped off the engine and could have headed for Coimbatore with Vandana – as he had earlier planned. But that idea of his hadn't clicked. It was his good fortune though that Elango had come out and had told him about what the woman heard. So things really were not all that bad. There was progress.

A few more hours passed. Yadu started to feel drowsy now. The stillness of the night, combined with the boredom of the passing hours was making him fall asleep, right there, astride the peepul branch. Yadu tried rubbing his eyes vigorously, but it had little effect. This worked for about five minutes. Then he started to fall asleep again. He decided there was no point staying up here. He would only fall down from the branch in his sleep. He decided to abandon his wait...for the time being. He would find a nice spot and rest, only for a *little* while, he promised himself. He thought of the inside of the jeep first. But that would be too risky if somebody came for it. He couldn't imagine sleeping on the forest bed for fear of snakes. Finally, he decided to sleep on the luggage carrier atop the jeep. He climbed on top, covered his body with the rug-like tarpaulin that he found there and then went to sleep.

~

Four hours and fifty minutes after Yadu had fallen asleep, just two hundred metres away from the jeep, Brian Hardaker stood facing the Arabian Sea, signal lantern in one hand and a torch in the other. He was standing, all alone, in the middle of the railway bridge. He was staring intently at the horizon hoping to see the sight that would guarantee him safety.

Hardaker had arrived by the bridge two hours back. He had been in Calicut all day making preparations for the next stage of their plans. He'd made a lot of phone calls – almost all of them international. He'd had to wait a long time to get through, but in the end he had managed every one of those calls.

As per their original plan it was Icy who was supposed to have done this signal duty. But since he had been in Calicut all day he had taken it upon himself to do this. Sethu would arrive shortly to take him back to Anchorpoint, which was their base inside the forest. A base that Hardaker was *very* proud of.

He now caught sight of the silhouette of the cargo vessel across the western sky. Yes, the vessel was finally here. The ship signalled that it was entering the channel now. Hardaker raised the lantern and started swinging it. The ship swung around slowly. Then it started to enter the river. Shortly, it was moving upstream in the direction of the bridge.

Hardaker felt a rush of excitement seeing the small ship. This was the culmination of all their planning. This was the culmination of his dreams. In a few hours he would be out of this damned country with the tag of the 'richest man in the universe'. If he somehow managed to get out of the country with the cargo, then all his hard work would have been worth it. He just hoped the last stage of his plans would go smoothly. There was no reason why it shouldn't. It had all gone like clockwork so far. The police had no clue what they were up to; the railways had no clue what they were up to. Nobody for that matter did. So what had he to worry about?

The ship was moving forward steadily. It would be under the bridge in a couple of minutes.

He sensed some movement to his left. He turned, and his eyes fell on the jeep that had just leapt out of the Keyyurli forest. It was still quite a distance away, but Hardaker was sure it was Sethu arriving here to take him to Anchorpoint. He looked at his watch. Half past four. Sethu was on time as usual. Things were going so smoothly he felt all this was divinely ordained. He felt it in his heart that destiny wanted him to be the richest man in the universe. Nobody had the power now to stop the juggernaut he had set rolling.

In twenty-four hours it would all be over, and he and his men would be out of here permanently – with the greatest treasure of them all.

37

Hardaker continued to wave the lantern until the ship had gone under the bridge.

Sethu now brought the jeep to a halt inches away from where Hardaker stood.

'Right on time,' Hardaker murmured.

Sethu got out of the jeep, went to the edge and peeped over to have a look at the cargo vessel. A couple of men waved to him from the bridge of the vessel. Sethu waved back.

'Let's go. We haven't got all day,' Hardaker said as he sat in the front passenger seat. 'We have to be in Anchorpoint by the time the ship reaches there.'

Sethu took one last look at the ship and then he headed back to the jeep. He started the ignition and drove the jeep in reverse gear until they were outside the bridge. He then pulled the jeep to the right and let it slide down the slope on to lower ground.

'Where are you going? The line's that way,' Hardaker gestured.

'To the peepul tree,' Sethu said. 'We'll take the other jeep. This one's low on petrol.'

Sethu negotiated past the bushes and slowed down the jeep as they neared the giant peepul tree. He parked the jeep right next to the one already standing there. They both got out.

Sethu's eyes went to the tarpaulin sheet on top of the jeep. 'That thing didn't look this bulky last time I saw it,' he commented.

'A python must have got inside,' Hardaker said. 'I hear they like to curl up inside snug places.'

Sethu ignored Hardaker's comment and slid into the driver's seat of the other jeep. Hardaker got beside him.

'Aren't you going to check?' Hardaker asked with a rare smile on his face.

'No way,' Sethu said.

'It's just your imagination running wild. Start the jeep, let's go,' Hardaker said.

~

Tuesday, 9 December 1947

Fifteen inches above Hardaker's head Yadu woke up from his deep slumber in a state of *utter* bewilderment. The jeep had started to move under him, and that's what woke him up. He sat up and looked around, unable to comprehend where he was for the first few seconds. The pitch darkness didn't help matters.

Then he saw the peepul tree as the jeep swung in a wide arc, and instantly he realised where he was. His palms went up involuntarily to his mouth.

Somebody had got into the jeep while he was asleep.

Yadu couldn't believe he had fallen asleep with so much at stake. He looked at his watch. It was half past four. He had slept for nearly five hours. What a stupid thing to do, *you fool*, he told himself.

God only knew what all had happened here during that time. Questions started popping into his mind now. He wondered who these people were inside the jeep? Were they Hardaker's men? If not, what were they doing near this forest at this ungodly hour?

Fortunately for him it didn't seem as if they had sensed his presence up here so far. He was glad the temperature had dropped during the night. Because it had got cold he had wrapped himself completely with the tarpaulin sheet, and that was probably what had saved him.

He noticed that the jeep was headed for the abandoned line. They were going into Keyyurli forest. Yadu had mixed feelings about this. On the one hand he was excited. It did really look as if one of Hardaker's men were driving the jeep. On the other hand he was anxious and uneasy. What was he getting into here? He was all alone. If these men caught him he was done for.

As the jeep swerved and swayed past all the bushes he realised that this was going to be one rough ride. They would be travelling on top of the abandoned line, and it would be quite a challenge for him not to make a sound. The jeep would keep throwing him up in the air and he would have to land softly every time lest he catch their attention. The last thing he wanted now was for them to wonder what was causing the bumps on their roof.

Yadu hung on to the carrier rails tightly and hoped things would work out alright.

The jeep now entered the forest through the tunnel-like entrance he had noticed earlier. Yadu looked in front with considerable curiosity as the jeep's headlights caught the dull glint of the steel rails. As the car leapt and bumped its way over the tracks Yadu noticed something that confirmed his suspicions that the engine had passed this way recently: the rail path was strewn with mutilated tree limbs. It was easy to guess what had happened here: The engine had bulldozed its way past the trees, snapping and ripping the branches that were in its path. Even the shrubs and bushes alongside the track had not been spared. The steel wheels had crushed the life out of them. The bushes that had escaped then were being crushed by the jeep's tyres now. Yadu looked all around him trying to register everything he saw in his mind. Every now and then he caught a glimpse of the river to his left. The track seemed to be hugging it in many places.

As time wore on they went deeper and deeper into the forest. The scenery soon got monotonous. Dawn was yet to break, so the forest was still dark. The men in the jeep now started talking. With a wild jolt Yadu realised that he recognised the voices. There were two of them. One man spoke in a loud confident baritone. His accent was unmistakably English.

Hardaker!

Yadu sucked in his breath and stopped breathing.

He guessed the other man to be Sethu. Yadu started sweating ice. *He had found them!* He had *finally* found them.

He didn't dare peep down and have a look, but he was sure it was Sethu in the driver's seat and Hardaker in the front passenger seat. They were still talking to each other, oblivious of his presence on the roof. Yadu strained his ears to see if he could catch what they were saying.

He tried to eavesdrop on their conversation by placing his ear on the roof. But that didn't work; he couldn't hear a thing. Then he tried leaning dangerously to one side. This worked better. He could now catch strings of their talk.

'Mostly,' Sethu replied to some question that Hardaker had posed. Yadu hadn't caught the question.

'What do you mean, *mostly*?' Hardaker then asked.

'We almost had a major mishap at Anchorpoint. Luckily, it was averted in time,' Sethu said.

'Mishap?' Hardaker asked.

'You know Mani, the fireman?'

'What about him?'

'He tried sabotaging the engine.'

'*What?*'

'Don't panic. We sorted it out,' Sethu said. 'It was our good fortune that the engine driver lost his nerve. Fearing for his life he came and told Dorai of Mani's plans.'

'The engine is safe then?' Hardaker asked.

'The engine is. The fireman isn't,' said Sethu.

'What did you do to him?' Hardaker asked.

'Dorai broke his leg. We have chained him and kept him isolated.'

'The *bloody* gall of the man. Wait till I get my hands on him,' Hardaker exploded. Then he said something in a low voice that Yadu didn't catch.

Leaning a little Yadu had caught most of what they told each other. He had a fair idea of who they were talking about. They were surely talking about the engine driver and the assistant of the Mangalore Express.

Below him the two ruffians fell silent, and Yadu had a quiet moment to reflect on what these men were up to. None of their activities made any sense to him. He hoped he would find out once they reached Anchorpoint – this place that they had just referred to. Though he had not even met the man Yadu was already thinking of the fireman as an ally in his fight against these men. If the man was brave enough to try sabotaging the engine, then surely he could count on him if the need arose. Not physically of course. From what Sethu had said it seemed as if the man was incapable of moving. Maybe he could fill him in on what these people were really up to.

They rode on in silence for another ten minutes. Then the sky brightened up a bit with the first light of dawn.

Sethu started to drop speed and Yadu realised that they must be nearing Anchorpoint.

It was the changing landscape that gave him the idea. As they drove on he started seeing tree stumps, hundreds and hundreds of them. Each was about ten inches high and poked out of the ground like ugly warts. The jungle started to give way to this enormous clearing by the river. Yadu didn't have to look too closely to see that the stumps were what remained of trees – trees that had been felled in the hundreds to create this large clearing.

However, there were more surprises on the way. The first thing that caught his eye were the four carriages in the distance. They seemed like empty coal carriages.

Hardaker and Sethu continued with their conversation below, but Yadu wasn't listening. His eyes were riveted to what was unfolding in front of him now. His jaw dropped as he took in the sight in front of him.

Yadu was certain this was what they called Anchorpoint because the name was so apt. Hardaker and his men had built a riverside harbour in the middle of this forest. With disbelief on his face Yadu looked at the riverside jetty, at the ship anchored in the middle of the river, and at the twin tugboats. Both the tugboats were crane-fitted. One tugboat stood alongside the ship, and the other one was moored near the jetty. Yadu was taken aback at the sheer size of the cranes. What did they need such big cranes for?

In the clearing itself there were half a dozen huts. Next to the huts was a vehicle park where a dozen vehicles stood. There were a few cycles, three motorcycles, a jeep, a car and even a railway handcar.

He couldn't help but notice the amount of work that had gone into this place. Here and there rocks had been blasted to form an even surface. North of the jetty, there were piles upon piles of a mud-clay mixture. It looked as if the river had been dredged at this point, no doubt to accommodate the ship.

Hardaker and his men had even built a rail track alongside the jetty. There was a train of railway carriages that stood on this track. Standing guard beside the coaches were two huge Alsatians. They had been tethered to the trunk of a tree.

It was just five in the morning but the jetty was already busy. A dozen men were working on the carriages attending to various jobs. One of them was uncoupling all the carriages. Three others had climbed onto the coaches and were unlocking the carriage lids. From the frenzied manner in which the men were working it appeared as if the ship had just arrived. The tugboat that was near the ship had started to drift towards the jetty. Yadu guessed that the men were preparing to offload the cargo of the carriages onto the ship.

Sethu, in the meantime, had brought the jeep to a halt opposite the four empty carriages. Yadu crouched low as Hardaker and Sethu got out of the jeep and strode towards the coaches.

'He is in the second coach,' Sethu said. Yadu assumed he was talking about the fireman.

He waited until the two of them had jumped into the carriage and then slid down from the roof and hid behind a tree. He would be asking for trouble if he stayed on the roof any longer. Yadu continued to watch the activities of the labourers from behind the tree. Both tugboats were now floating by the jetty. Their crane arms were swinging this way and that, readying themselves for a lift – much like weightlifters before their attempt. Yadu watched on as the crane arm was latched onto the first coach. The man operating the tugboat then used the crane to lift the entire coach off the ground. Carrying the carriage – like a stork carrying a baby – the tugboat now drifted in the direction of the ship. The second tugboat now got into action at the jetty.

He could now hear the groans coming from the second coach. Hardaker had started attacking the fireman. The poor man was wailing in pain. Yadu wanted to go to the rescue of the man; only he couldn't do that without jeopardising his own position. With pangs of guilt he shifted his gaze back to the river.

The cargo of the first coach had already been dumped into the ship's hold. The tugboat had come back to the jetty with the empty carriage.

Yadu had initially assumed that Hardaker and his men had holed up inside Keyyurli forest to escape police detection. Now, having seen the ship, the crane-fitted tugboats and the jetty he realised there was a far greater motive in their choosing Keyyurli forest as their hideout. They had a major smuggling operation going on inside here. But what they were smuggling he had no idea. Was it sandalwood trees? Was it elephant tusks?

While Yadu was trying to understand Hardaker's motive, inside the coach the fireman was still being given the third degree by the Englishman and Sethu. Yadu could hear the man pleading for mercy, but it didn't look as if these two were going to pardon him. Yadu felt mighty uneasy about being just a few metres away and yet not being in a position to help the man.

Then, just as suddenly as it had started, Hardaker's assault on the man stopped. Maybe he'd had enough. Yadu pulled his head back as he sensed that the two were finished with their business inside the coach. Sethu came out first. He walked briskly to the jeep and then got into the driver's seat. Even as he was starting the jeep Hardaker emerged, sweating profusely, slightly out of breath.

He got into the jeep and gestured for Sethu to start moving.

Yadu watched as the jeep sped off in the direction of the makeshift jetty. He waited for a full five minutes, making sure that they weren't coming back. Then he made a dash for the coach from where he had heard the groaning.

38

The coach was an iron-ore carrier type with an open top. An open wagon, in railway parlance. One had to climb up the coach and jump, to get in. Yadu climbed up the sides and looked in.

The sight that met him was not very different from the one he had visualised. Lying face down in the middle of the carriage was a young man who seemed to be in a semi-conscious state. He was chained to a cast-iron sidebar. There were streaks of blood on the coach floor. The young man was panting and sighing heavily. He was mumbling something in tamil that Yadu couldn't quite understand.

Yadu made a soft landing on the coach floor but he still managed to startle the man. The fireman whipped his head in obvious panic, perhaps thinking that the Englishman had returned.

'It's okay, relax. I have come to help you,' Yadu whispered in a reassuring tone, stretching out a friendly hand.

The man squinted his eyes and stared at Yadu for what seemed a long time. He had a cut just above his eyebrow from where blood oozed.

'Who are you?' he finally mumbled.

'My name is Yadu,' he said. 'You must be Mani.'

Yadu looked at the man with compassion. The fireman was young. He was probably not a day older than twenty.

He was short and slim, and looked like a boy who had grown into a man much too quickly.

'You are the fireman of the hijacked engine, aren't you?' Yadu asked, taking a few tentative steps in his direction.

It took the man some effort just to nod a yes.

'I was travelling on the Mangalore Express that night.'

Yadu could see a sudden spark of interest ignite in the man's eyes. He tried to get up and sit.

Yadu went to him, helped him to a sitting position and looked around for a cloth to stem the flow of blood. But there was no cloth around. He tore the man's shirt and used that to wipe away the blood from his face. Then he pressed the piece of cloth to the wound on his forehead and Mani winced in pain.

'Can I get you some water or anything?' Yadu asked. 'Are you alright?'

'I'll be okay,' Mani said moving slowly to the side of the coach. He sat resting his back on the sidewall.

'How did you get here?' Mani asked. His voice was weak.

Yadu told him quickly about his kidnapped father and how his trail had brought him here.

'Is anybody else kept captive here other than you?' Yadu asked. He doubted his father had been brought here, but thought that there was no harm in checking.

'It's just me and the engine driver here as far as I know,' Mani said.

Yadu then checked the chains to see if he could somehow break them and free this man.

'These are heavy. You'll need an axe,' Mani said.

'Where can I find one?' Yadu asked earnestly. He thought that if he could free this man and take him to Inspector Kripakaran, his case would then be strengthened.

'Look my friend, I know you mean well. But forget about freeing me from here. It's too dangerous. If you genuinely want to help me, just go to Calicut and bring the police here. These men have to be stopped at all costs.'

What the man said made sense. Even if he managed to find an axe it wouldn't be of much help. The moment the axe struck the chains the sound would carry all the way to the jetty. Hardaker's men would know immediately that someone was trying to free the fireman. Not only would he be putting this man's life in jeopardy, but in the bargain he too would get himself caught.

'You have a point. I ought to go get the police,' Yadu conceded. 'But you will have to fill me in on what's going on here. The police are sure to ask me about it.'

Mani nodded sagely, understanding Yadu's position. The police weren't going to shift their asses for a sixteen-year-old boy unless they had adequate reason to believe that this was a life and death matter.

'I'll tell you whatever I have found out so far,' Mani said.

'Are you up to it?' Yadu asked doubtfully. 'I mean, physically. Do you need a bit of rest?'

'I'll be okay, thanks,' Mani said. 'Tell me, where do you want me to begin?'

'You can start by telling me what exactly is going on here,' Yadu suggested. 'What is Hardaker up to?'

Mani swayed his head from side to side in an attempt to stop the throbbing inside. Yadu waited patiently as the man collected his thoughts. After a few minutes the fireman finally cleared his throat and began.

'For you to fully appreciate what's going on here I need to tell you about the geography of this place first.'

Yadu nodded to show he was okay with that.

'This abandoned line that we are on terminates at a point called Keyyurli, which is seventy kilometres from Calicut. It is roughly fifty kilometres away from this place. Are you with me so far?'

Yadu nodded.

'Okay. Now you only have to look around to get a feel of this place. From here up to Keyyurli it's just dense forests all the way through. There are no roads, no forest paths, nothing. The only link to Keyyurli is this abandoned railway line.'

'The line inspector at Calicut told me that,' Yadu offered helpfully.

Mani sighed deeply, then went on. 'Now, let me tell you at the very outset that there are certain things about this whole business that are still unclear to me. But what I have found out so far is that Hardaker and his men arrived at Keyyurli three months back and found a few goods carriages abandoned there. I am not yet sure if they knew about these abandoned carriages or if they just stumbled on it by pure chance. However it maybe, that they opened these carriages and found that they contained an *invaluable* cargo. What exactly these carriages contain I have not yet been able to ascertain. I have seen these coaches though, at Keyyurli, and I know for a fact that there are twenty two coaches in all.' Mani paused here to catch his breath. 'It's the cargo inside these coaches that Hardaker is after.'

'I see,' Yadu said.

'Hardaker found these carriages more or less around the time India got her independence. He had already decided he was not going to stay here in India any longer. So he decided to smuggle this cargo out of the country.'

Mani paused. 'But that's where all his problems began.'

'What problems?' Yadu asked.

'The problem of transport. Sometime in the past – maybe three months back, maybe five years back, I don't know – somebody brought all these coaches up to Keyyurli. An engine was used to haul these coaches up to that place. Whoever brought the train there left the carriages behind but didn't leave the engine behind. He no doubt went back to Calicut or wherever with the engine.'

'So Hardaker had all these carriages, but he had no engine to lug it. He had no idea how he was going to transport the cargo over a seventy-kilometre distance. Like I said, there are no roads from Keyyurli to anywhere. So transporting the cargo by road was ruled out. Building an airstrip and airlifting the cargo would take too long and would arouse a lot of suspicion. It didn't take Hardaker long to realise that he needed the services of an engine *urgently*.'

That was the precise moment the entire jigsaw fell into place in Yadu's mind. Suddenly it became crystal clear what Hardaker had been up to all this while.

Mani continued. 'If he got an engine then all his transportation problems would be solved. He could use the engine to lug the carriages from Keyyurli up to Calicut. Then he could smuggle the cargo out of the country without anybody's knowledge.'

Yadu felt choked for breath. He couldn't believe what he was hearing. Hardaker had sent the police, the railways, the media and the entire country on a wild goose chase.

'I see now why Hardaker staged the RBI coach hijack,' Yadu said softly, more to himself than to Mani. 'Everybody thought he was after the RBI coach. It was the *engine* he'd been after all along.'

'You are absolutely right,' Mani said. 'That's the reason he abandoned the coach outside Shoranur. That's the reason they didn't help themselves to all the RBI money. The RBI coach hijack was merely a diversionary tactic intended to hoodwink the police. Hardaker didn't want them to know what he was really after.'

'From what I see here, he has succeeded in his mission so far,' Yadu said.

'We have to hand him that. He has executed his plans to near perfection.'

There was something though that Yadu didn't quite understand. 'Couldn't he have procured an engine in a simpler fashion though?' he asked.

'Look, one can't walk into a shop and buy or rent a railway engine. One's got to request the railways for it. They would have asked a hundred uncomfortable questions as to his intent. It was all too complicated. Hardaker had decided that it was much safer to hijack an engine and then return it a few days later, like he is going to do with this engine. At first he planned to hijack it from a nearby station. But then he feared that the railways and the police would search all the abandoned lines first for the missing engine. That was something he could ill-afford. The last thing he wanted was the police stumbling onto his setup here at Anchorpoint. He decided on the RBI coach hijack after considerable planning, I must say.'

Mani had to stop for a couple of minutes because of a coughing bout. Yadu knelt down opposite him and asked him if he was okay. Mani nodded.

Above them the sky had started to clear. The birds had started their chirping in the trees. Yadu looked at his watch; it was a quarter to six now. He couldn't see the jetty from where he stood, but he could make out from the noise reaching his ears that the men were still busy with their loading operation. Some cargo this was! Twenty-two coaches in all. Yadu wondered what was inside the carriages.

'How did you manage to gather all this information?' Yadu asked, when Mani had recovered fully.

'I eavesdropped on their conversation. You've got to understand: I have been with them for two days now. Hardaker, no doubt, intends to kill both Devraj and me after their purpose is served, so they didn't mind me listening in on their conversations.'

'I take it Devraj is your engine driver,' Yadu said.

'I am ashamed to say that,' Mani said. 'He stabbed me in the back by telling Dorai about my sabotage plans.'

'Brave of you to even think on those lines,' Yadu said.

The compliment drew a smile on the young man's face.

Mani then said Hardaker built this makeshift harbour so he could load the cargo onto a ship surreptitiously. The engine would bring the carriages here to Anchorpoint. The cranes would then lift the carriages, take it to the ship and dump the cargo into the hold. And then the ship would leave the country with the cargo. Since the loading was done inside the forest, nobody would ever know about it, and their secret would remain safe.

'Hardaker has it worked out to the last detail,' Mani finished.

~

Vandana had made remarkable progress at her end since the time she had left Yadu by the bridge.

The previous evening Elango had dropped her off at the railway station. Finding out that the next train to Coimbatore was not due until half past ten, she had accepted Elango's advise and had taken a bus to Coimbatore. She arrived at the railway station just before eleven. Inspector Kripakaran was still on duty at the command desk, so she briefed him of what they had found at Calicut.

It's important to note that, by this time, Kripakaran was completely frustrated with the 'horses with blinds' approach of the police in the case. The police force was still clueless about the whereabouts of the hijackers. When Vandana told him that the goods train drivers were absconding he decided he'd had enough. He took Vandana to Wellington House and sought an audience with the commissioner of police. He told the chief the theory Yadu had propounded, and why he thought the boy was right. He laid particular emphasis on the fact that the station master Sukumar too believed in this theory.

The police commissioner agreed that this was a theory worth pursuing – especially in the light of the absconding goods train drivers. He sanctioned Kripakaran a team of ten and asked him to leave for Calicut immediately, to pursue the case further.

Inspector Kripakaran and Vandana left for Calicut at half past two. They arrived at Keyyurli railway bridge at six, so they could have a word with Yadu first.

Problem was, they couldn't find Yadu near the bridge. Vandana had no idea where he had vanished.

~

Just twelve kilometres to the east, Yadu sat raptly listening to Mani.

'The engine wasn't at the jetty when I landed here,' Yadu was saying.

'It's gone to Keyyurli for the last batch of coaches,' Mani explained. 'Devraj and I brought fourteen coaches here last night. Those are the coaches that are being loaded onto the ship now. The engine's gone for the final eight coaches.'

'How long before these people leave Anchorpoint permanently?' Yadu then asked.

'I reckon they'll be finished in a few hours. You have three, maybe four hours to get the police here.'

Yadu went quiet when he heard this. This was going to be touch and go. Getting to Calicut would take him a couple of hours. That was if he stole one of their motorbikes. If he went by cycle it would take even longer. Getting back here with the policemen might take another couple of hours – if he could convince them quickly. Did he have enough time to stop these men, he wondered.

Then he had a sudden flash of inspiration.

'How long before the engine gets back here with the next batch of coaches?' Yadu asked.

'An hour or so,' Mani said. 'Why? What's on your mind?'

'What if I completed the work of sabotage that you started?'

Mani's eyebrows went up on hearing this. 'You want to sabotage the engine?'

Yadu smiled. 'Not the engine, no. That's beyond me. What if I sabotage the railway line instead?'

It was Mani now who smiled. 'How do you intend doing that?' Yadu sighed and murmured. 'I don't know yet. Maybe I'll roll boulders onto the track. Maybe I'll unscrew the rails or something...'

Mani went quiet on hearing this.

The silence was punctured suddenly by the whistle of a steam engine coming from deep inside the belly of the jungle.

'That must be the engine returning from Keyyurli,' Yadu said. Mani nodded.

'You know what?' he said after some time. 'That idea of yours might just work.'

'You think so?'

'Not if you do it your way.' Mani said. 'If you do it *my* way though there is a chance that this might work.'

39

Mani told Yadu about the dynamite sticks that Hardaker's men had used at the time of dredging the river. He said that they might still have some left over.

'Where am I likely to find these sticks?' Yadu asked, getting all excited. He could see where Mani was headed with this idea. If they blew the rail track that led to Keyyurli, then there was no way the second batch of coaches could be brought here to the jetty. Hardaker's men would be forced to set right the tracks first. That might just give him enough time to go get the police from Calicut.

'It's most likely to be in the hut nearest to the vehicle park. That's where they usually keep all the tools.'

'Let me see if I can find it,' Yadu said, getting up on his feet.

~

As Yadu scaled the sidewall he heard the engine's whistle yet again. He had to hurry. There was no point in blowing the track *after* the train had arrived here.

'Be careful,' Mani said, waving to him. 'For the both of us.'

Yadu nodded and then leapt onto the ground.

The dozen odd men on the jetty were all still busy with the coaches. Nobody was looking this way. This gave him a shot of confidence. He needed that badly because reaching the hut was going to be a very tricky affair. Since most of the trees in the area had been cut there was nothing to provide him cover.

Yadu took a deep breath, and then he made a dash for the hut. It took him less than a minute to reach the bamboo and mud structure. Much as he wanted to check the jetty, he resisted the temptation. He opened the door, stepped inside and quietly shut the door.

The inside of the hut was lit by a hurricane lamp placed on a stool. Yadu cast a glance around the hut and made sure there was nobody inside. Then he went to the small window and looked out at the jetty. He breathed easy on seeing that the men were all still preoccupied with their jobs. Nobody was looking in this direction, which meant that nobody had caught sight of him dashing into the hut.

Yadu then turned around and had a proper look at the interiors. Mani had been right: this was indeed their storeroom. Everywhere he looked there were tools and equipment strewn all over the floor; there were tools stacked on a wooden shelf on the far side of the wall; they were even hung from the ceiling. Spades, shovels, toolkits, digging equipment, axes, sandbags, measuring tools...Yadu's gaze roved all over the room, and then it went to the shelf. It finally came to rest on what looked like a shoebox. He pulled the box off the shelf and looked inside.

Dynamite sticks!

There were four sticks in all, each seven inches long and two inches thick. He stuffed the sticks into his trouser pockets and then helped himself to the matchbox behind the hurricane lamp. His job done, he walked out of the hut just as quietly as he had come in.

Outside, in the vehicle park, he got onto one of the cycles, and then he started pedalling in the direction of the railway line.

He reached the line a few minutes later. Yadu couldn't have timed it any better if he had wanted to, because just as he got off the cycle he heard the engine's whistle again. In the far distance he saw a puff of smoke.

Yadu got off the cycle and let it fall by the wayside. He looked behind him just as a precaution. There was no one around. The jetty was not in his line of vision any more – because of the trees.

He got down on his knees and placed a couple of sticks under a rail. He tweaked their long fuses together. He had to get this right because this was his only chance. If the sticks blew and if they *didn't* damage the rails – then he was done for, because the sound of the blast would get all the men here.

He took out the matchbox from his pocket, and with trembling fingers he lit the fuse. Then he made a wild dash towards the trees.

Yadu was about twenty feet away from the sticks when they exploded, but it still wasn't enough. The blast was so powerful that it lifted him clean off the ground and threw him into the bushes. He rolled a few feet, then he hit the trunk of a tree and came to a stop.

There was a peculiar ringing inside his ears. Yadu thought he had lost his hearing. With some effort he pulled himself up to a sitting position. He felt dazed. He had heard soldiers use the term 'shell-shocked' to express what they felt when they'd nearly been hit by a bomb. That's how he felt at the moment: shell-shocked.

Somewhere in the deep recesses of his brain his survival instincts kicked in. He had to get out of here fast. They would have heard the blast at the jetty and they would all come running here to see what had happened. He had to make himself scarce.

It took some effort, but he managed to get up on his feet. His legs were trembling; he looked at his hands; they were trembling too. With that dazed look still on his face he looked in the direction of the blast. The debris was still settling down, but he could see that the dynamite had done its job. It had ripped the rails clean off the gravel stone bed it had been screwed to. The blast had sprayed the skies with mud, gravel stones and bits of beam ballast. He slapped his face a few times to get the wooziness off his head. For about fifteen feet both rails had been completely ripped away. The beam ballast had crumbled to flakes. There was a four-foot-wide, six-foot-deep hole formed at the point of explosion.

Looking at the hole it finally dawned on him what he had just done. A smile broke out on his face. *He had done it.*

Yadu took a few tentative steps towards the track. The dust from the explosion now started to settle. He could see a bit more clearly. It had registered somewhere in his brain that he had succeeded, but the feeling of elation was yet to sink in.

It now occurred to him that even if Hardaker had the steel rails and the tools he would still need at least half a day to set right this mess.

To his left he noticed the train slowing down. The engine driver had no doubt noticed the blast. To his right he could now hear some loud cries. He could hear an approaching jeep. His head was still feeling a bit woozy, but he forced himself to run. He sprinted a little distance and then entered the woods. Yadu hid behind a tree and waited for Hardaker and his men to arrive. He wanted to see how they would react to this.

A jeep now tore past him towards the explosion site. Dorai was riding the jeep and Hardaker was seated beside him. The look that Hardaker had on his face was something

Yadu would never ever forget in his lifetime. He had seen angry men before; but the look on Hardaker's face was something else: it looked like an African war mask, the bushy eyebrows, the pallid complexion, and the burning intensity in the eyes.

Yadu knew what would happen to him if he got caught now. But the temptation to stay here and watch their expressions was just too overpowering. He stayed behind the tree and watched on as the jeep came to a halt by the blast site.

A deep guttural groan left Hardaker's mouth as he looked at the hole. He had been the first one off the jeep, but now Dorai and Sethu too had jumped off. All three of them wore such gobsmacked expressions on their faces that Yadu decided that all this had been worth it just to see this.

Yadu watched as Hardaker whirled all around looking for the person who did this. There was such fury in his eyes that even Dorai and Sethu tried to evade eye contact with their boss.

'Who did this to me?' Hardaker roared at the top of his voice. 'Come on outside, you coward. Come and show yourself to me.'

As if Yadu would do such a thing.

Hardaker took an iron bar from the jeep. His pale complexion had gone a deep pink with all the blood that had rushed to his face.

'It must be that boy Yadu. He must have got here somehow,' Dorai ventured. He wished he hadn't a moment later, because the moment Hardaker heard Yadu's name he brought the iron bar crashing onto the jeep's windshield. The glass broke into a million pieces.

'That scum! How did he get here?' Hardaker asked.

By this time a few of the workers from the jetty had arrived. They all stood a safe distance away and watched their raving lunatic of a boss mould the front of his jeep into a shapeless lump of metal.

Hardaker now grabbed hold of Dorai's shirt collar. He locked eyeballs with Dorai and then asked how the boy had got here. The effect Hardaker was having on everybody was palpable. A couple of men sensing trouble started backing off. They slipped away and started walking back towards the jetty. Given a chance Dorai would have done the same.

'I...I have no idea, Brian,' Dorai stammered.

Hardaker let go of Dorai's shirt. 'What are you all looking at?' he thundered at his men now. 'Go find him. Spread out, get into the forest.'

Yadu now slipped away from behind the tree. If he stayed here any longer he would be asking for trouble. He started to run.

He made his way quickly through the woods heading in the direction of the vehicle park. He had already decided what he was going to do. He was going to steal one of their bikes, and then he would ride all the way to the police station at Calicut.

But getting to the vehicle park was easier said than done. To get there he would have to come out into the open again and that gave him the jitters.

Within minutes he had left his pursuers behind him and had arrived at the edge of the woods. He could see the vehicles now. Only two hundred metres separated him from his escape vehicle.

He looked in the direction of the jetty, then he looked to his left to see if anybody was on the abandoned line. Nobody was looking this way, so he broke into a wild sprint.

He arrived by the vehicles panting and gasping for air. He looked around, made sure nobody was watching and then he eased one of the motorbikes off its stand.

He had just started pushing the bike up the slope on to the line when it all started going horribly wrong for him.

The dogs at the jetty started to bark.

40

Not all the men on the jetty had gone to the blast site. About five of them had remained behind to oversee the lift, with Icy in charge. The moment the dogs started barking, Icy sensed that there was an intruder around; so he removed the leash off them. The two Alsatians, darted in the direction of the vehicle park, barking at a high pitch.

The loud barking not only got the attention of the men who had gone into the woods, it even got the attention of Hardaker, who was about three hundred metres away.

Yadu looked at the two dogs that were rushing in his direction, and he was rendered immobile for a few seconds. He had no idea what he should do next. If he started the bike then Hardaker would immediately hear it.

He decided he didn't have a choice. If he continued to push the bike the dogs would catch up with him and would rip him to shreds.

He sat astride the bike and tried to kick start it. He tried a few times but the bloody thing wouldn't start. Behind him the dogs were fast approaching. Hardaker's jeep – with its pug-nosed face – appeared in his rear view mirror. Several other men came running out of the woods realising the trespasser was out here in the open.

The motorbike finally sputtered to life. Yadu changed gear and then pulled away just as the dogs reached the line. Not a moment too soon. A couple of more seconds and the dogs would have sunk their fangs into his leg.

He whipped past the clearing and entered the forests. Yadu had broken into a cold sweat by this time. He looked at the rearview mirror and noticed a whole procession behind him: the two dogs were still after him; behind them was the jeep; and behind the jeep were a few motorbikes. Hardaker was leaning out of his seat goading Dorai to drive faster. The Englishman held a rifle in his arm.

Yadu focused all his attention now on the railroad ahead. If he lost his concentration now then that was it. One wrong turn or one fall is all that separated him from death at the hands of Hardaker. The man would surely not forgive him for what he had just done. He had *blown* the railway line.

In spite of the unfortunate situation he found himself in Yadu knew that this was one job he would be proud of for the rest of his life. It remained to be seen if he would come out of this situation alive. One part of him was proud of what he had accomplished here, yet there was another part that was worrying over what he had done. He had messed up Hardaker's plans alright, but what would the repercussions be? Once Hardaker got out of here he would surely go to where he had hidden his father, and he would probably take out all his fury on him. *That* thought troubled Yadu a lot. He would not allow that to happen. He had to get Hardaker captured by the police somehow or the other. For that he had to reach Calicut safely, and for that he had to concentrate on his driving.

The dogs had given up their chase, leaving it to their mechanically endowed bosses. Hardaker's jeep was still behind. In fact, the gap between Yadu's bike and the jeep had reduced considerably in the past five minutes. The three bikes remained close behind the jeep.

It was half past six in the morning and there was a nice breeze inside the forest. Yadu's shirt though was fully drenched with sweat. He was riding as fast as the motorbike would go, but the jeep kept gaining on him.

And now he had one more thing to worry about. Hardaker had just started shooting with his rifle. Bullet after bullet whizzed past him. Yadu realised that this was it. It was only a matter of time before one of the bullets lodged itself into his back. He still had a long way to go to civilisation. He was not even near the bridge, let alone the.....

That was when Hardaker finally got lucky with his shot as a bullet punctured Yadu's tyre, throwing him off onto the ground. Yadu rolled like a top and then crashed into a bush.

Hardaker let out a bone chilling war cry and Dorai brought the jeep to a halt within a few metres of where Yadu lay. All three of them – Hardaker, Sethu and Dorai – jumped off the vehicle and ran to where Yadu was lying. All three started to kick him with all the pent up fury of the last few days. Yadu was too dazed from the fall to even move, let alone provide himself any meaningful self-defence. He covered his head with his hands and cowered from their blows. That was about all he could do.

The kicking went on for a couple of minutes with their shoes making violent contact with Yadu's stomach, chest, his face. Blood started to spurt from his mouth. He sensed that his end was near.

In that moment of clarity, he managed to grab hold of somebody's leg. Instantly he grabbed the person's other leg and yanked. Sethu lost his balance and dropped to the ground. Yadu leapt onto him and started raining blows even as the other two continued to kick him.

Hardaker then grabbed hold of Yadu's collar and pulled him up. Yadu twisted and then punched the Englishman in the face. The man didn't flinch. He twisted both of Yadu's hands and then took him to the jeep. As Yadu struggled to get out of his hold Hardaker threw a powerful upper cut that caught Yadu just under his chin. He found himself airborne the next instant. A second after that he had crashed onto the already broken windshield. It felt like he had been caught in the epicentre of an explosion. That's how much it hurt. Blood started oozing from the cuts in his face.

'You scum, you are going to regret what you've just done. You are going to die such a slow, tortuous death that you'll...' Hardaker was so mad he couldn't even find the words to finish his sentence.

'How the hell did you get here? Who told you about this place?' Dorai bellowed, joining the party.

'Did this boy come alone into the forest, or was there somebody with him?' Hardaker asked, in his deep baritone.

'I have no idea, Brian,' Dorai said.

Yadu watched as a blur of a fist shot towards his jaw. He didn't even attempt to get out of its way. He had no more strength. These men were too powerful for him. Hardaker's iron fist rammed his jaw and then sent him crashing through the windshield again. The entire panel of glass crumbled on him this time. Yadu had seen the blow coming but he had been in no position to evade it. His reflexes simply refused to function, numbed by the dread this fearsome looking man caused.

Hardaker now pulled Yadu back towards him as if he were a rag doll. He propped him on the bonnet of the jeep. There were several cuts on Yadu's face and on his forearms.

Yadu heard Hardaker's voice as if he were talking from a mile away. The Englishman was saying, 'I warned you, didn't I? I warned you right at the beginning not to go to the police. I warned you to stay out of my path.'

For a moment he gazed into the Englishman's hatred filled eyes. Hardaker was cursing him for causing them so much anxiety over the past few days. Yadu was just inches away from passing out. Hardaker now caught Yadu's collar and made him sit upright.

'How old are you?' Hardaker now asked, holding him by his collar.

Yadu didn't answer for a while. Then fearing the hammer-blow that Hardaker would launch he whispered his age.

'Sixteen,' he said in what sounded like somebody else's voice.

'Sixteen,' Hardaker repeated, tightening his grip on Yadu's collar. He now looked around at his men. 'He is sixteen,' he told them. Then turning to Yadu he said, 'You are sixteen and you want to take on Hardaker? Have you *any* idea what an insult that is to me?'

Hardaker now lifted Yadu clean off the bonnet with both hands and then flung him onto the roof of the jeep. Yadu landed on the roof with a thud and then he slid down and fell onto the ground.

Yadu groaned as the back of his head slammed onto the hard ground. His head started to throb violently.

'Let's get this over with,' Hardaker then said, picking up his rifle from inside the jeep.

He walked about ten metres away and he took careful aim.

Yadu heard the rifle go. That was the last thing he heard.

41

What Yadu had heard before he fainted was not one but three rifle shots. If he had been conscious he would have seen Hardaker, Dorai and Sethu falling down onto the ground like heavy sandbags. He would have seen Inspector Kripakaran and his men running down the track, rifles in hand.

Vandana, Inspector Kripakaran and his team of policemen had decided some time back to leave their position by the bridge and head into the forest in search of Yadu. They had been travelling for about twenty minutes when they had heard the gunshots coming from deep inside the forest. Realising something was up they had speeded up. Then they had heard the approaching jeep and more gunshots. Kripakaran at this point had decided not to use the jeep anymore. He ordered everybody out of the jeep and they started running instead.

They had been running for a few minutes when they saw the jeep ahead. The occupants had got out of the jeep and were mauling somebody. Vandana recognised the men instantly and told Kripakaran who they were. The inspector then ordered his men into the woods so Hardaker and his men wouldn't know they were here. They had positioned themselves about hundred metres from the villains and had trained their rifles on the three men. Inspector Kripakaran waited until Hardaker had raised his rifle to shoot Yadu. Then he ordered his men to take down all three men.

All three bullets found their mark. Hardaker got hit on his shoulder; Dorai got hit on his left leg and Sethu was hit on his left arm.

The moment the three fell down Inspector Kripakaran and his army of ten ambushed the three men and took them captive. Hardaker didn't even know what hit him. He had no idea where the police had come from or how they had reached this place.

The three men riding the motorbikes tried to escape into the forest, but they too were caught. Kripakaran sent one of his men on a bike to Calicut to order for police reinforcements. Applying a little foresight, he asked the man to inform the coastguard too, so that Hardaker's other men wouldn't try to escape via the river.

Vandana, meanwhile, with the help of one of the policemen, carried Yadu to the police jeep. She started first aid on the badly bleeding, fainted figure that was Yadu.

~

Yadu Ranganathan was under sedation and Vandana was at the hospital by Yadu's side when all the exciting things happened at Anchorpoint.

Inspector Kripakaran, on finding Yadu injured and unconscious, had immediately arranged for him to be taken to a hospital in Calicut.

Then he got busy rounding up the gang. Hardaker, Dorai and Sethu posed no problems at all because of the condition they were in. All three were so grievously injured that they were in no position to run even though they had seen the advancing police party. Their injuries made their capture that much easier.

As for the hired hands in Anchorpoint, most of them fell into police hands quite easily. A few of them foolishly tried to hide inside the forest, but eventually they too were flushed out by the police force. Icy was the only one who escaped the police dragnet. He was caught a month later in Mangalore as he was boarding a train bound for Madras.

The ship and the crane-fitted tugboats that were anchored on the Keyyurli River tried to escape, but were intercepted by a fleet of coastguard speedboats. The crew were all detained pending further investigations.

Mani and Devraj, the engine driver and the fireman of the Mangalore Express were both freed and sent to Coimbatore for a police debrief.

Among the first things that Inspector Kripakaran did on rounding up the gang was to find out where they had kept Ranganathan. Hardaker and Dorai refused to cooperate, but Sethu blurted out the address in Madras where he was kept captive. Kripakaran lost no time in contacting the Madras police. He arranged for Ranganathan to be rescued immediately.

Two hours after all the arrests were made inside Keyyurli forest, All India Radio announced that the hijacked engine of the Mangalore Express had at last been found near Calicut. No other details were let out to the media at this time as the police themselves, including Kripakaran, were unsure of what exactly this grand scheme of Hardaker was. All Kripakaran had found out from the coastguards who had seized the ship was that the cargo Hardaker had been stealing was iron and nothing else. That's what they had found in the ship's hold, and in the second batch of coaches – tons of iron.

Kripakaran had been baffled seeing the cargo they had seized. He couldn't believe this was what Hardaker was smuggling out of the country. The police tried prying the truth out of their mouths but none of them, Hardaker, Dorai, or Sethu, cooperated.

The whole story came out of an unexpected person the next day: Ranganathan.

42

THE POLICE COMMISSIONER'S OFFICE, COIMBATORE
10 DECEMBER 1947. 6.20 PM

With the perpetrators refusing to divulge what they really had been up to the police had to piece together the whole story from the only people who knew something about the hijack and the smuggling operation. So Yadu Ranganathan had been brought here earlier that morning from the hospital in Calicut. Ranganathan had been flown all the way from Madras. Vandana had been taken to her home in Palghat, and after she had informed her parents she too was brought here.

Besides these three, Inspector Kripakaran was in the room, and so was the chief operations manager of southern railways. A couple of other senior police officers too were in the room. The media was the reason why all these people had been rushed to this office. They had been waiting outside Wellington House since the previous day to get their hands on the story. The police, after failing to learn anything of import from Hardaker and his men, had finally brought these people here since they were the only people who were in the know.

Inspector Kripakaran started things off by telling the commissioner how Yadu's 'goods train' theory had been bang on target. Hardaker had never been after the RBI money. It held no lustre for him because all he had wanted was the engine – so that he could transport the twenty-two coaches of cast-iron cargo from Keyyurli all the way up to Anchorpoint. He had found the coaches at Keyyurli minus an engine. As to where exactly these coaches came from and why there was no engine he said Ranganathan would elaborate in a little while.

Since there was no way of getting an engine legitimately without arousing a lot of suspicion, he had taken this route. He had tried hijacking an engine a month back from Calicut but it proved to be too difficult. Besides, he was frightened that the railway personnel would come looking on the abandoned line in search of the engine. If that happened, then they would see Anchorpoint, and would instantly realise that some major smuggling operation was going on here. He didn't want to risk such an eventuality, so he had gone for a more elaborate way of getting the engine. This way he could rest assured that the police and the railway people would be busy looking for the RBI coach. No one would suspect what they were really after.

Yadu was asked to take over at this point, to tell them about the Calicut-Mysore project, and how the line upto Keyyurli lay abandoned for the last eight years.

Earlier, in the reception, Yadu and Ranganathan had had a joyous reunion. Kripakaran had already informed Yadu the previous day that his father had been found and rescued by the Madras police. But he had deliberately not told him that his father too had been called to Wellington House. So, for Yadu it had been a wonderful shock to see his father there. Ranganathan looked off-colour and weak. He had a couple of bruises in his forehead and his elbow, but otherwise he looked alright.

Yadu had introduced Vandana to his father, and the three had done a lot of catching up as they waited for the commissioner to call them.

Now, in the commissioner's room, Kripakaran asked Ranganthan to tell them what he had learnt during the time he had been Hardaker's captive.

What Ranganathan said in the first five minutes, almost everybody in the room already had pieced together. It was not for this that he had been flown all the way from Madras. It was what he said later that they were all interested in: the story of the priceless cargo.

~

The cargo that Hardaker had been so desperate to smuggle out of the country was a consignment of gold. It was not *any* consignment of gold. It was *the largest* consignment of gold that had ever been lost in the history of mankind.

1100 tons of pure solid gold.

Worth hundreds of billions of dollars.

Worth thousands of billions of rupees.

Just as he had expected, everybody in the room let out loud gasps at this point. The police commissioner reserved his judgement. He wasn't going to believe any of this. 1100 tons of gold? Did that much gold exist in this world, he wondered to himself.

Ranganathan wanted them all to visualise the amount of gold he was talking about. So he broke it down into figures they could all understand. A kilogram of gold was 1000 grams of gold. It was not a kilogram of gold Hardaker was smuggling. It was not a 1000 kgs of gold that he was smuggling (which is one ton). He was smuggling a 1000 tons of gold. Enough to make him and his gang members the richest men in the universe many times over.

Ranganathan told the group about the night of his capture when a drunk Icy had bragged to him about their grandiose scheme. Icy had said that they had planned not just the biggest smuggling operation in India; they had planned the biggest smuggling operation the world would never know about. They were planning to buy islands in the Caribbean, which was no big deal for them, because, with the kind of money they would make selling this gold, they could buy whole countries if they so wished.

Since every single member of the small group was eager now to know where such a huge consignment of gold had come from in the first place, Ranganathan started to tell them the story of the gold. The gold, he said, belonged to the British government...

~

It all started in the year 1939 with the stirrings of the Second World War. Hitler started his campaign of terror in Europe. He started conquering the European countries one by one. Austria fell first, then Poland, then France. No country was able to withstand the onslaught of the marauding Nazi army. Countries started falling like ninepins. Only the areas ruled by Hitler's ally, Mussolini, were safe.

After France too had fallen to the Nazi might, Hitler set his eyes on Great Britain. In September 1940 the mighty Nazi troops started advancing towards Great Britain. Blitzkrieg after blitzkrieg followed, to make the British buckle and surrender. Thousands were killed in the air raids that Hitler had orchestrated as a terror tactic. There was a very real chance that Great Britain too would fall into Nazi hands sooner or later. The entire world watched with bated breath, because the outcome of this war would, in many ways, seal the fate of the world.

Everybody was worried because the Nazi army's might was growing exponentially with every country they took over. They would empty the coffers of every country they conquered, and they would pump in the spoils to strengthen their own army.

What most observers the world over feared was that if Great Britain was taken over, then Hitler would surely usurp every last penny in the treasury, and would pump all that money back into his war effort. Which is what the world did not want at that moment.

So, the leaders of Great Britain at the time, Winston Churchill, Prime Minister; Sir Kingsley Wood, the Chancellor of the Exchequer; and a few other war cabinet members decided, that for the safety of the world at large, they had to stash away their gold reserves in some safe place where Hitler would never be able to get at it even if Great Britain fell to the nazis. It wasn't long before they all agreed that the best place to hide their gold reserves was in India, their biggest colony.

The transfer was just meant to be for the next three-six months. If they held out against the Nazi might for the next six months then they would be safe. They could bring the gold reserves back to England. Everybody agreed that in the greater interest of the world this had to be done. Once Hitler got his hands on their gold reserves he would become invincible – because of the sheer might of his armed forces.

Preparations got underway in September, the year 1940, to send the consignment to Cochin, in India. Nobody was to know about the consignment, least of all the media. This was supposed to be a top-secret operation. If anybody, the enemy spies especially, got a wind of this transfer, then they would lose the gold forever.

In the interest of safety it was decided that the gold bricks would be melted, made into rods, bars and roundshots and then coated with iron. The entire batch of 1100 tons of gold was made to look like a consignment of iron. This was done so that even if the ship carrying this top secret cargo was intercepted in the high seas by German U-boats, or by pirates, they wouldn't care much for it since it was just 'iron' that was being transported. That was the idea. For the same reason it was decided to do away with escort ships. The larger the fleet escorting the vessel, the more suspicious the German U-boats would get, and that wouldn't serve their purpose. So they sent the ship to Cochin on its own, with a skeleton crew and with no escort.

Big mistake.

Two things happened a day before the ship was supposed to reach port. One, the ship was hit by a storm, and two, taking advantage of the weather conditions some pirates got aboard the ship. The pirates murdered the crew aboard. They ransacked the ship and stripped it of everything – except the iron. Then they made away with whatever cargo they could lay their hands on.

The group of five in England, meanwhile, had lost contact with the ship. They feared the ship had sunk in rough weather. They tried *desperately* to get in touch with the ship. Search parties were sent. Every available warship and frigate was sent to the Arabian Sea to look for the cargo ship. Nobody was told why finding the ship was so important. They were only told that the ship, *Invictus*, had to be found at all cost. The Royal Navy might have had a chance of finding *Invictus* if the weather had improved. But unfortunately for them it had only deteriorated, making things very difficult for all of them. The search for *Invictus* continued for many months but the ship was never found.

Back in Great Britain, the group of five who had decided to send the gold to India remained closeted for days wondering what they should do. Should they tell the cabinet of their monumental blunder and risk the wrath of the entire nation? Or should they keep mum and hope desperately that the MI6 would find the ship?

Afraid of the backlash at such a sensitive time they decided to keep the whole matter under wraps. They just hoped to find the ship in the days to come.

The ship itself, meanwhile, had drifted towards the port of Calicut. A group of fishermen who had gone into the sea braving the bad weather, saw the damaged, dangerously lurching ship about twenty-five miles outside Calicut. On returning they informed the harbour master of Calicut about what they had seen.

The harbour master of Calicut at the time was an Englishman called Oliver Woodbridge. Now, Woodbridge was an Indophile if ever there was one. He had lived in India all his life, had seen the oppression of the Indians under British rule and was greatly ashamed by it all. It's important to understand this particular aspect of Woodbridge's character, because if he hadn't been such an Indophile, the rest of what happened would never have happened. Things would have taken an altogether different turn.

Woodbridge, hearing about this lurching ship outside Calicut, went into sea and had a look at it. His only interest at this point of time was to make sure the ship didn't sink in the mouth of his harbour. Then he would be in great trouble as all incoming and outgoing vessels would be stuck wherever they were.

What Woodbridge did was, he boarded the ship, and guided it into his harbour. He then had a look in its hold to see what it held. Why he was interested in its cargo was because of the extraordinary number of telegraph messages he had been receiving from his higher in command in the last few days. Almost every single telegram ordered him to inform the high command in case he came across this ship called *Invictus*. No doubt Woodbridge was interested in the cargo.

Once the ship was alongside, he personally checked the hold once again, saw the extraordinary number of iron rods and round shots, and started to suspect that they might be more than what they appeared to be. So he took a sample, went to a local blacksmith and got the bar melted.

And found that it was pure gold inside! His hunch had been right!

It didn't take sixty-year-old Woodbridge to figure out what must have happened. He knew the gold had come from Southampton. He knew about the impending all-out attack by Hitler's Nazis. He also knew about the frantic search operations that the Royal Navy was conducting in the Malabar Coast.

At this point he could have done the right thing by calling his superiors and telling them that he had found the ship. (The Royal Navy were still assuming that the ship had already sunk somewhere in the Arabian Sea.) The only trouble was that Woodbridge wasn't sure whether this would really be the right thing to do.

Woodbridge thought it was divine providence that all this gold had come back to India in this fashion. He was one of the few British who readily accepted the extent to which the empire had bled India for more than two hundred years. Looking at this huge pile of gold that had arrived here, he thought this was indeed God's way of returning all the gold that his countrymen had looted from this place.

Woodbridge seriously started thinking of ways in which he could hide the gold until Indian independence. All this happened in late December 1940, and by this time Indian independence as a possibility was already being whispered about in political circles. Woodbridge knew all he had to do was hide this consignment for a few years. Once India got its independence he could let the Indian government in on his little secret. It would no doubt be a shot in the arm for the fledgling country to have, what looked like a few hundred tons of gold.

It must be noted here that Woodbridge never thought of usurping all the gold himself. The thought never even occurred to the man. Inspired by this idea of hiding the gold, he got to work immediately. He decided first of all that he wouldn't inform his British bosses about finding the ship at all. He understood the risk he was taking, but he didn't care about the consequences if he was found out.

Using his clout as harbour master he brought in fifty transient labourers into the docks. He arranged for as many open wagons as he could get without arousing anyone's suspicions. Then he started the onerous task of emptying out the ship of its cargo. The labourers worked night and day, in three shifts. In a week, the cargo had been unloaded.

Finding a place to hide the coaches proved to be easier than he had expected. In fact, it was because he knew of this place – Keyyurli – that he embarked on this dangerous mission in the first place. Having lived in Calicut for a few years he knew about the Calicut-Mysore project. He was around when it was abandoned. The project engineer, a friend of his, had even taken him on the line a couple of times. He knew hiding the coaches in Keyyurli was never going to be a problem. Most people had forgotten about the line. Very few people dared to venture into the place even if they knew about it. It was the perfect place to hide the gold for as long as he wished.

So, on the day that the last of the cargo was loaded on to the coaches he organised for the coaches to be taken all the way up to Keyyurli by the port's engine driver. Woodbridge went along on the ride, made sure the tops of all the carriages was sealed, and then he arrived back in Calicut after extracting a promise from the engine driver that he would never talk about this to anyone.

His work was still not done. He had to get rid of the ship. That night he steered the ship personally out of the harbour, into the Arabian Sea. Following behind in a trawler was his deputy who had no clue what Woodbridge was up to. The Englishman sunk the ship in a safe place, and then boarded the trawler to return to Calicut.

Then he started his long wait for Indian independence.

This was how the 1100 tons of gold had turned up at Keyyurli.

~

Ranganathan told everybody about how Woodbridge had been held captive in the same house that he too was held captive. It was from the Englishman that he had learnt of Hardaker's conspiracy. With much regret he then informed everybody how Hardaker had killed the man in cold blood the day before he set off for the hijack.

There was a long period of hushed silence after this as the extent of Hardaker's villainy sunk into everyone. Then the commissioner broke the silence, asking Ranganathan how Hardaker had found out about Keyyurli.

Ranganathan explained that Hardaker was an MI6 agent during the time contact was lost with the ship. He was operating in the Malabar Coast at the time. Some five years after the ship had been lost, Hardaker, by a stroke of luck, chanced upon the very fishermen who had first seen the lurching ship. He realised they had seen the ship he had been looking for five years ago: the *Invictus*. By this time it was MI6's best-known secret that the *Invictus* had contained a huge consignment of gold. Hardaker, smelling money, started investigating deeper and deeper. His investigations revealed that Woodbridge, the harbour master had offloaded the cargo and then had sunk the ship. At this point he resigned from his job and went after Woodbridge. He kidnapped the harbour master, and for months he tortured him in a bid to find out where he had hidden the cargo. And for months Woodbridge held on, not letting go of his secret. Indian independence was due any minute now. He didn't want all that gold to fall into the hands of a crazed maniac like Hardaker.

But in October this year, two months after Indian independence, Woodbridge finally succumbed to Hardaker's torture. He told him that the gold was in Keyyurli.

Now Hardaker knew where the gold was, but he didn't know how he was going to transport it through the seventy odd kilometres of forest. So he plotted the RBI coach hijack...

'...and that's how I came to be involved in all this,' Ranganathan finished.

Epilogue

After seven months of trial, Hardaker, Dorai, Icy and Sethu were sentenced to life imprisonment. The goods train driver Mathew, his fireman and the guide were sentenced to five years rigorous imprisonment for being accomplices in the crime.

The Indian government returned the 1100 tons of gold to the British two months later.

The police found out that it was Ranganathan's ex-boss (an Englishman) who had directed Hardaker to him for the transfer details.

The police dropped all charges against Ranganathan, as nothing was stolen.

Yadu Ranganathan failed in all his subjects in his half yearly exams, since he wasn't able to appear for even a single exam. It was indeed disappointing for him after all the preparations he had done. But his photograph, splashed across every major newspaper in the country, acted as a bit of a compensation.

As appreciation for the splendid job he had done in the case, Inspector Kripakaran was moved from the Erode police station to the district police headquarters.

When Vandana bid him farewell at Wellington House, Yadu thought, with some sadness in his heart, that that was the last he would see of her. Their paths had crossed briefly on a railway line, and now they would be going their separate ways.

What Yadu hadn't taken into account was the time a case like this would take in court to get resolved completely. As the public prosecutor's two star witnesses, Yadu and Vandana had to appear in court often.

It was unlikely that anybody else looked forward as eagerly to the trial dates as these two did.

Glossary

Abhistu	Idiot
Aiiyo Kadavule	'Oh my God!'
akka	Elder sister
appa	Father
banian	Light inner garment worn by men to cover upper torso
chappals	An item of footwear similar to a flip-flop with a toe strap
dhoti	A rectangular piece of unstitched cloth, usually around five yards long, wrapped about the waist and the legs and knotted at the waist.
edupudi	Man Friday/person or servant who does odd jobs
gopuram	A Gopuram is a monumental tower, usually ornate, at the entrance of a temple, especially in southern India.
goonda	Member of a crime gang; hired muscle
idlies	South Indian staple breakfast item. Idlies are steamed cakes made from a mixture of cooked rice and black gram, fermented with the aid of mould.

kutcheries	A katcheri (or kutcheri) is a gathering. In the context of Carnatic music it is a place where people gather to listen to classical music concerts of vidwans.
lathi	The word lathi means cane. A lathi is basically a six to eight foot long cane tipped with a metal blunt. It is the Indian police's most used crowd control device.
lungis	A garment worn around the waist
mridangam	The mridangam is a percussion instrument. It is the primary rhythmic accompaniment in a Carnatic music ensemble.
mufti	Civilian attire. Refers to ordinary clothes, especially when worn by one who normally wears a uniform.
nadaswarams	It is a wind instrument similar to the North Indian shehnai but larger, with a hardwood body and a large flaring bell made of wood or metal.
paati	Grandma
paavadai-dhavani	Half saree
paayasam	A rice kheer/pudding typically made by boiling rice with milk and sugar
panduranga	Hindu god. Manifestation of Lord Vishnu
pudina	Mint leaves
rathotsavam	Temple car festival
sappad:	Meal
tank bund	A short wall built to curtail water overflowing from the tank onto the streets.
thinnai	A raised platform with a roof, like a

verandah but only much smaller. A pyol.

tonga   Horse drawn carriage

vadai   A South Indian savoury snack shaped like a doughnut and made with lentil or potato.

vellayan   White man

zari   A type of thread made of fine gold or silver wire used in traditional South Indian silk sarees.

Acknowledgments

I would like to thank Mr P.C. Dhandapani, ex-RBI officer, and Mr S.S. Kumar, ex-Indian Railways officer for their valuable technical inputs. The expertise is theirs, the interpretation and mistakes, if any, are mine.

Siddharth and Siva, thank you very much for your valuable observations and suggestions. And John Scaria, thanks for making those extended vacations possible.

Many thanks to Trisha Bora and team at Rupa.

Most of all, to my wife Mamata. Without your patience, love and support, this book would not have happened.

6